GANGSTERS OF FATE

GANGSTERS OF FATE

JOSEPH JENKINS

This is a work of fiction. Names, characters, places, and incidents are either the product of the author's imagination or are used fictitiously. Any resemblance to actual persons, living or dead, or actual events is purely coincidental.

stratageminnovations.com

ISBN 979-8-9988548-6-6 (paperback)

The characters and events portrayed in this book are fictitious. Any similarity to real persons, living or dead, is coincidental and not intended by the author.

Printed in the United States of America

10 9 8 7 6 5 4 3 2 1

First Edition

CHAPTER 1

THE CARDS BEGAN to be dealt, and the game chips were distributed as the three players took their seats. The dealer moved quickly, slapping cards down with mechanical precision. Each player had no choice but to play with the hand they were dealt.

They examined their cards in silence, fingers twitching toward the chips in front of them. The only sounds in the small, drab room were the clatter of plastic chips and the slow, heavy rhythm of their breathing. Silence was the first layer of strategy. Time was the second on the stairway of a great plan.

But silence was a fragile commodity.

Outside the room, a party erupted with music that pounded against the walls like a beating heart. The muffled bass thudded through the silence, cutting into the players' focus like a blade. It was as if they were sequestered in the backroom of a riotous celebration—choosing isolation over indulgence, purpose over pleasure.

The dealer, his face unreadable, finished passing out the cards and moved to the door. He said nothing—never did. His role was simple: observe and distribute. He knew the hands each player held, yet offered no insight, no advice, no interference. He left as quietly as he had arrived, letting the roar of the party seep in through the open door. The club's chaos gushed in like floodwater—bright flashing lights, seizure-inducing strobes, and the unmistakable stench of sweat, booze, and regret.

The smell hit hard, as did the heat radiating from the dancing bodies just outside the room. The crowd outside moved like logs caught in a river's current—directionless, thoughtless. But the players inside were branches lodged into the bank, stubborn and unyielding, refusing to let the current write their story.

The door finally closed behind the dealer with a soft *click*. The game had begun.

A game with no real stakes. No prize. No loss.

But deadly serious to those who played it.

The first player reached forward, about to set his card, when the music outside surged again, louder, jarring him.

"You insisted on this party, Malcolm," he muttered, placing his card on the table. His voice was gravelly—low and rasping, like a growl from an aging wolf.

"It was Amanda's idea," Malcolm replied with a grin, throwing a wink in Amanda's direction.

Amanda didn't return the gesture. Her expression was cool, pragmatic. Silent.

"What's the matter, Rob?" Malcolm goaded. "Is it past your bedtime? Worried you'll miss the early bird special?"

Amanda chuckled softly, shielding her smile behind the cards fate had handed her. She laid down a card and moved her chips forward.

"Don't start with that senior crap, Malcolm. I'm only ten years older than you. If I'm old, then you're right behind me." Rob's tone sharpened. "You planned this, didn't you? You think you're clever—messing with our concentration. I can't even hear myself think!"

"Relax, Rob," Amanda said, eyes still on her cards. "The party was my idea."

Rob scoffed, twisting in his chair. "Stiff Amanda? Throwing a party?"

"It's called morale, Rob. We push our people any harder, they might start forming a union," she replied dryly.

Rob rolled his eyes and gestured at Malcolm. "Go. Your turn."

Malcolm fidgeted, a grin spreading across his face. "Mandy's the serious one in our little trio," he said. "I'm the face, and Rob's the proverbial muscle."

Rob scowled. He flicked his card toward the center of the table with a touch too much force. "Amanda, you're up."

Amanda examined the cards already played, then studied her hand. She rubbed her temple, clearly struggling to focus through the booming beat outside.

"The damn music, Malcolm," Rob growled.

Malcolm just laughed and adjusted his bow tie. "I told you. Amanda's party."

Rob muttered. "Take your turn already. We should have a damn timer."

Amanda placed her card. Malcolm followed swiftly. "Jackpot!" he shouted, dragging a pile of chips toward his side of the table.

"Hold on!" Rob barked, reaching out to stop him. "Let me see that."

"Check it, old man," Malcolm said, smugly pointing to the pile.

Rob muttered to himself, inspecting the stack of cards.

Amanda pressed her fingers to her temples. "He does this every time, Rob. He riles you up so you'll lose focus."

"I call it the charades tactic," Malcolm said, wiggling his eyebrows and dancing in his seat.

Rob chuckled despite himself. He tossed another card and pushed more chips into the center.

"My tactic for Amanda," Malcolm said, starting to unbutton his shirt, "is what I call the sexy play. A little chest hair—"

"Don't flatter yourself," Amanda said, smirking. "You're not my type. That flabby stomach won't seduce anyone."

"Come on, Mandy, we'd make beautiful mixed kids. Goofy white dad, strong Black mama."

Amanda rolled her eyes but grinned. She played her card and won the round. Malcolm whooped, throwing down his card with flair.

"Damn," Rob muttered, pointing accusingly. "You two are cheating."

Their laughter said otherwise.

Suddenly, a couple slammed into the window behind them, locked in a passionate embrace. The players jumped. Rob stood and stormed to the door, cursing.

"I got it, sir," said a voice from the corner.

"No, Cassandra. Let Rob handle it," Amanda ordered, gesturing to hold her position.

Rob pounded on the glass until the couple staggered away.

"I can't stand young people," Rob grumbled, returning to his seat. He glanced at Cassandra. "Sorry, not you—I didn't mean—"

"Spoken like a true old man," Malcolm teased, rocking in his chair.

"Malcolm—" Rob warned, pointing a finger.

"It's alright, sir," Cassandra replied. "I'll try to keep people away from your game."

"How old are you, Cassie?" Malcolm asked. "Twenty-two? Twenty-three?"

"You're a walking lawsuit," Amanda snapped. "Never ask a woman's age. You really are a clown."

"He has no filter," Rob muttered, waving at Malcolm. Amanda and Rob both complained as Malcolm smugly collected more chips.

"I just turned thirty," Cassandra said, trying to diffuse the tension.

"See? She's cool. You'll get a nice tip—probably from Rob," Malcolm said, pushing Rob's chips with his fingers.

Rob swatted him away. "Did you just steal my chips?"

Malcolm shook his head with a guilty smile.

Amanda waved Cassandra over. "You don't have to be so formal with these two."

"I'm here to do my duty, ma'am," Cassandra replied.

"Drop the ma'am and sir crap," Rob said, locking eyes with her. "You're not with the government anymore. You work for me now. We're not like them."

Cassandra stiffened, then quickly nodded. "Yes, sir—" She caught herself. Rob gave her a look.

"You should keep doing it," Malcolm said, mock-clapping. "Rob's just a teddy bear."

"My apologies. This environment is . . . different from my last," Cassandra replied carefully.

"Well, you don't want to be a rebel for *this* job," Rob muttered, shuffling the deck.

"How 'bout drinks?" Malcolm offered. "Mandy? Rob?"

Amanda handed Cassandra some cash. Malcolm did the same.

"Rob?" Malcolm asked.

Rob shook his head. "I don't drink."

Before Malcolm could respond, Cassandra slipped out the door. Noise and neon flooded in like a tidal wave. The players leaned back, overwhelmed.

Amanda leaned close. "Sweet girl. Rob, you found a good replacement."

The men couldn't hear her. Rob slammed the door, sealing off the noise. He stomped back to the table.

"I said Cassandra's a sweet girl. You know how to pick them."

Rob didn't answer. He stared into space.

"Rob? Earth to Rob," Malcolm snapped his fingers.

Rob blinked, shook himself, and returned to focus.

"Where'd you go? Back to the prairie?" Malcolm joked. Amanda shot him a look.

"Rob used to be a shepherd," Malcolm said. "Tilling fields, real man's work."

Rob's face fell, as if weighed down by memories. After a long pause, he nodded.

"I climbed my way through trenches to get here," he said quietly. Amanda leaned in to hear him better. "You and I—we bootstrapped it. No handouts. No support. And sure as hell . . . no mercy from fate."

"Fate," Amanda said, half scoffing, half lost in thought.

"I remember my bootstrap story—" Malcolm started confidently, puffing out his chest like he expected applause from the other two players.

"Please, Malcolm," Rob interrupted with a smirk. "When was the last time you flew commercial? You were born with a silver spoon in your mouth. What do they call you on the news? 'Malcolm the Tech Mogul'? Must be a tough life—you've got maids who call you 'sir.' The only boots you've ever touched are the ones you pay someone else to shine."

Amanda chuckled, and Malcolm blushed.

"He's so out of touch, he probably doesn't even know how much a loaf of bread costs," Amanda added.

Rob laughed, and the two swayed with laughter as if in rhythm, exchanging jokes like a practiced routine. Malcolm looked away, face souring.

"Alright, alright. Let's get back to the game," he muttered, eyeing his cards.

"Look at him, Amanda—our little 'socialite silver-dollar' is embarrassed," Rob teased, reaching out to pull Malcolm's seat closer.

Malcolm forced a smile, cheeks reddening. "Guys, I'm not—" he squeaked, then laughed awkwardly again, clearly rattled.

The friendly ribbing filled the room with warmth and levity—until it didn't.

A heavy thud cut through the air.

All three players jumped. They turned toward the window. The club lights flickered. The music had stopped. Then came the screams. And another loud crash followed.

Chairs scraped back as they stood. Malcolm crouched near the corner where Cassandra had been stationed earlier. Amanda knelt beside him, while Rob took position by the window.

The unmistakable click of a cocked gun pierced the air.

"Rob, no—wait," Malcolm hissed.

Rob took a quick glance through the window, then dropped back down. His hand tightened around the grip of his pistol like a viper coiled to strike.

He reached for the doorknob, his gun pressed tightly against his cheek.

Just as he began to open the door, Malcolm grabbed his wrist. Their eyes locked—one defiant, the other desperate.

Rob shoved Malcolm off and stepped into the hallway. The club was eerily silent.

Malcolm let out a grunt, frustration etched on his face as he watched Rob race into the crowd. Concern overtook him. He dashed back to the table and rifled through his bag.

"Mandy," he said, pulling out a handgun and holding it out to her.

"No," Amanda said, calm but firm. Her eyes locked on the weapon.

"Amanda, this is serious. Please—"

"I don't need the damn gun, Malcolm. I can handle myself." She bolted through the door before he could argue.

A scream tore through the silence, followed by the sharp crash of glass.

Malcolm threw off his blazer and raced after them.

The club flickered with sporadic lighting—as if trying to continue the party—but the illusion was broken. The once-ecstatic crowd stood frozen, revealing just how bland and poorly decorated the club truly was. The stench of sweat, stale alcohol, and vomit crept through the room. Faces of pleasure soured into discomfort.

The crowd had formed a circle around something—or someone.

Malcolm caught up to Amanda as she pushed through the bodies. Across the room, Rob struggled to push through the crowd. People made no effort to move. The lack of empathy made the tension worse.

Another glass shattered in the center of the crowd.

Screams from frightened women mixed with shouts of encouragement.

"Come on, baby! Give me another drink!" a loud, arrogant voice rang out from the middle of the circle. It echoed through the entire club.

Rob's face darkened. He recognized the voice.

Cassandra's reply was clear and forceful. "This is your last warning. Leave. Now."

Rob finally made it to the front, Amanda and Malcolm flanking him. "Dunkin," Rob growled. "And his thugs."

"Cassandra!" Rob called out, his voice sharp. The people closest to him turned to look.

"What am I paying you for if you can't handle this Neanderthal—"

"Robbie!" Dunkin interrupted, slurring his words mockingly. "Still letting women fight your battles?"

Dunkin was a hulking, bald brute—leaning lazily on the bar, knocking over glass after glass. His boots sprawled across the bar stools like he owned the place. Two goons stood at either side of him, flexing under their tank tops and scowling like professional thugs.

"Get your feet off the furniture," Rob barked. His pistol remained steady in his hand.

Dunkin laughed in his face, exaggerated and cruel. He knocked another glass to the floor just to watch it break. The bartender yelped.

"I just want another drink, Robbie. But your bartender? She's rude. Won't serve me or my boys?"

"You're not welcome here," Rob snapped.

"Oh yeah? And why's that?" Dunkin turned his attention to Cassandra, eyeing her with sick curiosity. He gestured lewdly, his breath foul. "What a crew you've got now, Robbie. The nerd, the bitch, and the old man." His words slurred but still hit with venom.

Dunkin rose from the bar and approached with a swagger, each step heavy like a drumbeat. The circle widened in fear.

"What do you even call yourselves, huh? What kind of coalition is this?" he slurred.

His cronies followed behind, towering and menacing. Rob's hand began to tremble.

Amanda and Malcolm noticed the change immediately. The tension in Rob's face. The fight behind his eyes.

"The old man beat me up," Dunkin announced to the crowd, spinning in a sloppy circle. "He tortures everyone! And the bitch—she's got her little black goons doing her dirty work. And the nerd . . ."

Dunkin grabbed a drink from a stranger, chugged it, then smashed the glass.

"Hey!" the drink owner shouted.

One of Dunkin's goons started to reach beneath his shirt. The other stopped him with a whisper. The crowd muttered, the atmosphere primed to explode.

"What did you say?" Dunkin asked, slow and dangerous.

Saliva rolled down his chin as he loomed.

The man repeated himself angrily. Dunkin ignored the words—until the stranger grabbed his arm.

That was a mistake.

Without even facing him, Dunkin clamped a meaty hand around the man's face and twirled him in place. "Have a nice trip," he muttered, and flung him like a toy. The man slammed into bar stools and crumpled. "Damn. I wanted to throw him like a football," Dunkin said with a chuckle, turning back to his gang.

"GET OUT, DUNKIN!" Rob roared. "Get out in the next five seconds or—"

Dunkin dropped into a mocking crouch. "One . . . two three…" he counted, swaying like a drunk dancer.

Rob squared his shoulders, planted his foot, ready to charge like a bull.

"Robbie…" Dunkin sang mockingly, drawing closer. "Come on, old man. Show everyone what you're made of." He stretched his arms out wide, daring Rob to strike.

Cassandra stepped in front of Dunkin as he approached the players.

"Well, well... pretty little princes," he slurred.

"How'd Robbie smuggle you across the border, huh? Huh?"

He spun his arms in exaggerated circles, eyes flicking from Cassandra to Rob. His tongue dragged across his lips in a lewd gesture.

"Oh, I see . . ." he purred. Then back to Cassandra: "I hope I get a turn after Robbie's done. How much are your services, sweetheart? Robbie likes his girls dressed like cops, I see."

Laughter rippled through the crowd. Dunkin basked in it, dancing on wobbling feet like a drunken king.

Cassandra locked eyes with the man twice her size. Her fists clenched as he mimed rubbing his belly, pretending he was starving. The quiet soldier took a step forward.

With one lazy swing, Dunkin swatted her aside like an annoying fly. The crowd gasped as she flew across the room, crashing onto a bar table. Glasses shattered around her as she rolled to the floor.

The room fell into stunned silence. Rob's eyes blazed. His hand flew to the pistol under his coat.

Amanda gripped his arm. "Wait," she said calmly her eyes never leaving Cassandra. Rob shot her a furious glare. "She's got this," Amanda added.

He yanked his arm away, nostrils flared, and turned back to the chaos.

"Robbie, Robbie, Robbie," Dunkin sang like a circus clown, his fingers mimicking a piano. His two cronies laughed, drunk on power and whiskey.

Then—

CRACK!

A bottle smashed over Dunkin's skull. The laughter cut off like a dropped mic. He dropped to the floor with a crash that echoed.

Cassandra stood tall, brushing shards off her suit jacket. She took a deep breath, then calmly pulled her long brown and golden-streaked hair into a tight bun.

Rob smirked, eyes drifting to Dunkin's unconscious body.

But it wasn't over yet.

The two men flanking Dunkin charged. Rob stepped forward, but Amanda grabbed him again.

He threw her a glare.

She answered with a steady nod.

Again, Rob shook her off.

One of the goons lunged at Cassandra, throwing a wild punch. She sidestepped and drove her elbow into his gut. He folded.

She swept his legs in one swift motion and sent him crashing to the ground.

The crowd exploded—cheering like it was the Super Bowl. Rob pumped his fist in the air.

Amanda and Malcolm exchanged amused glances.

The second thug vaulted over his fallen leader and rammed into Cassandra with his shoulder. She hit the ground hard, groaning in pain.

He lifted his foot to stomp her— She caught it mid-air, twisted, and brought him down beside her.

In one motion, she rose and drove her heel into his crotch.

He screamed.

Cassandra backed off, panting, as the crowd roared again.

"What are you waiting for? Finish it!" Rob shouted, stepping closer.

She nodded slowly, eyes fixed ahead.

Across the room, Dunkin stirred—using two by-standers to help pull himself up.

Rob's hand went back to his pocket. This time, he drew his pistol.

Cassandra saw it.

She bolted forward, sprinted past Rob, and launched herself at Dunkin. Her boot met his chest with a thud. He toppled backward like a bowling pin, taking several partygoers down with him.

Rob scowled, reluctantly slipping the pistol back into his coat.

Then—Sirens.

Red and blue lights flashed across the club walls.

Chaos erupted. The floor trembled under the stampede.

"Sir, we need to go," Cassandra said urgently.

Dunkin groaned again.

Rob gave him a swift kick for good measure.

"Sir!" Cassandra shouted louder.

Police burst through the doors. Glasses flew, chairs toppled, people screamed and shoved.

Cassandra stepped in front of Rob and extended her arm, guiding him toward the back.

Malcolm and Amanda pushed through the panic, with Rob and Cassandra close behind.

Rob cursed under his breath as Cassandra shoved open a back door.

A uniformed officer stepped over Dunkin's body, who was still groaning on the floor.

"That's Dunkin—the city's clown," he muttered to his partner.

All around them, partygoers were being tackled to the ground. Some hurled bottles. Others pushed to escape. It was like watching a beehive explode.

The older cop turned to his rookie partner, who was crouched over Dunkin, checking for a pulse.

"Don't waste your time. That idiot's been picked up more than half the gangsters in this city."

"He's hurt bad," the rookie said. "Shouldn't we get a medic?"

"Kid, this is his fifth brawl this month. He'll be fine."

The older officer squinted across the room. "It's those three we should be worried about."

The rookie stood, radio in hand. "Dispatch, multiple disturbances—club incident in progress—"

The older cop rolled his eyes. "They'll be here in five."

"They brought you in to help clean this mess. Jessie, let me give you some advice—grow a spine. These people would watch you bleed and laugh about it."

Jessie frowned.

"Don't look at me like that," the older cop snapped. He pointed behind him.

Jessie turned.

Dunkin was somehow upright, holding his head, staggering toward a barstool.

"Dunkin," the officer said with disdain.

"Hey, man," Dunkin grinned through a busted lip.

"Officer Dan!" His voice rose with a drunken sparkle. "I had a dream... your boy was massaging me. Real sensual."

He puckered his lips and made kissing noises toward Jessie.

Jessie recoiled.

"Alright, alright," Officer Dan barked, motioning for backup. Two officers stepped in, helping Dunkin and his crew off the floor.

Officer Dan scanned the room again, his face hardening.

"Something wrong?" Jessie asked.

"Yeah," Officer Dan muttered. "Where the hell are those three?"

Rapid steps echoed through the stairway as the four rushed down the steps. The bright moon peeped through the square windows as the four made their way to the back door. The quiet night was cool and the calmness of the moon made the parking lot almost feel heavenly compared to the heated room the four just departed from.

Rob continued to gripe as he reached the door to exit the club. Cassandra held the door open for the three of them to exit.

"Next time shoot the bastard," Rob ordered right in her face as he passed Cassandra holding the door. The two were so close they almost touched noses. Cassandra nervously nodded and moved back further for Rob to pass.

"Forget him, Cassie, you did great," Malcolm slammed a wad of cash in her hand as he passed behind Rob.

Amanda held the door, smiled at Cassandra, and motioned her to go in front of her.

"Nope, nope!" Malcolm yelled. He pointed to Rob beginning to limp in another direction. "We still have to finish the game." Malcolm boomed.

"The game you cheated," Rob snarled.

"Guess we'll have to finish it to find out," Malcolm said.

"We have to play chess. You can't cheat at chess."

The group turned toward the club as more commotion was heard. The bright lights from the club's window continued to flash. The noise of the partygoers ceded however screams and frantic cries were faintly heard from the parking lot. Cassandra noticed some burnt marks on the club as if parts of the building had been reconstructed previously.

Amanda looked at her watch. "Malcolm I'm going to head in for the night."

Malcolm giggled and playfully slapped her hand. "You can't even see your watch out here. Come!" Malcolm persisted.

Amanda's face made a surprised expression from Malcolm's passion. "Is Daisy at home now?" Amanda asked.

Malcolm's voice grew louder and he started to sway left and right. "No . . ." Malcolm spoke fast. "She's in India right now. On a humanitarian venture, I sponsored." Malcolm looked at the street, his eyes became lost in thought. Realizing he'd been unresponsive for too long Malcolm moved his arms in a playful way. "I just realized my house is empty but ready for some players. Come on, guys! No one has school tomorrow." He pointed to Cassandra. "Even you Cassie. You have to play."

"I would be honored but I have—"

"One game Malcolm, one game," Rob said, interpreting Cassandra. "Let's get one thing straight, none of your tricks."

Joyous anticipation filled Malcolm's face. The wily player called the valet to bring his car around. The others began to walk toward the other side of the parking lot when a limo pulled around.

"Malcolm, you did not drive this here?" Rob laughed examining the long black car.

Amanda and Cassandra walked toward the limo as well.

"Get in, get in," Malcolm insisted, holding the car door open.

"Our cars are here Malcolm—" Amanda began to say.

Like a child anticipating opening gifts at Christmas Malcolm spoke fast and with excitement. "My driver will take you back. Come on. One game. One game."

Amanda folded her arms not budging from the wily players heckling. After making pouting faces and seeing Rob and Cassandra examine the limo she gave into Malcolm's begging. Rob, Amanda, and Cassandra followed Malcolm into the limo.

The long black car drove smoothly. The four leaned back into their seats enjoying the luxury of the interior.

Malcolm noticed Cassandra looking at the bottles on the side of the door. "Have!" He began to reach for one.

"That's quite alright sir. I was looking—"

"Nope. I insist Cassandra." Malcolm gently handed her a bottle. "You saved us from Dunkin tonight." Rob scoffed at Malcolm's words and folded his arms. "You're our protector."

Rob snatched the bottle before Cassandra could take it. The three watched as he struggled to try and open the bottle.

"Need some help?" Malcolm said with a bashful smile. He reached over to take the bottle from Rob but Rob turned away.

Without warning, the limo honked and jerked to the side. The passengers lurched in their seats, gripping whatever they could as the car swerved hard.

The bottle flew from Rob's hands and clattered to the floor, rolling beneath the seats. The limo pitched again, harder this time.

It felt like the vehicle was skidding on ice.

Momentum tossed them from their seats. They hit the floor with a thud, limbs colliding. Amanda scrambled upright, gripping the seat handle, trying to steady herself. She strained to peer through the darkened windows.

A violent revving sound filled the air.

Amanda ducked instinctively.

Then—*crash*.

Another car slammed into the front of the limo with brutal force. The impact jarred the entire vehicle. Glass exploded as the windows shattered. The limo screeched to a halt.

In a daze, the passengers groaned on the floor, stunned, battered. Jagged shards of glass glittered in the moonlight above them, the cool night air pouring in through broken windows.

Rob lay on his back, gasping.

Malcolm was the first to react. He crawled over, gritting his teeth through the pain, and propped Rob up against the seat.

Blood dripped from Rob's hairline, pooling down his cheek like sweat. He clutched his chest, breaths shallow and rapid.

"Stay with me, man. Stay with me!" Malcolm patted his shoulder, voice strained and panicked. "Rob! Keep your eyes open!"

But Rob's eyelids fluttered. His head lolled to the side. His breath slowed. His body slumped, heavy and lifeless.

Malcolm grabbed him by the shirt. "Rob! ROB!"

No response.

Then—they heard it.

Footsteps.

Slow. Steady. Getting closer.

A shadow moved across the cracked glass of the limo's roof—tall, broad, deliberate.

The three remaining passengers froze.

A hand reached for the limo door handle.

And began to pull it open.

CHAPTER 2

THE *CLICK* OF the limo door creaking open made all three of their hearts jump. Their wide eyes locked on the crack of light slowly spreading into the darkness. The anticipation was unbearable. The fear of *what* was on the other side… even worse.

Moonlight poured in as the door opened fully—only to be blocked by a looming silhouette. A dark figure filled the frame, its face obscured, but two glowing red dots—like eyes—pierced the darkness.

The shadow slithered forward, its red eyes scanning the interior like a predator sizing up its prey.

The three inside the limo could barely breathe. Their chests rose and fell like they had just run a marathon. Fear rooted them to the floor as the figure crept further into the vehicle. It moved slowly, deliberately, like death itself reaching for Rob.

Then suddenly—it convulsed.

The figure spasmed violently, thrashing its limbs like it had touched a live wire. It stumbled, twisting with pain, eyes wide with shock. Malcolm turned and saw Amanda on the floor, arm outstretched, taser crackling in her grip.

Amanda lunged again, but the figure dodged. She advanced, closing the distance, her arm drawing back for another strike. The red eyes flared as if surprised.

Trapped between Amanda and the back corner of the limo, the figure twisted and flailed. Amanda jammed the taser into its side once more, and the attacker howled—high-pitched and primal—like an animal caught by a predator giving its last breath.

Then it lashed out.

The figure grabbed Amanda's wrist, yanked the taser to the side, and shoved her hard. She tumbled across the limo floor as the figure bolted out the door into the night.

For a brief moment, silence returned—until *more* footsteps echoed. Dozens of them.

They all froze, dread tightening their throats.

The limo swayed under sudden weight. Someone—or something—had jumped on top.

Malcolm, wheezing and pale, reached across the floor and pushed his pistol toward Cassandra. She met his eyes. Hesitant. Then took it.

Amanda let out a sharp gasp.

Outside—circling the limo—were *more* red eyes.

Like owls in the dark, their glowing eyes peered through the shattered windows, cutting the shadows like laser sights. Their faceless forms prowled, slowly closing in.

Cassandra crouched beneath a broken window, raising the gun toward the red eyes closest to her.

"Put that away," a low voice called from the dark.

The three tensed. The voice was calm. Too calm.

"We just want the old man."

They scanned the shadows, searching for the speaker.

A hand shot in from the side and grabbed Cassandra's wrist.

She shrieked and instinctively pulled the trigger. The gunshot cracked through the night. The figure retreated, and the red eyes outside blinked back—but only for a moment.

Then one stepped closer.

With moonlight glinting off its form, the figure came into view. A black plastic mask covered its face, with two glowing red glass lenses where the eyes should be. A black hood concealed its head, and its body was wrapped in tactical gear—sleek, armored, and silent.

It pressed one gloved hand against the window.

"Give us the old man," the voice said again, colder this time.

Suddenly—*thump*. More bodies landed on the roof.

Malcolm struggled upright, voice trembling but defiant. "No . . . go to hell."

The masked figure leaned forward, ignoring Amanda's taser now just inches from its face. It reached inside and grabbed Rob, trying to drag him out.

Malcolm clutched Rob's jacket. "No!"

The attacker yanked Rob hard. His limp body crashed to the floor, slicing across broken glass.

Amanda raised her taser again, jamming it toward the figure's face.

"Pathetic," the masked man muttered.

Then he spoke louder, calling into the night: "*Psalmists.*"

More glowing eyes moved closer to the windows. Arms emerged—each holding a glinting blade. Medium-sized, curved, and deadly. The tips scraped against the broken glass.

"I'll ask one last time," the masked leader said. "Give me Rob . . . and the rest of you walk away."

"Go. To. Hell," Malcolm rasped, trying to sit up.

The attacker chuckled, amused. "Already have."

Cassandra's voice was firm, despite the tremor in her breath. "Who are you? What is this?"

The masked man turned to her, still breathing hard. "We are the Spirit of Change. We are the Anointed. We proclaim good news to the poor, freedom to prisoners, recovery of sight to the blind, and liberty to the oppressed."

His followers—"Psalmists"—remained frozen outside, their red eyes gleaming like ritual flames.

"You haven't been enlightened yet," he added. "But don't worry. That's why we're here." Then his voice hardened. "This man . . ." He pointed to Rob's body. "Has transgressed. He must answer for it."

Malcolm shouted hoarsely, "He's *dead*! He's dead—just leave him alone!"

The psalmist leader shook his head. "It takes more than a car crash to kill a man like Rob."

While Amanda's eyes flicked toward Malcolm, the psalmist lunged—knocking the taser from her hand. He reached in again, grabbed Rob's limp form, and started dragging him out the door.

Cassandra surged forward, tackling the psalmist to the ground. They both scrambled to their feet. Cassandra threw a punch, but he blocked it effortlessly, spun, and kicked her square in the stomach. She fell back, wheezing, then sprang up again.

The psalmist leaped away—quick, agile, controlled.

She followed.

More red eyes crowded the window. From inside, they looked like vultures perched at the edge of a corpse.

Cassandra attacked again—an elbow strike this time. But the psalmist caught her wrist mid-motion.

"You'd make an excellent addition to our order," he said smoothly. "You fight with heart."

Then—*sweep*—his leg took her out from under.

Back in the limo, Malcolm slid lower into his seat, arms trembling. "They're just . . . staring at us."

"I know," Amanda whispered, lifting Rob again.

"They're surrounding us," Malcolm whimpered. "I have to call Daisy." He fumbled in his pocket, hands shaking. "They're going to kill us . . ."

"Malcolm!" Amanda snapped.

Outside, Cassandra screamed and hit the ground again.

The psalmist leaned into the limo once more, his grip tight with frustration as he yanked Amanda away from Rob.

With a grunt, he seized Rob by the arm and dragged him out of the vehicle.

"He's a heavy one," the psalmist muttered.

Two other figures emerged from the darkness, lifting Rob's limp body and slinging his arms over their shoulders.

"No!" Cassandra shouted from the ground.

Several psalmists closed in around her, daggers drawn and pointed as she crouched defensively, eyes darting between the glinting blades.

The lead psalmist approached her calmly, almost casually. Behind him, Rob was being carried off, barely conscious.

"You've got heart," the masked man said, his voice oddly respectful. "What's your name?"

Cassandra stayed silent, her eyes defiant.

Without warning, the psalmist drew his dagger and pointed it toward Amanda, who was still looking out the limo window. The threat was unmistakable.

Cassandra's glare hardened. "It's Cassandra," she growled. "Cassandra Chavez."

"Well then, Cassandra Chavez," the psalmist said, almost smiling under his mask. "Our order is open to anyone willing to convert. You've got strength… something rare. Much more than these three corrupt gangsters you protect."

A sudden *scream* broke the tension.

Everyone turned toward the source.

One of the psalmists carrying Rob had collapsed to the ground. Rob now stood—barely upright—blood running down his face, a dagger trembling in his hand.

The second psalmist quickly disarmed him, knocking the blade to the ground. Rob fell again, collapsing beside the one he'd managed to stab.

The lead psalmist chuckled, shaking his head.

"I told you—Rob's too damn stubborn to die."

He motioned to the others. "Pick him up. Let's go."

Suddenly, police sirens wailed in the distance—loud and close. Flashing red and blue lights pierced the shadows. Tires screeched.

The psalmists froze. Their heads turned toward the oncoming cars.

The lead psalmist looked at his soldiers, then gave a sharp command. "Disperse!"

He knelt briefly beside Cassandra, his voice low and cold. "Watch your step around these gangsters."

And then—just like that—they vanished into the night.

By the time the police cruisers skidded to a halt, the psalmists were gone.

Malcolm stood frozen as paramedics lifted Rob's stretcher into the ambulance. He trailed beside them, arguing with the medics even as they secured Rob inside the vehicle.

Nearby, Amanda sat silently on a folding stool, wincing while a medic dabbed antiseptic across the bleeding cut on her temple.

"You get into it with the wrong person tonight?" Officer Dan sneered, looming over her with his hands shoved in his coat pockets. "Your pal Rob bite off more than he could chew again?"

Amanda shot him a glare but said nothing.

The din of flashing lights, shouting officers, and clattering equipment filled the air. Chaos surrounded the crash site—squad cars, spectators, and a second vehicle embedded into the limo's side.

Another medic leaned toward Officer Dan and whispered something in his ear. Dan's expression shifted.

"Damn," he muttered, wiping his face. "Hey, Malcolm!" he called out. Malcolm looked up from fussing with the medics at the ambulance. "Get your butt over here."

Malcolm approached slowly, still glancing back as the ambulance doors slammed shut.

"They're telling me your driver didn't make it," Officer Dan said bluntly.

Malcolm looked away. He didn't respond.

"What, cat got your tongue?" Officer Dan continued, voice rising. "You waiting for your lawyer to show up or something? Why the silence?" He cast a glance at the retreating ambulance. "Don't worry about your buddy. Rob's not a dog, he's a damn fat cat—with nine lives."

Amanda clenched her fists. Malcolm glared at the officer. Even the medics tending Amanda paused, startled by Officer Dan's cruel tone.

"You were just at the club, right?" Officer Dan asked, shifting his attention. "You three came from there?"

Silence.

"Fine. I can run your tags. I just need to know what happened here."

"Did either of you see who was driving the car that hit you?" Officer Jessie asked as he walked up, tucking his notebook into his jacket after finishing his scene photos.

Dan scoffed. "Don't waste your breath, kid. These lowlifes don't talk."

Amanda gave a crooked smile. "You've got quite the handsome new officer here, Dan. A refreshing change from the pale-faced ones who used to arrest me for driving while Black."

Dan narrowed his eyes at Jessie. "He's new. He'll learn what trash he's dealing with soon enough."

Jessie stepped forward, his expression stiff. "Mind if I take this from here?"

Dan grumbled but backed off. Jessie crouched beside Amanda, holding out his tablet computer.

"Can you tell me anything? Anything at all?" he asked gently.

Amanda smirked. "You're not *that* handsome, kid."

"For God's sake, Amanda," Malcolm snapped. "Quit flirting and tell him what you know."

Jessie held up the tablet again, showing an image of a blood-streaked dagger. "Do you recognize this? Do you know who it belongs to?"

Amanda said nothing. Her eyes drifted away—toward Cassandra, who was now pushing through a crowd of reporters, their mics shoved in her face.

Jessie lowered the device, still waiting.

Dan chuckled from behind. "Don't waste your time, kid. These three like playing hardball. But I always get answers eventually."

Amanda rolled her eyes. "Stop filling his head with lies, Dan."

The officer stepped forward, raising his hand like he might strike her.

Jessie quickly intervened. "We've got what we need," he said firmly, standing up. The irritation in his voice was clear.

As the officers walked past Cassandra, Jessie glanced back to see her helping Amanda to her feet as the medics packed up.

"Jessie, let's go!" Officer Dan barked, already climbing into the patrol car.

Jessie hesitated, then followed.

The hospital room was unnervingly quiet. Malcolm sat beside Rob's bed, twiddling his thumbs. Machines beeped softly behind him, blinking with robotic rhythm. Rob lay unconscious, his face wrapped in bandages, covered in scrapes and bruises.

A knock broke the stillness.

"Come in," Malcolm called.

Amanda and Cassandra pushed past the curtain. "You've been here all night?" Cassandra asked, taking in Malcolm's wrinkled clothes and the dried blood staining his shirt.

"Yeah . . ." Malcolm replied wearily.

Amanda sat on the edge of the small couch next to the bed. "You really are like a little brother to him," she said gently.

Malcolm gave a faint smile, his eyes glassy. His exhaustion was plain—his shoulders sagged, his movements slow. It was clear he hadn't slept.

"I just had to make sure they didn't harvest his organs or something if he croaked," Malcolm joked, avoiding Amanda's gaze. But his voice cracked under the attempt at humor, betraying his worry.

"Sir, with all due respect . . . maybe you should get some rest," Cassandra offered softly.

"I'm fine," Malcolm replied, his tone gaining energy. "Didn't you hear Officer Dan? I've got nine lives. I'm like a fierce lion."

"I believe he was talking about Mr. Rob, sir," Cassandra corrected gently.

"Nah—he meant me," Malcolm smirked.

A raspy voice chimed in: "The only thing you do like a cat is piss in a box."

Everyone turned toward Rob as he stirred in the bed, blinking up at Malcolm. "You . . . you stayed all night?"

Malcolm turned away. "No. I was in the other room. Just came to check on you."

Amanda and Cassandra exchanged amused smiles, knowing he was lying.

Rob looked around the room, momentarily speechless. Then suddenly, he touched his chest, noticing the pulse oximeter on his finger and the oxygen tube in his nose. "Where are my clothes? You let them take my clothes? My swimsuit area is on full display! They put me in this . . . this gown?" he grumbled.

"Rob," Amanda said sharply, snapping his attention back. "You know why we're here."

"To make sure I'm okay," Rob deadpanned.

"Rob. Who were those men?" she asked firmly.

Rob tried to sit up, winced in pain, and collapsed back onto the bed.

"Rob!" Amanda warned.

"Fine," he wheezed. "It was the Psalmists."

All three leaned in, listening.

"They parade around like some soft-hearted, all-welcoming organization," Rob continued, then jabbed a finger at Amanda. "Kind of like your buffoon of a brother."

Amanda narrowed her eyes.

"They're a cult," Rob said coldly. "And I confronted them. They took something from me . . . and I took something back."

"What are they after?" Malcolm asked.

"Don't worry about it," Rob muttered. "I'll handle it. They're after me—not you."

"Just *Nightmare*," he added under his breath.

Cassandra leaned closer, puzzled. "Sir?"

Rob scowled at her, making her pull back slightly.

"With all due respect," Cassandra said cautiously, "the man I fought . . . he knew about all three of you."

"That's why I hired you," Rob shot back. "You do your job, this works itself out."

"Rob, this isn't that simple," Amanda pushed. "They could've killed us."

"But they didn't. We're alive. They want me—not you. I'm sure of it. Just . . . go on with your lives and let me handle this."

Amanda's patience thinned. "This bravado is getting old. We need the truth, Rob. What are we really dealing with?"

Rob exhaled heavily. "They're like . . ." He paused, searching for the word.

"Ninjas?" Malcolm guessed.

Rob rolled his eyes. "The group's called the Psalm Society. They act like some spiritual, enlightened movement—schools, churches, social outreach. But anyone paying attention knows they're a cult. A powerful one."

"You were part of it?" Cassandra asked. "They fight like demons."

"You calling me vulnerable?" Rob snapped.

"No, sir!" Cassandra raised her hands quickly.

Rob sighed. "They've got soldiers. Assassins. Like the ones who jumped us."

Amanda leaned in. "What do they want with us?"

"They don't. Just me."

"Rob . . ." Amanda urged.

"They stole someone I loved. She wouldn't come back. They'd already brainwashed her. So I took their symbol. Now they want it back."

"Then give it to them, man," Malcolm said.

"I did," Rob said flatly.

They all stared at him.

"I gave it back. But they think otherwise. It's a misunderstanding, and I'll fix it. Simple as that." He looked directly at Amanda, then Cassandra. "And no, we're not calling the cops. The Psalm Society's been operating outside the law for years. Police won't help, and they won't believe us anyway."

"So what do we do?" Cassandra asked.

"Nothing. Let me get out of this hospital. They'll come find me. I'll explain. It'll be handled."

The others exchanged looks. None were convinced.

After more debate, the two women eventually left the hospital.

Outside, Cassandra drove while Amanda sat quietly in the back seat, watching the city roll by.

"No offense, but I'm not sure about this plan," Cassandra said. "These people fight like terrorists. The police need to be involved."

Amanda remained silent, eyes still on the window.

"I think we coordinate with law enforcement. Get Rob some kind of security detail—"

"He knows what he's doing," Amanda cut in. "Cranky as he is, he's a strategist. His plans are . . . unorthodox, but they work."

Cassandra didn't respond. Amanda could tell she wasn't convinced.

"And these Psalmist people?" Amanda continued. "They should be more afraid of us."

Still, Cassandra said nothing.

Amanda tilted her head. "What do you think we do, Cassandra?"

"Do?" she repeated.

"I'm sure you've heard things . . . about Rob, Malcolm, and me. Strange things, haven't you?"

"I . . . I've heard many things, ma'am."

Amanda smiled softly. "You're sweet."

"Ma'am, are you sure we're going the right way?" Cassandra asked, growing nervous.

Amanda chuckled. "You're headed downtown, right?"

"Yes, ma'am."

"Then yes, you're going the right way."

The scenery changed as they drove. The clean, suburban glow gave way to rougher streets, older buildings, and tighter homes.

"Welcome to the ghetto, Cassandra," Amanda said with a smirk. "Pull over up there."

They stopped in front of a small house. A wired fence separated it from others. The yard was patchy, the windows barred. Several men stood in the front, their eyes shifting to the car. Chains glinted on their necks. Their expressions were hard, alert, and aggressive.

Amanda rolled down the window.

"Mandy!" one of them shouted. His face lit up as he rushed over and kissed her cheek. The others followed, crowding around the car with joy.

"I've got a friend," Amanda said coolly. "Wondering if you could take him for a walk."

A grin broke across the man's face. "Yeah?"

"My place. Maybe fifteen minutes?"

"Bring the boys?"

"All of them." Amanda smiled.

The man turned to the others, and they began chanting like a team preparing for kickoff.

Amanda rolled up her window. "You can go," she said to Cassandra.

"Ma'am . . . your house isn't fifteen minutes from here."

"We're going to my other house," Amanda replied calmly. "I'll direct you there."

Cassandra drove for about five minutes before reaching an older, freestanding house tucked into the corner of the neighborhood. Several cars lined the street outside. The front door was already open when she and Amanda approached.

Inside, a front desk sat in the middle of a large common area, with two open spaces branching off to either side.

To the left, a group of teenage girls sat at desks typing on laptops. A woman paced at the front, tossing out computer jargon as if she were leading a tech class. The room was cluttered with wires, devices, and cardboard boxes marked with a logo that read *Armory*.

On the right side, younger girls were either reading books or squabbling over tablet computers at small tables. Their playful learning atmosphere was abruptly shattered by the raised voice of a man yelling at the woman at the front desk.

"I want my daughter now!" he shouted, his words laced with profanity. The girls froze and turned toward the outburst, startled.

"Amanda, Mr. Brown is here again—he's demanding to see his daughter. I . . ." the receptionist stammered.

"You bitches can't keep me from my own child!" Mr. Brown bellowed, knocking over a nearby trash can. Several younger girls scattered upstairs in fear.

Amanda's face remained calm and composed. She stepped forward slowly, her tone measured.

"Mr. Brown, you know why you can't see your daughter. You remember what the social worker said."

"I don't give a damn what she said!" he shouted, stepping closer—so close their breaths mingled. Cassandra instinctively tightened her fists.

Amanda held up her hand, signaling Cassandra to stay put.

"He won't touch me," she said. Her voice remained firm. "Mr. Brown is a sorry excuse for a father who sees his child as a paycheck. She's nothing but government assistance to him."

"You don't know me, bitch!" he snapped, waving his arms as he loomed over her.

Amanda's eyes didn't even blink. "You need to leave."

"Or what?" he growled, clenching his fists.

"I'll make you leave," Cassandra interjected sharply.

"Easy, Cassandra," Amanda said coolly. "This small man is nothing but bark. He's the real female dog here."

Mr. Brown's jaw tightened. "Man, I don't need this. You're insane!" He turned toward the door. "Crazy—look at you. Covered in bruises. Looks like your man finally lost his patience. Can't say I blame him."

He stormed toward his car.

"Don't come back here harassing my staff," Amanda called after him.

"I'll be back tomorrow! Call the cops. I'll bring my lawyer."

"You probably can't even afford one," Amanda replied dryly.

"I don't need a lawyer. I got my boys—boys who handle bitches like you."

"They must be real tough guys—ganging up on women," Amanda shot back.

"Shut your mouth!" he shouted.

A new voice spoke up.

"You talk to a lady like that?" Mr. Brown turned. It was the man Amanda and Cassandra had met earlier—the ruffian with the streetwise crew.

"This him?" he asked Amanda.

"Take him for a walk," she said casually, turning her back and walking into the house.

Mr. Brown's yelp echoed through the air as the thuggish men tackled him. They pummeled him quickly and shoved him into a car. Moments later, the vehicle screeched off down the street.

Amanda smiled faintly as she heard it disappear.

Cassandra stared, wide-eyed. She couldn't believe what she had just witnessed.

"Amanda, I . . . I didn't know what to do," the receptionist said shakily.

"It's handled," Amanda replied. She reviewed a lesson plan with the woman, as if the confrontation hadn't just happened.

Meanwhile, Cassandra wandered, watching girls in various rooms giggle and work with devices. Two girls chasing each other accidentally bumped into her.

"Sorry!" one of them squeaked, then ran off after her friend.

"Girls, go do your homework," the receptionist called out, still talking with Amanda.

Amanda turned slightly. "Ms. Mary, can you call Esperanza to come here?"

Mary nodded and gestured to two older girls to go fetch her.

"Cassandra," Amanda said suddenly. Her tone was serious now.

Cassandra turned from the hallway.

Amanda reached out, and Ms. Mary handed her a tablet. Scrolling, Amanda continued, "I want you to understand something about me. My philosophy is simple: education and technology are the keys to true mobility. Especially for those born without access. Especially for Black and Brown children who are too often overlooked."

Cassandra nodded slowly, trying to process Amanda's words.

A small girl waddled into the room beside Ms. Mary.

"Ms. Amanda would like to speak with you," she said softly.

Amanda knelt. "Hi, sweetheart."

"Yes, Ms. Amanda?" the little girl said sweetly.

"I want you to meet someone." Amanda waved Cassandra over. "This is my friend Cassandra. She's very sweet."

Esperanza studied her carefully. "Is she my mommy?" she asked innocently.

Amanda and Ms. Mary both chuckled.

"No, sweetheart. She works with me," Amanda said, brushing the girl's hair back.

Cassandra stood frozen. Her body remained stiff, but her face revealed she was moved. Slowly, she knelt down to Esperanza's level.

She glanced at Amanda, who gave her a small, knowing nod.

Then Cassandra and Esperanza began speaking softly in Spanish. Esperanza giggled as Cassandra asked her questions, and soon, the two were laughing quietly like old friends.

"Okay. It was nice to meet you, Ms. Cassandra!" Esperanza said brightly in English before darting off after another girl who raced past them.

"Esperanza, we're not finished!" Ms. Mary called out, half-scolding.

"It's alright," Amanda said, waving her off gently.

Cassandra stepped closer, eyes scanning the space around them. "Do all these girls . . ."

Amanda raised an eyebrow, her mouth curling into a sly grin. "What?"

Cassandra hesitated. "Do they all live here?"

Amanda folded her arms and leaned slightly against the desk, her smile widening.

"The only one who lives here," she said with a hint of mystery in her voice, "is me."

A police car sat idling outside the hospital. Officer Dan slurped his coffee while Jessie typed into the onboard computer. Every now and then, they both glanced up as someone exited the building—but none of them were the person they were waiting for.

"I'm not sure this is legal," Jessie muttered, eyes still on his screen.

"Legal? Sure. Ethical? Not a chance," Officer Dan replied with a snort. "You wouldn't believe how far this city bends over for these lowlifes."

"I'm here to help, Officer," Jessie said sincerely. "That's why I joined up."

Dan gave a dry laugh. "I admire the enthusiasm. Hell, I even envy it. But I brought you out here so you could see what you're really dealing with. These gangsters? You and your team are in way over your heads."

They watched silently as a family wheeled a patient out of the hospital, the wind tugging at the automatic doors, forcing them open and closed like a haunted breath.

"That man from last night—Rob—he's a thug," Dan continued, his tone low and sharp. "Don't let that limp fool you. He has no respect for the law, the badge, or the country. He's tied up with Amanda and her crew from downtown... and Malcolm."

"Malcolm's the loudmouth with the flashy suits?" Jessie asked, half-distracted by his typing.

"Yeah. Daddy Warbucks. Runs that million-dollar military contractor. Lives up in Shiloh Heights."

Jessie raised a brow.

"That's where the rich folk live," Dan clarified. "Our salaries wouldn't cover a dinner reservation up there. And that spoiled trust fund punk is just as dangerous as those two street thugs. They think they run this city."

"What about the car crash last night?" Jessie asked, the edge in his voice hinting at irritation.

"Could've been Dunkin and his crew. Or Amanda's crowd—her kind always bring trouble. You think the city's dirty now? Wait until I show you downtown."

"Don't you find it odd no one was found in the car that hit them?" Jessie pushed.

"Rob probably scared 'em off. He tortures people, you know. He's not just a thug—he's an animal."

"Does Rob or Amanda actually lead a gang?" Jessie asked, glancing over.

"No," Dan growled. "And that's what makes them so dangerous."

Suddenly, the hospital doors slid open again—and Rob emerged, limping down the steps. The wind swept through his hair as he walked. Officer Dan leaned forward, squinting at the direction he took.

"Hey, Officer Dan!" Malcolm's voice came from Jessie's side of the car. He leaned casually against the window, startling both officers.

"Looking to arrest Rob again today?" he grinned.

"Get the hell away from my car," Dan barked, leaning over Jessie to shove the door.

"I don't think we've met," Malcolm said smoothly, extending a hand toward Jessie.

"Don't fall for the charm, kid," Dan snapped. "This one's got the mayor and half the city council eating out of his hand with those so-called humanitarian projects. Makes me sick."

Malcolm chuckled awkwardly. "Officer Dan, you're giving the kid the wrong impression."

"No—just the true one," Dan shot back. "Scum like you in high places makes it damn near impossible to clean out scum like Rob in low places."

"Now that's deep, Dan. Real poetic," Malcolm quipped.

"Damn it," Dan muttered, looking past him.

"Problem?" Malcolm said, that familiar mischievous grin creeping onto his face.

Dan's lip curled. "You . . . you better keep your wits about you, rich boy." He started the engine. "You, Amanda, and that old dog are in deeper than you think."

The squad car pulled away as Malcolm waved, mockingly cheerful.

Rob limped over. "He was watching, wasn't he?"

Malcolm nodded. "Just like you said."

Rob tossed a plastic bag filled with blood-streaked and wrinkled clothes into Malcolm's arms. "Where's the car? I'm going home. I need a real shower. I'm not staying in that hellhole another second. I'm not paying that hospital to lay in bed and eat trash food."

"I've got some clothes at my place," Malcolm offered.

Rob sighed. "Fine." He followed Malcolm toward the car, limping, tired, but determined.

CHAPTER 3

RAPID GUNFIRE CRACKED through the air.

Rob's body tensed as goosebumps crawled across his arms and legs. A chill ran through him, and he began to shiver. He gripped his weapon, but his arm wouldn't move—frozen. He could hear them coming. Louder. Closer. But from where?

Another burst of gunfire.

Still frozen. His heart pounded. He looked down at his camouflage uniform, trying to recall his training. His mind blurred. The presence of the enemy was unmistakable now—he could feel them, smell them. Rob's legs finally obeyed. He bolted in any direction his instincts pushed him, knowing they were on his heels.

A bullet grazed his arm. He hit the ground hard, face-first in the mud. Wind knocked out, he scrambled for his rifle—fingers clawing the earth—but instead clutched his bleeding arm.

Screw the gun.

He crawled.

Just crawl.

Then—a boot slammed into his side. Rob tumbled down a muddy incline, rolling. Shouts surrounded him, voices barking orders in a language he barely understood.

He was surrounded.

The fear of death choked him. Rob gave up. In that moment, the feisty player, always defiant, folded inward. He covered his face.

A gun clicked.

The chamber fired.

Rob squeezed his eyes shut—

He woke, gasping.

Sweat soaked the sheets. His hands trembled, heart racing like he'd just escaped hell itself. He sat up, wiping tears from his face, chest heaving. Still half in the dream, Rob staggered to the bathroom, one hand pressed to the wall for balance.

He collapsed to the floor.

Mouth open, lungs straining, he stared at the tile.

Rob lifted the toilet lid and dry-heaved, body convulsing. After a moment, he wiped his mouth, resting his head against the porcelain seat, breathing like he'd run a marathon.

Eventually, he stood and faced the mirror.

His reflection was a wreck.

Bags under his eyes, bloodshot pupils, half-healed wounds stretched across his chest where the stitches had torn. He lifted his shirt and traced one with his fingers. Then he grabbed a washcloth and wiped the sweat from his face. He turned back to the mirror and saw it. A reflection of a supernaturally being, not of reality but of nightmares. A being of terror, with its red piercing eyes, and its dark thirst for violence. This reflected being dawned a mighty medieval knight's suit of armor and hellish smoke radiated from its very presence. This was Rob's reflection, a reflection he saw only in the dark but for the last couple of years he witnessed it in the light.

Rob placed his hand on the mirror and this demonic medieval knight did as well. A slow calm came over Rob and his breathing returned back to normal. It was if Rob's true self, this hellish chaotic entity, was calming him, bringing him peace.

Something clattered behind him.

Rob froze.

His eyes darted around the counter. He snatched up a hairbrush, crouching low, heart thudding. Another sound—closer. He peeked out into the hallway. Nothing.

He turned—The hellish medieval knight was gone as he looked the mirror.

Rob hurled the brush into the glass.

The mirror shattered.

Silence followed.

Shards of the mirror cascaded onto the sink and floor. Rob leaned over the counter, panting, his reflection now a mosaic of broken edges.

He pressed against the wall and stumbled out.

"Mr. Rob?" a maid called gently as he passed her in the hall. He didn't respond.

Down the long staircase he went, slowly, weakly, clinging to the banister, one shaky step at a time. He reeked—of sweat, of vomit, of fear—but refused any offer of help from the staff who stared as he passed.

In the parlor, Malcolm was mid-argument on his phone.

"No, reschedule the damn meeting! I said I'm not going! I don't care what—" He looked up, palm on the speaker. "Business stuff."

Rob nodded, then collapsed onto the couch like a ragdoll. Malcolm eyed him warily.

"What do you mean, what do you tell them?" he barked into the phone. "Tell them something came up! I'll reschedule. Everyone's replaceable, Karen—even you." He hung up and turned back to Rob. "Good help's hard to find these days."

He studied Rob, now hunched and holding his chest, trembling as if he were about to vomit again.

"You okay?" Malcolm asked, more seriously now.

"Fine," Rob muttered, barely audible. "Daisy's coming home?"

"Yeah," Malcolm said, more subdued. "It's safer here. Those freaks are still out there. I'm not taking chances. This place is locked down—monitored twenty-four seven. Everything's connected to my phone."

"This stupid house . . ." Rob wheezed. "I could barely make it down here."

Malcolm chuckled. "Next time I'll install one of those automatic chairs for the stairs. Like in old folks' commercials."

Rob didn't even flinch at the joke—just kept breathing hard.

"Seriously though, you look worse than when we got hit."

"When was that again?" Rob asked faintly.

"What do you mean?"

"Never mind," Rob whispered, slumping lower.

Malcolm stared at him. "You were out cold, man. In and out for two days. I thought you knew."

Rob's eyes widened.

Malcolm's phone buzzed again. He answered, then waved two maids over. "Please get him some food," he said, covering the receiver. Then, lowering his voice further, he added with a smirk, "And try to get him in a bath. He's ripe."

As the maids scurried off, Rob looked down at his shaking hands, trying—and failing—to calm the tremors.

Like the crowded streets of New York, people bustled through the airport in streams—left, right, in clusters and pairs. Over the intercom, the phrase *Welcome to Shiloh City* played like a broken record, repeating as passengers disembarked from their planes and entered the infamous city.

Malcolm patted his thighs anxiously and glanced at the overhead clock. He rocked back and forth on his feet, nerves practically oozing from his body.

Rob, growing irritated, folded his newspaper higher to shield himself.

"You think the flight got delayed?" Malcolm asked, reaching over and crumpling Rob's paper to get his attention.

Rob pushed his hand away, then tried to smooth the wrinkles out of the page.

"Should I ask the airport staff again?"

Rob said nothing. He simply unfolded his paper again and resumed reading.

"Good morning," Cassandra said as she approached.

Rob sighed, clearly losing his patience. He lowered his paper again, his reading completely disrupted.

"Hey," Malcolm greeted without turning. He patted his thighs one last time, then hurried off. "I'm just gonna go check!"

"He's really excited to see his wife," Cassandra observed. "Does she travel often?"

Rob set the newspaper in his lap, giving up. He looked at Cassandra, her face full of curiosity.

"Daisy is Malcolm's daughter."

"Oh—sorry, I didn't mean to assume—"

"She's a sweet girl. But spoiled as hell," Rob said flatly. "Malcolm's little flower. Delicate Daisy. Pampered. Privileged. Completely out of touch with reality. Must be nice being pretty and rich."

He crossed his arms and looked away.

"Fate always favors the privileged," he added, quieter. "Well . . . sometimes. Then there's Malcolm."

Cassandra smiled gently. "He really loves her, though."

Rob looked down and muttered, "She's the only thing he has left."

Just then, Amanda appeared with a sharply dressed young man walking beside her. His hair was trimmed in a trendy, angular cut, and his box beard was manicured to perfection. His sneakers were loud. His clothes looked fresh off the rack.

"Don't forget, Manda," the man said cheerfully. "We still need to lock in two more venues this month. I sent you the schedule—you never replied."

Amanda didn't respond. Her eyes were elsewhere.

"Manda, Manda. Let me guess—you went on a date! You found a man? Girl, get it! Get it!" he laughed, bumping her hip playfully.

"Calm down," Amanda groaned. "I've been . . . preoccupied."

"All you do is work. You need to come out! Hit one of my shows. Stop bossing people around and update that wardrobe. We need to *exude* sexy."

Suddenly, the young man gasped and froze in his tracks, stretching an arm out in front of Amanda like a security barrier.

"What?" she asked, eyes scanning the airport.

"You didn't tell me Rob was going to be here," he whispered, visibly shaken.

Amanda chuckled under her breath, amused by his sudden anxiety.

As she stepped forward, he blocked her again.

"Wait—wait. Is that the new hire you mentioned?" He pointed toward Cassandra. "Damn . . . she is *fine.* Fine like a wine."

Amanda sighed and brushed past him.

"Don't even think about it," she said with a smirk. "You're not her type."

"Unless her type isn't sexy, I think I've still got a shot."

"The buffoon returns," Rob said, standing and limping over. "Mikey, the self-help guru."

Mikey instinctively stepped back. Rob gave a crooked smile and held out his hand.

"I hold no grudge. You stole my car. That was the past."

Mikey hesitated, then shook it. "Yeah, man . . . I'm glad to hear that."

Rob pulled him in for a hug.

Amanda and Cassandra watched Mikey's eyes widen in fear.

Rob whispered just loud enough to be heard: "Without you, I never would've met your sister. She tells me to lighten up all the time. So I'm telling *you*—lighten up, man."

Mikey stiffly nodded.

"Daisy's flight just landed!" Malcolm called, spotting them. "Mikey!"

Mikey quickly broke free from Rob's embrace and did a quirky handshake with Malcolm.

"I don't think we've met properly," Mikey said, turning to Cassandra. "I'm Mikey—Amanda's baby brother. I got the looks; she got the brains."

Amanda rolled her eyes.

"Nice to meet you. I'm Cassandra," she replied, shaking his hand.

"*Cassandra.* What a beautiful name." He kissed her hand dramatically. "Amanda didn't tell me she hired such a powerful, stunning woman. You saved her, didn't you? And even grumpy over there?" He pointed back at Rob. "That's real courage. If I may say—you're like a superhero and a runway model rolled into one."

Cassandra blushed, a shy smile forming.

Rob grunted. "He talks as much as Malcolm. Don't fall for it. He charms for a living."

"I didn't know Amanda had a brother," Cassandra said, clearly amused.

"Don't let the youthful glow fool you. I'm only a few years younger than her. But *you*—you make my sister look like she's from the Stone Age. This pantsuit is *everything.* My stylist would lose his mind if he saw you. Let me get him on the phone right now."

Cassandra giggled. "No, I've had these forever."

"Mikey, *cool it,*" Amanda warned.

"Big sisters—am I right?" he said, nudging Cassandra. "Listen, if you ever get tired of guarding grumps like these or Malcolm's mansion, give me a call." He fished around and handed her a card. "Call me if you want to vent about my sister. Or just, you know . . . call me."

Amanda and Rob glared at him.

"I'd love for you to come to one of my shows. I can get you backstage," Mikey added, winking.

Malcolm pointed to a door where passengers were beginning to exit.

He broke away from the group and waited anxiously.

One by one, passengers came through.

None were Daisy.

Malcolm groaned after every wrong face. "That's all the passengers, folks," the airport staffer called, closing the gate.

"No! That can't be!" Malcolm shouted. He began to climb over the barrier, prompting nearby security to step in.

"She was supposed to be on that flight!"

Heavy footsteps echoed down the hall.

A man carrying a tower of luggage emerged, panting.

"Daisy! Daisy!" Malcolm cried.

Behind him, a young woman adjusted her sunglasses. "*Daddy!*" she squealed, running into his arms.

"You need to get back behind the barrier," a guard warned.

Malcolm ignored him, wrapping a protective arm around Daisy as they approached the group.

"You can bring those over here," Daisy told the man still struggling with her bags.

"Aunt Amanda!" Daisy greeted, hugging her.

"Did you help a lot of people, honey?" Amanda asked, kissing her cheek.

"Yes! My team and I went to so many places. Look—I have pictures." She pulled out her phone.

"Hey, girl!" Mikey chimed in, reaching for a hug.

"Mikey, Mikey," Daisy smiled. "See you at your next show." They did a matching handshake.

Malcolm beamed and turned to Cassandra. "Daisy, I'd like you to meet Cassandra. She's a real warrior."

"Hello," Cassandra said, extending her hand.

"Get in here," Daisy said, swatting it away playfully and pulling her into a hug. She leaned back and snapped a selfie. "I'm tagging you. My followers need to see the woman who saved my dad."

"She's a goddess," Mikey added.

"I like it!" Daisy agreed.

Rob groaned and turned to walk away.

"Uncle Rob—you came too!" Daisy said, holding her arms out. Rob allowed a quick hug, giving her a soft pat on the back.

"Didn't think you noticed anyone but yourself," Rob said sarcastically.

Daisy laughed. "Uncle Rob," she said, gently pushing his chest. "When are you finally going to let Dad and me do something about this shaggy hair?" She playfully tugged on a strand.

A few feet away . . .

Cassandra leaned toward Amanda and whispered, "You think it's safe for her here?"

"A lockdown will be in place at the manor," Amanda replied. "But it'll feel like a prison to her."

Cassandra glanced at Daisy, confused.

Amanda continued, "Malcolm . . . he's overprotective. Maybe too much. Daisy's been sheltered most of her life—confined to the manor."

Cassandra looked to Mikey, who was chatting animatedly nearby. "And your brother?"

"I'm not worried about him. Mikey and Daisy are practically celebrities. Social icons. The Psalmist group wants to stay low-key—Rob and I agree on that. They attacked us at night, then vanished when the cops showed. They could've struck in broad daylight, but didn't. Influencers like those two? They're too visible. The group won't risk exposure." She paused, watching Malcolm laugh and chat with his daughter. "Malcolm, though . . . he's just too protective."

Cassandra quietly pulled out her phone and began researching the Daisy and Mikey on the web.

"Shiloh City," Daisy muttered, taking a slow look around the airport lobby. "Can't say I missed it."

"It's where home is," Malcolm beamed. "Where family is."

Daisy didn't respond. Her eyes drifted to her pile of luggage. "Daddy, let's have someone grab my bags. We should go out to eat. Just us—we can catch up."

"*Out?*" Malcolm chuckled. "We can eat at the manor. Have a nice dinner there. Everyone can come."

"No, Daddy," Daisy said firmly. "I mean *out.*"

The two locked eyes. Neither budged.

An announcement echoed over the intercom, and a crowd passed between them. As the people moved, it almost looked like Daisy was drifting farther from her father—physically and emotionally.

Before Malcolm could say another word, a voice called out: "Daisy!"

A group of young women rushed over, squealing and hugging her. Laughter erupted as they gathered around.

Malcolm tried to speak, but his voice was drowned out by the commotion.

"Come on, girl—let's go out!" one of Daisy's friends said. The group began to pull her away.

"Daisy! We need to go back to the manor—now!" Malcolm barked. His face reddened; his voice cut through the crowd like a whip.

"Daddy," Daisy said with an embarrassed laugh, placing her arm around him. Her friends went silent, the tension hanging thick. "I know you're happy to see me. I'll make time for *everyone.*"

"Say goodbye to your friends. You'll see them later. We're going home."

"I'm thirty, in case you forgot—"

"I don't give a damn how old you are. I *said* we're going back."

Daisy gave him a cunning smile and began typing on her phone. "Maybe Mom should weigh in on this."

"Daisy, don't bring your mother into—"

"Hey, Mom . . ." Daisy said into the phone.

Rob groaned nearby and motioned Amanda and the others to follow him. "This won't end well."

Malcolm clenched his fists. "Daisy, stop this—"

"If I can't get through to you, maybe she can."

"Daisy, what's going on?" her mother's voice came faintly over the line. Background noise suggested she was at a party.

"Dad's being a control freak again!" Daisy shouted into the phone.

"What?" her mother yelled. "Daisy, this isn't a good time!"

"Is Rob there? Is *Rob* with you?" her mother asked, her voice now tinged with fear.

Rob smirked when he heard his name.

"No," Daisy lied, glancing at Rob.

"Malcolm!" her mother shouted through the noise.

Malcolm leaned toward Daisy's friends. "Ladies, why don't you wait for us outside."

"No, Daddy. Don't dismiss them. You *always* do this."

"I'm trying to protect you."

"From *what*? Spending time with my friends? Living my life?"

"Malcolm, stop being so controlling!" Daisy's mother's voice cut in—louder now. She must have stepped away from the party.

Malcolm's shoulders stiffened. He smiled nervously at the group.

"Ladies, please. We'll be with you shortly."

"Malcolm," Daisy's mother snapped, "don't try to hide who you are. Let Daisy live her life. If you're not strong enough—"

"*I'm not strong enough?*" Malcolm shouted, suddenly grabbing the phone. "Don't *you*, of all people, lecture me about strength!" He turned to Daisy. "If you want to go out with your friends get your own place and find a job."

"Don't listen to your *weak* father, Daisy!" her mother shouted.

SNAP.

Malcolm crushed the phone in his hand. Gasps rang out as the shattered pieces dropped to the floor.

"You're coming home *now,* Daisy," Malcolm growled, grabbing her arm and pulling her through the group.

"Let go!" Daisy yanked herself free.

"You like the manor? The clothes, the jewelry, the life I pay for? It all ends. Right now."

Cassandra's eyes widened. The shift in Malcolm's demeanor was disturbing. His voice—his energy—it was as if someone else had taken over.

"Let's go," Malcolm ordered, motioning for Daisy to walk ahead.

Daisy paused, flicked her hair out of her face, and stepped past him. "It won't always be this way," she said with a hard stare.

Cassandra drove Rob through the heart of Shiloh City. In the rearview mirror, she saw him slowly drifting to sleep. Their eyes briefly met before she looked away.

"We're going the right way," Rob muttered, half-asleep. "Don't worry."

"Yes, sir," Cassandra replied.

Rob flared his nostrils. "Do me a favor?"

"Yes, sir."

"Drop the soldier act. You and I—we're no longer in uniform. The red, white, and blue never did a damn thing for us."

Cassandra's tone stiffened. "I'll always serve my country—no matter where I am."

Rob leaned forward from the back seat, a teasing grin on his face. "Ah. There it is. Some fire in you. You get a little grit when the flag's insulted."

She said nothing.

"I hope you use that grit in the job. That's why I hired you. I saw you. I *was* there—when you punched that guy for disrespecting you and your comrade. When you stood up to hypocrisy."

Cassandra's attention faltered. She swerved slightly, correcting the wheel.

"I was there," Rob repeated. "Saw what they did. You, of all people, who've never been truly welcomed here—how can *you* still believe in that flag?"

"This country gave my family a chance they never would've had," Cassandra said, her voice steady. "It's not perfect, but I still believe in the bigger picture."

Rob leaned back. "Everyone forgets the little pictures. But those make up the big one—the ugly underbelly.

That's what allows the Psalmist Society . . . or Amanda's idiot brother . . . to do what they do."

"We're out in the open. Do you think they'll attack?" she asked, steering the conversation back.

"You already know the answer. Amanda told you our theory. They hit us at night, when we were isolated. They won't strike now. Not out in the open."

Cassandra sighed, gripping the wheel tighter as Rob continued.

They pulled into a lot beside an older building. Rob opened the door and stepped out.

"You're about to see what Shiloh City is really made of," he said. "The filth isn't just in the ghettos or the mansions. It's *here*—in the gut of the city."

He pointed at a rundown trailer office up the hill.

"Watch my back. And remember your training."

Cassandra looked toward the nearby street. The club wasn't far. Her eyes shifted back to Rob, who surveyed the area like a soldier entering a battlefield.

"Where are you going?" she asked.

Rob grinned. "Getting bold, are we?"

He limped away from the car. "I'm going to talk to Dunkin. If there's anyone who knows what's happening, it's him."

The wind whipped around him as he walked off.

"Need backup?" Cassandra called.

"I'm fine," he said, barely glancing back. Then under his breath: "Time to give fate the finger again."

Some time passed . . .

Cassandra waited in the car, concern growing. She reached for her phone to call Amanda, then stopped. Doubt clouded her.

The sun dipped lower. The day was almost gone.

She opened the car door and climbed the hill toward the trailer. The wind hit her like a wave, nearly knocking her off balance. She slipped one hand under her jacket, gripping the handle of her firearm.

She crept up the stairs and peered through the trailer window.

It was empty.

Disappointed, she turned back. The wind howled again. She crossed her arms, bracing against the cold, and headed back to the car—alone.

Suddenly, a man burst out of the old building.

Cassandra jumped, drawing her gun instinctively. The man sprinted past her, clothes torn, face scratched and bloody—he looked like he'd been mauled by a wild animal.

Without hesitation, the quiet soldier moved toward the entrance, gun raised. She stepped inside, her boots quiet on the dusty floor. The sound of labored breathing echoed from deeper within the structure.

Room after room revealed illicit activity: men counting stacks of cash, others drinking, laughing, watching sports on flickering TVs. Smoke curled in the air. A haze of chaos and corruption hung heavy.

Following the sound of strained gasps, Cassandra approached a larger chamber at the back of the building.

Inside, Dunkin was on the floor, bleeding from his mouth, yet grinning wildly like he enjoyed the abuse.

"Robbie, I don't know anything!" Dunkin pleaded.

Rob stepped on his foot, pressing down hard.

"Stop holding out on me!"

Dunkin screamed, panting between laughter. Rob turned away in disgust, wiping sweat from his brow.

Dunkin leaned forward, slowly reaching for the table in the center of the room.

BANG!

Rob fired a shot inches from Dunkin's hand. The blast echoed through the walls.

Dunkin flinched but then cackled. "My men will be here soon, Robbie."

Rob rolled his eyes, still aiming. "They're probably passed out drunk—just like you."

He kept his gun fixed on Dunkin while rifling through papers on the desk.

"Didn't think I'd ever see *Nightmare* looking scared."

Rob froze.

His jaw clenched. His eyes darted like something personal had just been unearthed.

"*That's what they called you,* after the military," Dunkin continued, licking blood off his lip. "The gun-for-hire. The man in the mask. A soldier with no allegiance to country or code—only to the green."

He grinned wider.

"You tortured captives. Burned them. They said a monster haunted the night—a knight in a black mask. Pretentious? Sure. But fitting for you."

"Shut up." Rob turned to leave.

"I've been wondering what those guys wanted," Dunkin called louder. "Those men in black. The red eyes."

Rob spun back around.

"They came looking for something . . . didn't they?"

Rob's patience snapped. "Tell me what you know."

Before he could react, a man appeared from the shadows, gun drawn.

"You've got nerve walking onto my turf, Robbie," Dunkin sneered. "No partners this time. Just a limping old dog waiting to be put down." He danced mockingly on one leg. "Well, your master's here. *I'm* your master now."

Rob dove to the ground and fired.

BANG!

The gunman dropped. Rob scrambled over and grabbed the weapon off the floor. He now had one gun pointed at Dunkin, the other sweeping the room.

"Tell me what you know. Now. Or I'll make you wish I killed you."

"You won't kill me," Dunkin smirked. "Who else would you use as a punching bag?"

Rob growled. "Keep talking and you'll find out."

Suddenly, he felt a sharp jab at his back.

A Psalmist had snuck up behind him, pressing a dagger against his spine.

"Drop the weapon!" the masked man barked. "You've transgressed!"

Rob's hand tightened around the grip.

"Drop it, now!"

In one swift move, Rob twisted, angled his arm behind him, and fired.

CRACK!

The Psalmist howled as the bullet hit his foot. Rob pivoted, now aiming one gun at Dunkin and the other at the fallen attacker.

"Enough, Rob."

The voice was calm and commanding.

The Psalmist *leader* entered the room, face hidden behind a cold, emotionless mask. Behind him, Cassandra was marched in, two more cult members close behind, daggers at her back.

Rob's lip curled. His nostrils flared as he stared down the masked man.

"Drop them, Robbie. Drop them!" Dunkin laughed.

"I'll drop *you*, you fat—" Rob muttered.

"Please," the Psalmist leader said evenly. "We don't want to do this."

"I don't have the necklace," Rob said, eyes locked with the leader. "I gave it to your Dr. Jonathan. I'm not lying. You've already taken enough from me." His voice lowered. "Fate's dealt me bad cards my whole life."

He raised a gun slightly as Dunkin tried to inch away.

Dunkin, trying to taunt, wiggled his hips suggestively.

The Psalmist leader moved like a flash—knocking one of Rob's guns to the floor.

Rob countered, swinging the other gun toward him, but the leader grabbed his wrist. The two struggled in a tense standoff, neither giving ground. The leader pulled a dagger—Rob slapped it from his hand.

They grappled again.

The leader shoved Rob, knocking him to the floor. His gun skidded across the room.

From the sidelines, Dunkin cheered like a fan at a wrestling match. Rob rolled, snatched a dagger from the man he had shot earlier, and clashed blades with the leader. Metal rang as they fought. The leader kicked Rob back. Rob slashed but missed—his opponent struck first, slicing Rob's wrist.

The dagger clattered to the floor.

Rob clutched his bleeding arm.

The leader lunged, aiming a punch.

Rob surged forward, headbutting him with all his strength.

The leader staggered back, then kicked Rob down.

Rob hit the floor hard—motionless, arms sprawled out.

The Psalmist leader reached down, grabbed Rob by the collar, and yanked him upright.

Rob coughed . . . and smiled.

The gun he had retrieved was now pressed against the leader's chest.

The Psalmist looked down slowly—his own gun was now aimed directly at Rob's *groin.*

Everyone in the room froze.

Even Dunkin stopped laughing.

"Sometimes you just have to accept the cards fate has dealt you," the Psalmist leader said quietly.

That sentence—simple, cold—hit Rob like a hammer.

A tear rolled down his cheek.

Memories exploded in his mind.

The wind outside howled again, echoing through the building.

Time slowed.

His body trembled.

His heart pounded.

And for the first time in a long time . . . Rob remembered.

CHAPTER 4

"ROBERT," A TIRED, lugubrious voice called out. "Robert!" the man shouted, his tone now edged with irritation.

Rob stirred. The dry hay beneath him rustled as he shifted from sleep, startled by the sudden change in tone.

"Yes, Father," he mumbled.

"It's time to get up."

Rob's father pulled open the barn doors, and the morning sunlight pierced through like a blade. Rob winced, shielding his eyes from the blinding light.

"We're late," his father muttered.

"Daddy, may I please lie down for just a few more minutes?" Rob begged, his voice pleading.

"No. We're already late—didn't I tell you?" his father snapped. "Now come on. Grab the tools."

The man's eyes sagged with exhaustion, his face drawn and lifeless. Young Rob tried to keep a polite expression, but the early morning weight was too much. He let out a quiet whine, following his father out of the barn.

The moment they stepped outside, the heat crept up on them, thick and smothering. For a brief second, they both hesitated, glancing back at the barn—their shelter, now behind them.

The sun rose quickly, beating down on them as they worked the land. Time stretched, an eternity of shoveling, tilling, and wiping sweat from their brows.

By midday, the sun hung high overhead, casting sharp shadows across the vast, dusty field. Rob's father leaned heavily on his rake, wiping his forehead with a trembling hand. "Hey, Robert . . ." he breathed, pausing to catch his breath. "I think that's enough for today."

Rob's eyes lit up with surprise and gratitude. He looked at his father, unsure what had prompted the sudden generosity.

"Why don't you clean up in the barn," his father said, "and we'll go for a drive."

Rob's surprise deepened. His father's tone had shifted again—softer now. Almost kind.

They climbed into their old grey car, rust climbing up its sides like ivy. One window was cracked, the seats torn, the floor stained from years of hard living. Rob's father cursed under his breath as he turned the key, pounding the dashboard until the engine sputtered to life.

The car jostled over the uneven field, Rob bouncing in his seat.

They stopped in the middle of the field. Rob looked at his father, puzzled.

"Hey, buddy, I'm too tired to drive back," his father said. He stepped out and circled to the front of the car. "You want to take us back to the barn?"

Rob's face lit up again. He scrambled into the driver's seat as his father slid into the passenger side. Rob could barely see over the steering wheel, his excitement almost too much to contain.

"Hang on, son. You've got to put it in drive first," his father reminded him, chuckling. He reached into the back and pulled out a couple of old pillows. "Sit on these."

Rob hopped out, letting his father stack the pillows on the seat.

"Once you shift into gear, just press gently on the gas. Let the car do the rest. Got it?"

Rob nodded, wide-eyed with youthful wonder.

"Slow though, Robert. Take it slow."

Rob eased the car forward, carefully navigating the bumpy field. His father smiled, watching the barn grow closer through the windshield.

"Good job, boy. Just park it right over there," he said, pointing.

They stepped out and walked back into the barn.

"Wash up," Rob's father instructed, opening a small cabinet as Rob sank onto the pile of hay, exhausted.

"How many chickens do we have over there?" his father asked, pointing out through a small hole in the barn wall.

Rob squinted through the slat. "In the pen? I count three."

"Go outside and check. You can't count them from in here," his father snapped.

As Rob stepped out, he heard his father rummaging through the cabinet. Bottles clanked together.

"Damn . . . Empty. Why the hell would I put it back if it was empty? Damn it."

"Three chickens," Rob reported as he re-entered.

His father grunted, still hunched over the cabinet.

"Well . . . I guess we're having chicken tonight," he said, grabbing an axe and heading for the door.

Rob froze. His breath caught in his throat as he saw the axe hanging behind his father's belt. His hands trembled.

But then, as Adam opened the barn door, he caught sight of his son's pale face.

"Heck . . . we got that diner in town," he said suddenly. "Let's see if the old girl can make it."

Rob's face lifted, but unease lingered in his expression. He watched silently as Adam slowly removed the axe and placed it by the door.

The town diner was a small, worn-in place, usually filled with farmers and tired townsfolk.

"Hey, Rob," called a woman in an apron, smiling as the boy darted inside.

"My father let me drive again today," Rob beamed, hopping onto a stool at the counter. He launched into a vivid retelling of his day.

The waitress listened fondly, until her eyes drifted to the door. Her smile faded. "Rob, where's Adam? Did your dad come in with you?" she asked, concerned.

Rob hesitated. His smile vanished.

"He went over to the gas station," he said softly.

Just then, Adam entered—swaggering, laughing, his face plastered with a crooked grin. He ruffled Rob's hair. The boy stiffened, eyes darting nervously around the room.

"He tell you he drove today? Boy's getting better every time," Adam said proudly.

He leaned over to kiss the waitress. She recoiled slightly. Rob could she was very uncomfortable with Adam's advancements. Almost as if she were afraid of him.

"Adam, you smell like you've been rolling around with your chickens."

"That's because I have," he said, grinning as he planted a quick kiss. Adam held the kind waitress tight wrapping his arms around her waist.

"Let me get you two some menus," the waitress said, clearly uneasy.

Rob sat stiffly, his eyes locked on the counter.

"What's the matter, son?" Adam asked, eyes still trailing the waitress.

"Daddy . . . I changed my mind. Let's just eat one of the chickens at home."

"Why?" Adam's voice turned sharp.

"I'm worried . . . Last time we couldn't pay—"

"Who makes the money, son?"

Rob stayed silent.

Adam's smile disappeared.

"I handle things around here. You don't tell me what—"

"Adam, Adam," the waitress said quickly, trying to de-escalate.

"Damn." Adam stood abruptly. The diner quieted. Eyes turned toward them. "Is what I do not good enough? Are you not satisfied?"

Rob didn't answer.

"Tell me, son!" Adam shoved him lightly—enough to make the boy catch himself on the edge of the table.

"Adam," the waitress snapped, helping Rob back to his seat.

"Not good enough for him. Not good enough for myself," Adam muttered, pacing.

"I'm sorry, Daddy. Please . . ." Rob's voice broke.

"No, no—let it out. That old farm, waking up before sunrise—it's not good enough?"

"Daddy, I'm sorry," Rob cried.

"Adam, stop!" the waitress commanded.

"You all taking his side now? Fine. Let him find his own way home!" Adam barked.

Tears streamed silently down Rob's cheeks as the diner buzzed with murmurs and scornful glares.

"Shut up! All of you—shut up!" Adam shouted, sending everyone recoiling in silence.

"These people ain't doing nothing for you," Adam growled, gripping Rob's shoulders and turning the boy toward him. "They ain't paying no goddamn bills. They sure as hell ain't putting a roof over your head."

The tension in the diner swelled as a few of the patrons edged closer, faces tight with anger.

"Get out of my face. Get out!" Adam shouted, shoving through the crowd and storming outside.

The clatter of the diner returned slowly as customers turned their attention to Rob, who sat quietly wiping tears from his eyes.

"Here, sweetie," the kind waitress said gently, placing a plate of warm food on the counter in front of him.

Rob picked up a few biscuits from the plate and stuffed them into the pockets of his dirty overalls. Then, without a word, he slipped off the stool and ran toward the door, ignoring the voices calling after him.

Outside, Adam cursed under his breath, slamming the trunk of the car. He rummaged frantically through its contents.

"Damn . . . they're all empty," he muttered.

"Daddy . . ." Rob approached cautiously, his small hand holding out a crumbled biscuit. "I . . . I got you something. I'm sorry."

Adam didn't respond. He slammed the trunk shut and walked to the driver's seat.

"Sometimes you just gotta accept the cards fate deals you," he muttered, his eyes distant. "You're gonna have to learn that the hard way, son."

The engine sputtered and roared. Smoke choked the air. Rob stumbled back as the tires spun, and Adam tore down the road, leaving his son standing in the dust.

Night fell.

The summer air thickened, and the sound of crickets harmonized around Rob as he trudged the long road back to the barn. Open farmland stretched endlessly under the star-scattered sky.

When he finally reached the barn, Rob paused. Several unfamiliar cars were parked outside.

Inside, voices murmured and laughed.

"How much you need now, Adam?" a man called out.

"Just a few, come on," Adam replied, his tone defensive.

Rob slowly pushed open the barn door. Candlelight flickered against the walls. A group of men sat in a rough circle on logs, their faces half-lit and half-shadowed, giving them a ghostly appearance. The air was thick with the scent of sweat, tobacco, and labor.

"I used to have ten chickens out there," one man teased, sipping from a cup. "Now I count three. You're eating me out of house and home, Adam."

"You should come watch me. I let the chicken run and time it just right with the axe," Adam chuckled. The group laughed with him.

Another man leaned forward, his suit crisp against the contrast of the others' sweat-stained clothes. His blue jacket rested neatly on the log beside him—clean, pressed, out of place.

"Adam, how much of a freeloader are you?" he asked, voice like smooth gravel. "You chew my tobacco. Live in my barn."

"I work your land," Adam grunted, bristling.

Suddenly, the group froze. A soft rustle came from the haystack in the corner.

"You learn your lesson, boy?" Adam called.

Rob lay on his side, using his hands as a pillow. He said nothing.

"I heard you drove today, Rob. Your dad's always breaking the rules," the man in the suit said with a smirk. He was the only one not drinking. His presence demanded attention.

Rob nodded faintly.

"Answer your Uncle Alex," Adam snapped.

"It's alright," Alex said, raising a hand. "Kid's probably just tired."

"Tired from being ungrateful. Tired from being a nuisance," Adam said, his voice sharp as he stood suddenly, rage flickering in his eyes.

He clenched his fists and began to walk toward Rob.

The men rose with him, urging calm.

"Sit down, Adam," one of them said quietly.

Adam shoved a man aside. The tension mounted. Candlelight shook with every movement. Shadows danced along the wooden walls like violent spirits.

Then Alex spoke.

"Sit down."

His voice was calm, but it cracked like a whip through the barn.

The scuffle stopped. One by one, the men returned to their seats.

Even Rob, hidden in the hay, leaned forward, something inside him awakening—some deep, unfamiliar curiosity flickering to life.

Adam was the last to sit. His stare burned into Alex.

He picked up his cup and drank in long, angry gulps. The barn was silent except for the sound of swallowing.

Alex waited, then leaned forward, fingers steepled.

"I command respect," he said with a quiet smile.

Adam shifted, eyes darting around the circle.

"You think you can tell me what to do because you think you own me," Adam said slowly.

"Adam . . . don't," Alex warned, the grin vanishing from his face.

"What if I quit, huh? What if I stopped picking your cotton? Stopped working your land? I ain't your damn slave—I didn't come off your goddamn boat."

Alex sat still for a moment. Then, quietly:

"You quit, Adam, and no one will hire you. You're a nightmare. A liability. It's by God's grace I keep you around. A goddamn nightmare, that's what you are."

Rob's eyes sharpened. He didn't blink. It was as if Alex's words sliced open something inside him. He caught them in the air and folded them into himself like sacred truth.

"You don't know my life," Adam muttered.

"No," Alex said, leaning forward. "But I know your kind. You piss in your pants every time life hands you manure. You accept the hand you're dealt. You beg for it. You stretch out your cold, dirty hands and take whatever scraps you're given."

Adam stood again, furious, his body trembling.

The men around Alex rose, bracing themselves.

But Alex raised a hand. "Let him," he said. "Let's see what he does."

"You need me," Adam seethed. "You can't do jack without me."

"No," Alex said, rising slowly, his voice low but deadly. "You can't work without me. You can't *survive* without me. So, what are you gonna do?"

Adam stopped, fists clenched but unmoving. Slowly, he slumped back onto his log, defeated.

"You . . . you . . ." he muttered, eyes narrowing. "Gangster."

"What was that?" Alex leaned in. "What did you say?"

Adam didn't answer.

Alex slapped him hard across the face. The sound cracked through the barn like thunder.

Adam clutched his cheek, stunned, eyes wide.

"I asked you a question, Adam," Alex said coldly. "What did you say?"

Adam's lips pouted and his eyes became watery.

"Cry me a damn river, Adam," Alex scoffed, his voice sharp as broken glass. "We all got problems. Maybe you just haven't learned your lessons. Or maybe—just maybe—you're not strong enough."

He glanced toward young Rob, who was still watching wide-eyed from the shadows.

"Come here, kid," Alex commanded.

Rob hesitated, but eventually shuffled over, nervous and cautious. His eyes flicked to his father, whose face had turned beet red. Veins bulged from his neck like cords pulled too tight. His expression was so intense it looked as if his head might burst.

"You don't have to take what life throws at you," Alex said, his gaze fixed on Adam. "That's one lesson your old man never learned."

Alex reached into his coat pocket and pulled out a wad of bills. He slapped the cash into Rob's hand.

"Your dad gets none of it. You hear me?"

Rob blinked in surprise. A sly, almost disbelieving smile began to form—until he looked at Adam. His father's face was twisted in fury, his eyes wide and unblinking, trembling with rage and humiliation.

"Look at me," Alex said, drawing Rob's gaze back. "Don't worry about him."

He gave a nod, and the men around him began to rise, gathering their belongings.

"You leaving?" Adam muttered, swaying on his feet. He leaned back suddenly and collapsed to the ground. "I can't enjoy anything. The goddamn earth takes everything from me . . . it's red, blood-red, 'cause it keeps cuttin' me. It takes everything. My wife. My job . . ."

"Piss off, Adam," Alex muttered as he stood. "We're not gonna sit here and listen to you whine."

"What am I supposed to do? Huh?" Adam groaned, his voice cracking. "Rob's stuck here. I'm stuck. One move, another move—it don't matter. It's the same damn result. These are the cards I was dealt."

Alex and the others were nearly at the door.

"Stop being a damn coward and grow a pair," Alex snapped.

"No!" Adam suddenly shouted.

He lunged toward the wall, grabbed the axe, and hurled it with all his strength. The blade slammed into the wooden wall with a heavy thud, burying itself deep. The men flinched.

Silence fell.

Adam stood there breathing heavily, eyes wide as if realizing what he'd just done. He raised his hands slowly, palms out, as if to apologize.

Alex, calm and cold, reached behind his back and drew a pistol.

"I didn't mean it," Adam whispered, backing up, panic overtaking him.

Rob's eyes went wide. His knees locked. His heart pounded.

Alex advanced, slow and deliberate. Adam tripped over a log and fell to the dirt.

"Please . . . man . . ." Adam whimpered from the ground, staring up at the barrel of the gun.

Rob squinted, as if bracing for the blast. The silence stretched until the deafening sound of a single gunshot rang out. For a moment, Rob couldn't hear anything—just the fading echo bouncing inside his skull.

Then came the moaning.

Rob opened his eyes. His father writhed on the floor, holding his chest and gasping. But there was no blood.

No bullet wound.

"Let's go," Alex ordered, tucking the pistol away. He held the barn door open for his men, then turned to look back at Rob. "You know the difference between your old man and me?" Alex said, eyes sharp. "He accepts the cards life deals him."

He shut the door behind him. The gust extinguished the candle flames, and the barn was plunged into darkness.

Rob ran to his father's side. Adam was on the ground, panting heavily, clutching his chest. Rob examined him—filthy, sweaty, angry—but unharmed.

"This damn red earth!" Adam roared, punching the dirt beside him. He scooped up a handful and threw it. A dusty cloud blew into Rob's face, making him stagger back, coughing and rubbing his eyes. "I can't escape its toil. I can't escape," Adam groaned, crawling over to one of the discarded cups. He took a long drink and slumped against a log, head tilted back.

Rob wiped his eyes—and when he looked again, something had changed.

The barn was still.

His father lay sprawled on the dirt, mumbling incoherently, half-drunk and defeated. Rob watched in silence as Adam turned and lazily spilled liquor onto the ground. The liquid formed a dark trail, glinting under the faint moonlight streaming through the barn's holes.

The puddle reached Rob's feet. He stared into it. His small reflection stared back.

Something stirred inside him.

A breath. A choice.

Without a word, Rob walked over to the old cabinet and gathered everything he could find of value—worn tools, coins, scraps. He bundled them into a blanket, tied it to a stick, and slung it over his shoulder.

He took one last look at the barn—the moon now its only guardian—and stepped into the night.

He didn't look back.

CHAPTER 5

SHOUTS AND CRIES echoed through the vast chamber, crashing against every wall like a rising storm. Chaos reigned as the psalmist members pleaded with their leader—his weapon drawn, locked in a deadly standoff with the feisty player. Neither man moved. Neither blinked. Both were ready to die before backing down.

"Squad leader, please—put down the gun," one member begged, stretching out a trembling hand. "You know we don't use those."

"You heard him," Rob sneered, cocking his head with a defiant grin. His gun stayed trained on the leader's chest. He stood so close that his forehead brushed the cold surface of the leader's mask.

"You first," the psalmist leader snapped, trying to shove Rob back.

From the sidelines, one of the psalmists broke formation. He lunged from Cassandra's side, charging at Rob.

"Nope. Nope." Rob waved the pistol slightly, eyes never leaving the leader. The would-be attacker froze in place, hands half-raised.

Across the room, Dunkin casually retrieved his chair and dropped into it like a spectator at a prizefight. He leaned back and chuckled.

"Robbie . . . Robbie," he sang in a slow, mocking tone. "Don't let these freaks rattle you."

"Shut up!" Rob barked, flashing him a deadly glare without breaking his stance.

Dunkin looked at Cassandra holding up her hands with a psalmist member holding a dagger behind her back. "You're the bitch that nailed me in the head." Dunkin stood up from his chair. The behemoth stomped over toward her.

"Stop!" the psalmist member yelled to Dunkin still holding a dagger to Cassandra's back.

Cassandra elbowed the psalmist member in the face. The psalmist member held their head and moved away from Cassandra. She kicked the psalmist member and then twirled her attacker into Dunkin's pathway.

As if he was swatting a fly, Dunkin pushed the psalmist aside. The massive giant put both of his fists together slamming them into Cassandra. The quiet soldier dodged him just in time as he smashed his fist into a pillar in the room. Dunkin left a huge dent in the pillar.

"Come here," he began trying to grab Cassandra but she dodged his massive hands that tried to grab her. The behemoth chased Cassandra around the room.

"I can help your friend. Please just drop the gun," The psalmist leader said, putting more force toward Rob.

"Help her to the grave," Rob exerted more force.

"We're never going to budge," the psalmist leader pleaded.

"Never," Rob said almost to a whisper in the psalmist leader's mask. "But here's the thing, you won't shoot me." The psalmist leader's eyes focused on Rob. "If you wanted to shoot me you would have already. And seeing your cult doesn't believe in guns, the question is what am I waiting for?" Rob smiled his sly smile at the psalmist leader.

The psalmist leader's eyes lit up, then darted toward the floor.

Rob pulled the trigger. The shot cracked through the room like thunder, ricocheting off the walls. The psalmist leader rolled swiftly, taking cover behind a nearby pillar. Another shot rang out—Rob's bullet sparked against the stone.

"Are you insane?" the psalmist leader barked from behind cover.

"A little," Rob replied with a crooked grin, stalking closer. "I told you—I don't have the damn necklace. Your cult's pet doctor, Jonathan, took it from me. That's the truth."

Rob heard a soft mechanical click from behind the pillar.

A small black cylinder rolled toward him. Blue smoke hissed out, thick and fast.

"Shoot—" Rob fired again, blindly. But the smoke engulfed him. In the fog, the psalmist leader burst forward, slamming into Rob and knocking the gun from his hand. Rob swung, but the masked figure ducked and countered with a clean jab to the jaw.

They both went crashing to the ground, grappling.

"You fight like me . . ." the psalmist leader muttered, standing.

Rob spat blood and pushed himself up, eyes never leaving his opponent. He said nothing, but his expression spoke volumes. There was recognition there—something almost primal.

Meanwhile, Cassandra tore through the building, Dunkin in hot pursuit.

"Here, Chicka . . . here, Chicka," Dunkin sang mockingly, lumbering through the corridors.

He barged into a side room and spotted men below, shifting crates. "Boys! Robbie's in the big room, throwing fists with one of those masked freaks."

"You want us to take him out?" one called up.

"Nah," Dunkin sneered. "Just break his legs. I've got a spicy señorita to handle."

Cassandra leapt from the shadows and slammed a metal pole against Dunkin's skull. He collapsed with a grunt. Below, the startled men scrambled up the stairs.

Dunkin groaned, holding his head, rising slowly. His eyes locked on Cassandra. Fury flashed across his bruised face.

She didn't hesitate—rammed the pole like a lever, sending the behemoth tumbling into the men charging up behind him. The pile of bodies crashed to the floor in a heap of grunts and curses.

Cassandra paused, breathing hard. But a new sound caught her ear—footsteps. Dozens. Psalmist reinforcements stormed the building.

She bolted, racing back toward Rob.

"Get that woman!" Dunkin yelled from the floor, still reeling. His men scrambled to obey.

"Go!" he barked. "I need a damn minute."

The room emptied. Dunkin dragged himself to his feet, cursing as he leaned against the wall. He stumbled into a small room and yanked open a mini-fridge, pressing a frozen pack to his head.

"Damn woman," he muttered. "I can't beat her. I'm never gonna be happy again."

He punched the fridge door, denting it.

Then he froze.

Someone sat in his chair, back turned.

"Who the—" Dunkin's face changed as the chair slowly swiveled around. "Oh," he said, a crooked smile creeping across his face. "So you're the one behind this."

Back in the main hall, Rob and the psalmist leader both heard the rising thunder of boots—dozens of them, closing in fast.

The two fighters glanced at the doors, calculating. They knew time was running out.

Without warning, Rob lunged.

His fist cracked against the leader's mask. The figure staggered. Rob hit him again, driving him back step by step. A third punch landed squarely, nearly toppling him.

But the psalmist leader regained his footing—and shoved Rob back with an open palm strike.

Rob stumbled. Another shove. He retreated further.

The psalmist leader advanced.

He grabbed Rob's arms, halting his momentum. Rob gritted his teeth, trying to overpower him, but the leader held firm.

"Who . . ." Rob gasped, straining in the deadlock. "Who taught you that technique?"

"I don't know what you're talking about," the psalmist leader said evenly.

"No . . ." Rob exhaled, breath ragged. "Don't play dumb. Someone had to teach you that. That style. That way of fighting." He narrowed his eyes. "I watched your moves—you fight like me. I was trained in that technique, and I passed it down to only one other person."

"I said I don't know what you're talking about," the psalmist leader insisted, shoving Rob away.

Rob stumbled back, then steadied himself. His voice dropped, tight with suspicion.

"You know exactly what I mean. You take hits on purpose. You bait your opponent—make them think they've got the upper hand. Then you strike. It's subtle. Calculated. I called it . . . well, *he* called it . . . 'deceptive fighting.'"

"I don't know what you're talking about," the psalmist leader repeated, firmer this time—but his eyes flickered.

"Squad Leader," a voice echoed across the chamber.

Rob, the psalmist leader, and the injured all turned toward the entrance.

A hooded figure stepped into the room.

She wore the same psalmist garb, but her robes were brown—a color of distinction—and her mask mirrored the leader's, though its carvings were deeper, more intricate. Authority radiated from her.

"Elder," the psalmist leader said, quickly dropping to one knee.

"Why has this man not been apprehended?" she asked, her voice sharp and controlled. "Is this limping old dog too difficult for you?"

Rob's nostrils flared. He stared her down. She stared right back. The tension between them ignited like a spark to dry wood.

"Tell her," Rob demanded, his tone biting. "Tell her I don't have the necklace. I'm done with your cult. That god-forsaken place took everything from me."

The elder stepped forward, her voice calm but cold. "We've taken nothing from you, Rob. Don't insult us."

She raised her arms slightly, as if preaching to an unseen congregation.

"The Psalms Society is the spirit of change. We are the anointed. We proclaim good news to the poor, freedom for the prisoners, recovery of sight for the blind . . ." She paused, then met Rob's gaze again. "And we set the oppressed free."

"Save your religious nonsense for hell!" Rob snapped, stepping toward the elder psalmist. "I don't have your damn necklace. I gave it back to your Doctor Jonathan—ask him."

"Yes. I know," the elder psalmist replied calmly, beginning to circle Rob as he froze in place.

"Then why are you after me?" Rob demanded. "Why are you in my city?"

"Elder?" the psalmist leader asked hesitantly. "Our mission?"

"Your mission," she said, turning sharply toward him, "was to capture *Nightmare.* Which"—her voice turned ice-cold—"you failed to do."

She turned her gaze to Rob. "Tell me . . . has your son tried to contact you?"

"My son?" Rob's voice cracked as rage flooded his expression. He took a step forward. "How do you know about my son? Your cult took Mara—and my boy—away from me!"

"You pushed them away, *Nightmare.* And now your son leads a rebellion against us."

Rob stopped in his tracks, stunned.

"My son is in the city?" he muttered to himself.

Before he could react, the psalmist leader shoved him hard, sending him crashing into the table at the center of the room.

More psalmist members poured in from every doorway, daggers drawn and ready. Cassandra darted to Rob's side, helping him up as he leaned heavily on her shoulder. The psalmists encircled them, arms raised.

"Tell us what your son said to you," the elder psalmist demanded.

Rob clutched Cassandra, barely able to stand. She scanned the room, unsure what to do next. But Rob—his battered face locked on the elder—wouldn't look away.

Police sirens wailed in the distance. The room tensed.

Moments later, officers stormed through the doors.

"Freeze!"

"Damn," the elder psalmist hissed under her breath. Her followers threw down small black canisters. Smoke hissed and billowed instantly, filling the room.

Rob and Cassandra used the chaos to slip into the haze, inching toward an exit.

"My son is here," Rob whispered repeatedly, staggering beside her. "My son is here in the city . . ."

"You're bleeding," Cassandra said, trying to stop and check his wound.

"I don't care. Just get me out. I need to find him."

"Sir—"

"*Now,* Cassandra. *Now!*"

Down the hallway, the psalmist leader emerged from the fog. Rob leaned weakly against the wall, barely conscious. Cassandra stepped in front of him, shielding his body with hers.

The psalmist leader advanced slowly, dagger glinting in his hand.

Cassandra reached behind her for her gun.

"Not there," Rob whispered hoarsely, breath shallow. "I lost it . . ."

The psalmist leader closed in.

A gunshot cracked through the hallway. The psalmist leader crouched, startled. Rob and Cassandra flinched, turning toward the sound.

"Don't move!" Jessie shouted, gun aimed at the psalmist leader.

He placed a steadying hand on Rob's back, then moved past him, shielding Cassandra as well.

"Squad Leader," the elder's voice echoed sharply from farther down the corridor. The psalmist leader hesitated, looking in her direction.

More shouts and movement thundered through the building—officers clashing with Dunkin's men.

The psalmist leader began to crawl backward toward the corner.

"I'll shoot again," Jessie warned, tightening his aim.

"Squad Leader, we are *leaving!*" the elder psalmist barked, this time with unmistakable irritation.

The psalmist leader locked eyes with Rob—barely conscious, slumped against the wall—then disappeared into the shadows. His red eyes were the last thing to vanish.

Jessie turned to Rob. "What the hell was that?"

"...None..." Rob mumbled, already slipping. "None of your damn business."

He collapsed. Cassandra and Jessie caught him and dragged him outside. Police cars surrounded the block. Dozens of detained men sat on the curb, wrists zip-tied, while others were hauled into patrol vehicles.

"I can't fall asleep," Rob muttered, panicking. "If I fall asleep, they'll come back. They never stop coming—" He slammed a fist against his head.

"Sir, it's okay," Cassandra said, trying to steady him.

"He fights like me . . . He fights like me . . ." Rob rocked back and forth. He dropped to his knees, about to vomit.

"Sir, please—calm down—"

"I'm not *Nightmare* anymore . . . I told her," Rob said, grabbing Cassandra's arm, trembling. "I told her, but she wouldn't listen . . ."

A tear slipped down his cheek. He pushed her away and staggered backward.

"I have to find my son," he whispered. "I *have* to find him."

Then he collapsed.

Cassandra dove, catching him just before he hit the ground. Jessie quickly joined her, helping lift Rob as his body went limp in their arms.

The feisty player sat in the back of the ambulance, a blanket draped over his shoulders and an oxygen mask covering his face. His breathing was shallow. His eyes were fixed on the ground, unblinking.

"You had me worried sick," Malcolm said as he arrived, Amanda right behind him.

All around them, officers secured the area. Dunkin's men were either being arrested or desperately making excuses to avoid it.

"The doctor said he'll be fine," Cassandra assured them, standing beside Rob.

Amanda nodded, then turned to Cassandra. "Are *you* alright?"

"A few bruises, but I'll live, ma'am."

"Rob," Malcolm tried to lighten the mood. "You gonna tell me, 'You should see the other guy'?"

Rob didn't respond. His eyes stayed locked on the pavement.

"This isn't a joke," Cassandra said, her voice low and serious. She motioned subtly toward the cluster of police. "Those people—those *psalmists*—attacked us. They were working with Dunkin."

Amanda and Malcolm immediately focused on her. Rob remained silent, the steady hiss of his mask the only sound from him.

"They weren't after some stolen necklace. They wanted to know . . ." She looked over at Rob. "They wanted to know about his *son.* I guess . . . he's important to them. They were trying to find out if he's contacted Rob."

"Rob?" Amanda asked gently.

Still nothing. Rob didn't look up.

"Okay, enough with the secrets," Malcolm cut in. "My guys at the lab have something for you to wear—tech that can help protect you. We need to handle this, *now.*"

"Malcolm's right," Amanda added. "Rob, has your son—" She sighed and pinched the bridge of her nose. "You can't keep playing this lone wolf. What if Cassandra had been seriously hurt? Or you?"

"Can I speak to you all for a moment?" Jessie asked, walking up.

"Not now, Officer Handsome," Malcolm muttered dismissively.

Jessie ignored him and stepped closer. "Rob, I need you to come down to the station. Just to answer a few questions." He placed a hand on Rob's shoulder.

Malcolm slapped his hand away. "Read him his rights first. Otherwise, he's not going anywhere."

Jessie's face tensed. "I just want to talk."

"Then talk here," Malcolm snapped. "I don't trust what kind of crap you'll pull in a backroom."

"Grow up, Malcolm. I'm doing my job."

"It's past your bedtime, kid—"

"Sir, he helped me," Cassandra interrupted.

"Cool it," Amanda added quickly to Malcolm.

Amanda and Cassandra tried to defuse the rising tension, but Malcolm's face reddened with anger.

"Listen to your friends," Jessie said. He turned back to Rob and began to lean him forward slightly. "Just come with me for a bit, alright?"

"I said don't touch him," Malcolm barked, shoving Jessie backward.

Jessie stumbled. Surprise flashed across his face. "Don't do that again," he warned.

"Malcolm!" Amanda shouted.

"We don't know if he's some undercover psalmist. We can't trust anyone."

"This isn't a damn spy movie," Amanda snapped.

"I'll make sure you're out of here by tomorrow, you—"

Jessie cut him off. "Will you shut up? You're the rich scum who's part of why this city's rotting. I've watched people like you long enough. You and your little gangster club are part of the problem."

"Oh, you hear that?" Malcolm shouted, his voice rising. "Everyone hear that?" He grabbed Jessie by the collar. "Say something else and I'll sue you into the grave—and then send my lawyers to hound your corpse."

"Malcolm!" Amanda snapped again.

Malcolm shoved Jessie back.

Jessie wiped the spit from his face as Amanda and Cassandra turned on Malcolm, berating him. Rob finally looked up from his mask and focused on the scene unraveling.

"That's what people like you do," Jessie said bitterly.

"Let's just end this," Cassandra pleaded. "This isn't helping."

"No. He needs to hear it." Jessie pushed Cassandra gently aside and pointed at Malcolm. "You don't know what real people live through. You're just a rich snob with nothing but money. Strip that away, and you're nothing."

Cassandra had to physically hold Malcolm back as he charged toward Jessie. The two men began shouting and swearing, drawing the attention of nearby officers.

"I *know* that was him . . ." Rob said, his voice hoarse. He pulled off the oxygen mask. "Ezra's alive."

Malcolm froze.

Amanda looked at Rob, eyes wide.

Malcolm straightened, brushing his coat and glaring at Jessie, whose chest was still heaving.

"You've lost too much oxygen, Rob," Malcolm said. "Ezra's dead. We buried him."

"Did *you* see the body?" Rob barked, wincing and clutching his chest.

"Not this again," Malcolm muttered, wiping his face in frustration.

"Rob, stop," Amanda warned. She pointed at him, her eyes shimmering with emotion.

"He's alive," Rob said, softer now. "I fought him."

Amanda threw her hands in the air, exasperated.

"Who's Ezra?" Cassandra asked, glancing between them. "What's he talking about?"

Neither Amanda nor Malcolm answered. They looked away.

"It's him . . ." Rob repeated weakly. "It's really him."

"He's just delirious," Malcolm said, shaking his head and brushing at his coat again.

"I don't know why he's bringing this up now," Amanda muttered, rolling her eyes.

"What is he talking about?" Cassandra asked again, louder this time, her voice edged with urgency.

Rob stirred, struggling to sit upright. His voice was hoarse but determined. "Ezra . . . used to have your job."

Cassandra's eyes narrowed. "What?"

"They thought he was dead," Rob continued, his breath shallow. "But I know he's alive."

Amanda and Malcolm exchanged a glance—sharp, silent, loaded with unspoken history. Both turned away from Rob, their expressions tightening into masks of irritation and unease.

Frustration flared in Malcolm's eyes. Amanda's jaw clenched.

Something unspoken lingered in the air.

And Cassandra could feel it—there was more to the story. A lot more.

Phones rang endlessly and officers buzzed up and down the corridors of the precinct like hornets in a hive. Rob and Cassandra were escorted to a bench. Rob shivered beneath a blanket, pale and visibly rattled.

"Be careful what you say," Amanda warned, standing beside them with arms folded. Her eyes scanned the busy station floor. "We don't know who's clean. Some of these cops could be dirty."

"Yes, ma'am," Cassandra replied softly.

Amanda touched her shoulder, voice softening. "Hey. We've been through tighter spots than this. You'll be fine."

"You mean like when we lost Ezra?" Rob snarled from his seat, still trembling. His words made them freeze. "He's alive."

Amanda rolled her eyes. Rob pointed at her.

"He's alive," he repeated, voice strained. "I taught him those moves. Alex passed that technique down to me, and I passed it to Ezra. I couldn't even teach my own son, but Ezra? He was like a son to all of us."

"Rob, I was there," Amanda said, her tone weary. "Please, just stop."

"Don't tell me to stop! I *know* who I fought. I know my own damn teachings."

Amanda pinched the bridge of her nose. "Then explain why he's with the cult, Rob. If it's really him—why is he working for *them*?"

Rob's nostrils flared. He didn't answer.

"Can the dead come back to life?" Amanda asked.

"Why don't you ask your brother," Rob shot back. "He's the one always preaching metaphysical crap at his shows. Or better yet—ask that preacher boy who worships the ground you walk on. But don't stand there acting like *I'm* the crazy one!"

"Rob," Amanda snapped, pointing sharply at him.

Just then, Officer Dan approached with two other officers flanking him. He gave them a disgusted once-over.

"Why am I not surprised?"

"Go to hell, Dan," Amanda said, turning her back to him.

Dan sneered. "Already there, sweetheart. Right alongside you three gangsters running this city into the ground." He looked down at Rob, who still trembled in his seat. "But not for much longer. The day I see even *one* of you locked up for good? That'll be a damn good day."

He muttered something under his breath as his colleagues motioned for him to leave.

"Malcolm's making a scene in the chief's office," Dan added, turning back. "Damn jackass thinks he can get us all fired. Let him call every overpriced lawyer in the state—see if I care."

He disappeared down the hallway.

Jessie stepped in behind him.

"Get away from me," Rob snapped, raising his hand before Jessie could speak. "I don't know you. And I *do* know just about every officer in this city. I'm its eyes and ears—but *you*? You're a ghost. So why don't you tell me what the hell you know about the people who attacked me?"

Jessie raised his hands slightly. "I don't know anything."

"Sure," Rob scoffed. "I'll find out. I always do."

"Rob," Cassandra said gently, trying to calm him.

"What? You think he's Officer Handsome too?"

Jessie blushed slightly. Cassandra avoided eye contact.

Jessie stepped closer and offered Cassandra a small smile. "It's Cassandra, right? That's a beautiful name. You seem a lot more level-headed than him. What you did back there—how you handled everything—that's the only reason we made it out."

Cassandra smiled, faint but sincere, and gave a nod of thanks.

"Don't try your tricks, pretty boy," Rob growled.

"Rob," Amanda warned.

"She saved your life," Jessie said pointedly. "Did you even thank her?"

Rob just glared.

Jessie turned back to Cassandra. "I'm not trying to pry. I just want to protect this city—protect all of you. Please, work with me."

He reached out, gently touching her arm. Her heart skipped and her face flushed.

Amanda smiled knowingly. "Why don't you and Cassandra talk over there for a bit. I'll have a word with Rob—"

"Tell him nothing," Rob interrupted, staring hard at Cassandra. He nearly fell out of his seat as he leaned toward her.

"Uncle Rob!" Daisy's voice rang out. She rushed up and threw her arms around him, nearly knocking him over.

"You should be at the manor," Amanda said sternly.

"I'm not letting Dad trap me in there," Daisy shot back. Then, noticing Jessie, she smiled. "Oh—hello." She extended her hand.

Jessie's bashful grin returned as he shook it. "I've heard you're the princess of Shiloh City."

Daisy laughed, a soft, unfiltered laugh. "Let me guess—he's in there ranting and raving?" She pointed toward a hallway.

"He's in there threatening to fire the whole department," Jessie replied.

"He's such a man-baby," Daisy smirked.

"Go back to the manor, Daisy," Rob ordered. "There are people after your father."

"I'm not a child, Uncle Rob. And besides, I'm the queen of sneaking out." Her grin widened with pride.

"There are people after your father," Cassandra repeated, this time more urgently.

Jessie raised an eyebrow, stepping in. "So you *do* know who they are?" he asked, inching closer to Cassandra.

Rob shot her a look, nostrils flaring again.

Amanda stepped between them. "Can we have a moment, Officer?"

"I'm here to protect you," Jessie replied, trying to hold his ground. "That's my job."

Rob chuckled bitterly. "Sure it is."

"Cassie?" Daisy asked curiously. "Who do you bodyguard, anyway?" She pointed between Rob and Amanda. "Uncle Rob, I thought *you* used to be my dad's bodyguard?"

"Ezra's after me," Rob muttered darkly.

Daisy's expression dimmed with sudden sorrow.

"Does this Ezra person even know—" Jessie began.

"If you don't leave us alone . . ." Rob clenched his fist, his voice trailing off into a threat.

Daisy tried to lighten the mood, nudging Amanda playfully. “I think about him all the time. Ezra was special.” She gave a soft blush. “Uncle Rob and he would do all that combat stuff together. They used to—”

Rob pointed sharply at her, his gesture forceful enough to silence her mid-sentence.

Daisy giggled awkwardly, then drifted off into thought.

“Daisy, wipe the privilege off your face for five minutes and listen. Go home,” Rob snapped.

“My dad’s a jerk, but I don’t want anything to happen to him. He needs me.”

“You just want to be in the middle of the action,” Rob growled. “You never could stand not being in the spotlight.”

“And is that a problem?” Daisy teased with a smug smile.

“Damn . . .” Rob rubbed his face in frustration.

Cassandra leaned over to Amanda and whispered, “Why does she call him Uncle Rob?”

Amanda gave a faint smile before Daisy cut in. “He used to love my aunt. They were kind of a cute couple—for old people anyway.”

Rob turned his gaze directly to Daisy. His voice low and brittle. “She’s dead now. The only woman who ever loved me. Gone . . . just like Ezra.”

Daisy’s posture straightened, the smile wiped from her face. “If you don’t want your dad ending up in the same place, I suggest you go home. Now.”

“That was uncalled for,” Jessie cut in.

Rob groaned, trying to rise. “Damn . . . can’t get this twerp to leave us alone.”

Daisy flipped her hair back and leaned forward dramatically. She cleared her throat. “Jessie, was it? Could you get me something to drink? I’m a little shaken up, you know . . . worried about my dad and all.”

Jessie blinked, visibly flustered. “Yes, I—I’ll be right back.” Practically hypnotized, he rushed off.

Daisy smirked. “Men always think they’re in control, always trying to tell us what to do.” She looked directly at Rob. “But we stand our ground. And we brush the haters off.”

Rob opened his mouth to respond, but Malcolm’s voice boomed through the corridor.

Three men in suits scrambled to get out of his way as Malcolm stormed down the hall.

“They’re not going to stop me again,” Malcolm grumbled. “As long as they’re on my payroll, I don’t care what time I wake them. This is war.”

“I’ve never seen him like this before,” Cassandra murmured. “Is he okay?”

“You mean because he’s acting more like *me* than his clownish self?” Rob smirked. “Now you see why Officer Dan calls Amanda and me gangsters—but not Malcolm, huh?”

Cassandra nodded, processing the change.

“Don’t let his polished act fool you. He’s a ruthless businessman under all that charm. This? This is just the surface.”

“He didn’t always used to be like this,” Daisy said quietly as she stepped closer trying to hear Rob better.

Malcolm’s pace quickened when he spotted Daisy among the group. Jessie had just returned, handing her a water bottle.

“Daisy, you have no idea how furious I am right now. Go home,” he said, barely holding back his temper.

“Dad—” she tried.

He grabbed her hand roughly, teeth clenched. “People are after us. You know your life is in danger.”

She yanked her hand away. “I can take care of myself.”

Rob let out a derisive scoff. Daisy turned sharply toward him, clearly hurt.

Amanda stepped between them, placing a calming hand on Malcolm's chest. "Sweetheart, we need to speak with the police. Why don't we all meet back at the manor?"

Malcolm wasn't listening. "How the hell did you even get here? All the cars are locked down—I had the place sealed."

"It's called a *bus*, Dad. People use them when their father tries to control their life."

Malcolm wiped his face and exhaled heavily. Amanda leaned in close, whispering, "Malcolm, not here. Don't lose it here."

"I can take her home," Jessie offered.

"No damn way!" Malcolm exploded, shoving Amanda aside. "What did I tell you? Get out of here!"

"At least *someone's* treating me like a person today," Daisy muttered, shooting Malcolm and Rob a bitter glare.

Malcolm turned red with rage, barely holding himself together.

"Thank you, Officer," Amanda said calmly, gently pushing Jessie aside. "But that's not necessary."

She nudged Daisy toward the door and handed her some cash. "Please just take the bus back. I promise I'll explain everything when I get there."

Daisy folded her arms. Amanda met her eyes with a firm look. After a beat, Daisy let out a long, loud sigh. She glanced past Amanda and her fuming father to Rob—who watched her with quiet judgment.

"Do you see me the way *they* do?" Daisy asked softly, eyes locked on Amanda. "Are you just like them?"

"Daisy, I know things don't make sense right now," Amanda tried.

"I'm more than what any of you see in me," Daisy said, her voice shaking. "More than *any* of you give me credit for."

She turned and walked away.

Amanda stood still, her back to the others. She closed her eyes and took a long breath. Malcolm stepped up beside her.

"Thanks," he muttered, touching her arm gently.

Amanda gave him a small nod.

Daisy waited at the curb, pacing under the flickering lights of the bus stop. The cold air of Shiloh City night bit at her arms, and she hugged herself for warmth. The empty street and silence made the shadows feel alive.

"Princess," a voice called.

Daisy flinched, spinning around.

A car pulled up to the curb slowly. The passenger window slid down. Jessie smiled at her from inside.

"Need a ride, princess?"

She hesitated, then walked to the car.

"It's not fancy," Jessie said, "but it beats the bus."

Daisy leaned on the window. "My dad would freak if he knew you gave me a ride."

Jessie's smile faltered.

Daisy opened the door, sliding into the seat. "Guess that's a bonus, then."

CHAPTER 6

THE WINDS OF Shiloh City blew uncharacteristically soft this morning. Loose papers and litter danced across the cracked pavement like tumbleweeds in a desert, brushing against graffiti-covered, rust-stained walls. Downtown Shiloh always seemed to carry the scent of mourning—its black and brown buildings exhaled fatigue and decay, worn down by generations of toil. There was no time for self-care here. Just struggle. Just strain. Survival in this part of the fractured city meant keeping pace or being left behind.

Each morning, when the sun rose, it felt more like a reluctant grace than a full blessing. Its rays barely reached the streets, overshadowed by the biting winds that swept through like a reminder—of place, of burden, of bondage. The wind blew now on Amanda as she sat at a bench outside an aging brick building, rubbing her arms against the chill. Then, as if pausing to catch its breath, the wind stopped.

From her bench, Amanda watched the long line of people waiting at a service window. The queue snaked far beyond the length of the building. Men in oversized coats shuffled in place, tugging up sagging pants. Teenage girls with babies on their hips gossiped, bright braids cascading down to their waists. Amanda glanced to her right and saw a group of grown men rolling in on children's bikes, wearing ripped jeans and t-shirts despite the chill. They leaned against the chain-link fence, lit up cigarettes, and laughed, the smoke drifting up into the heavy air.

A low cloud passed overhead, casting a shadow that seemed to drain the life out of everything it touched. The temperature dropped; people shivered. But after a moment, the cloud moved on, and sunlight spilled down again, warming the concrete just enough to be noticed.

Amanda shifted as more men came hobbling down the hill toward the line, holding up their pants as they passed her. One man's do-rag flapped behind him like a tattered flag in the wind. Amanda cleared her throat and straightened her posture, watching them until they passed. Her gaze returned to the line, lingering on the young mothers and their children.

"Mandy!"

Malcolm's voice broke the silence as he bumped her shoulder and sat across from her.

"What are you doing here?" Amanda asked, glancing around nervously.

"I'm here to give you this." He slid a burgundy jacket, still wrapped in plastic, across the table. "It's a new prototype. The guys at Armory have been working on it."

He adjusted his own jacket, pointing to the right side of his chest. "There's a tracker here. And a camera, too."

Amanda frowned. "What are you talking about?"

"This'll help us keep track of each other—just in case those cult guys come at us again."

She peeled back the plastic and held the jacket up. "Try it on," Malcolm urged, grinning. "Come on, try it on."

Amanda chuckled, then stood and slipped her arms into the jacket.

"Here," Malcolm offered, helping her slide it on properly.

"Fits perfectly," Amanda said, moving her arms. "Maybe too perfectly. Malcolm, you already seem to know where Rob and I are half the time without a tracker."

Malcolm smirked. "I know, right? I had them make Rob's in black. Matches his whole moody, end-of-the-world thing."

Amanda's eyes drifted back to the line of people.

"Ohhh," Malcolm teased, raising his eyebrows. "You're waiting for *Mr. Preacher Boy* himself, huh? Childhood crush Josh?"

Amanda blushed. "Malcolm . . ."

He leaned back into his seat. "Want me to make him jealous? I'll pretend to be your old lover. He'll see you've developed a taste for white chocolate."

Amanda rolled her eyes. "I'm surprised you'd even come downtown. Aren't you worried someone might steal your cufflinks? You didn't bring your Porsche, did you?"

Malcolm chuckled. "Oh, Cassandra's circling the area. Yep—there she goes." He waved as a tinted car passed.

"I see you brought the Range Rover. Nice. All blacked out for . . . *the terrain*," Amanda said, sarcasm thick in her voice.

"Exactly," Malcolm said, moving his arms dramatically. "It's all about blending in with the environment."

Amanda shook her head. "Malcolm, you sound so ignorant when you talk like that."

He grinned. "Mandy, I'm good in the hood. I know the culture. Plymouth Rock didn't land on us. Jackson Five. Soul Train. All that jazz . . . or rap . . . or hip-hop."

Amanda groaned and covered her face. "Please stop."

Malcolm leaned forward, peering past her. "Ohhh, here comes Preacher Boy now. He's been after you since you guys were kids. Been praying for some *love*. And I mean—*love, love*," he sang playfully.

"Malcolm . . ." Amanda's face flushed deeper.

"He's like a Sunday School choirboy, right?" Malcolm teased. "All gospel and virtue. 'Thou shalt not look at a woman,' and if you do—gouge your eyes out. That whole bit. Gospel, or . . . jazz, or maybe hip hop," he added, smirking, waiting for a reaction.

Amanda just glared at him.

Malcolm raised an eyebrow, feigning a devious, inquisitive look. "Wait—do you think Preacher Boy Josh is still a virgin?"

Amanda pointed at him sharply. "Don't."

Malcolm chuckled, undeterred. "Why haven't you two hit it off? He's around our age, right? Forty? Forty-three? Maybe he's never even kissed a woman. Maybe he's waiting for *you* to be his first." He wiggled his eyebrows suggestively, then placed a hand on his chest. "Mandy, if you're holding out for me, I'm flattered—but romance? I've got too much going on for that."

Amanda gave him a tight-lipped scowl, her lips pursing upward in warning.

"Tell you what," Malcolm said. "I'm gonna help you out. You need my expert love advice."

Amanda's eyes widened, equal parts annoyed and embarrassed.

"Mandy, real talk—you never show emotion. Like, ever. You're a statue. I get it—you're the no-nonsense powerhouse, the glass-ceiling-breaking, woman-warrior type. But you deserve happiness too. You don't always have to be strong. Lean on someone once in a while. Even Rob does—and that grumpy old goat barely has a pulse."

Amanda bit her lip and clenched her fist. Malcolm's face softened as he noticed her struggling.

He began to speak, but she raised a hand to stop him. "I'm alright," she said, her voice steady. "I just have a mantra I repeat to myself. It got me this far."

She tapped her chest. "I'm strong here." Then her forehead. "And here."

Malcolm nodded, his voice gentle now. "I know you've been through a lot."

Amanda managed a soft smile. "What would *Silver Spoon Malcolm* know about the slums, anyway?"

He chuckled, relief washing over him as he saw some of her pain ease.

Just then, a cold gust of wind swept through the area, silencing them both.

When it passed, Malcolm's smirk returned. "Alright, I'm going to pretend to be your old lover. Desperate. Longing. Begging for love from my cold, overbearing ex."

Amanda groaned, glaring at him again.

"Come on, Mandy—you're my friend. And yeah, you can be a little motherly. But most of the time, you're serious, you're stern. You need to let loose once in a while. Have some fun. Find what makes you feel alive. Mikey does—he's always lit up. You? You need a little jazz in that gumbo personality. A little hip hop. Something."

He started poking her playfully.

Malcolm perked up suddenly. "Up! He's coming this way."

Amanda turned slightly to look behind her.

"Okay—kiss on the forehead and I'm gone." Malcolm leaned across the table.

Amanda began swatting at him just as Joshua arrived.

"Hey, Amanda," Joshua said, concern in his voice. He carried two plates stacked with fried chicken, square cuts of macaroni and cheese, and green beans.

"Hey, Joshua," Amanda replied, her eyes darting away, her face tilted downward.

"My dad's getting napkins," Joshua said, setting the plates down. He glanced at Malcolm.

Malcolm extended his hand. "Malcolm. How do you do?"

Joshua shook it cautiously. "I know who you are. You're in the news. The tech mogul from Shiloh Heights."

"I'm also Mandy's old flame. She just broke my heart," Malcolm said with a dramatic sigh. "Turns out she loves someone else."

"Malcolm," Amanda growled, gripping the bench and gritting her teeth. "Leave."

Just then, a tall, broad-shouldered man approached with a plate in hand. His voice was deep and smooth.

"Hello there. Amanda." He sat beside her, placing his plate on the table and wrapping one arm around her.

"Malcolm, this is Reverend Anthony. Joshua's father," Amanda said.

"Get out of town," Malcolm replied, eyeing him up. "What are you—six-five? These hands belong on a basketball court," he joked, opening the Reverend's palm and holding it in front of Amanda.

The Reverend laughed. "You look familiar. Have we met?"

"He's in the news, Dad," Joshua explained. "CEO of Armory. High-tech military contract company."

Reverend Anthony raised a brow. "He's not from around here." He glanced at Amanda. "You two dated?"

"No!" Amanda shouted, waving her arms, blushing furiously.

"It's true, Preacher Boy," Malcolm added with flair. "We were passionate. Spontaneous. But she always loved another."

"Okay!" Amanda snapped, pushing Malcolm off the bench toward the street. "Say goodbye to Malcolm," she told the Reverend and Joshua. She whistled sharply. "Cassandra!"

Cassandra driving Malcolm's car rolled by. Amanda waved as she guided Malcolm to the curb.

Back at the bench, she rejoined the father and son, brushing away the embarrassment from her face.

"Sorry about that," she said with an awkward smile.

"That's alright," Reverend Anthony said warmly. "He seems like a good friend—coming all this way just for you."

Joshua, however, stared silently at his plate, jabbing his food with unnecessary force.

"How's Mikey doing?" Reverend Anthony asked, breaking the tension.

"Mikey is . . . Mikey," Amanda chuckled. "Always busy—working on his shows, doing motivational talks. He's been speaking at churches, too."

"You're doing a great job managing him," the Reverend said, rubbing his chin. "Amanda, ever since I met you, I knew you were something special. Your father may not be around anymore, but I'm proud of everything you've done."

Amanda's eyes widened. Her fist balled instinctively, and she had to hold it down with her other hand before it struck.

Reverend Anthony and Joshua exchanged concerned glances.

"I—sorry," Amanda said. "Just a muscle spasm. Happens sometimes."

"Joshua's been looking forward to seeing you," Reverend Anthony said, smiling at his son. "Forty years old, still moping around the house. I told him—go meet up with someone. Get some sun."

"Dad," Joshua groaned.

"I think your friend Malcolm might've had a point," the Reverend teased Amanda with a wink.

"How do you know Malcolm?" Joshua asked. "Did he meet Mikey on tour?"

"Malcolm's . . . an old friend," Amanda replied with a soft smile. "The way we met—let's just say it's unforgettable."

Joshua's expression darkened, his eyes drifting away.

Amanda caught it and winced.

"I'm happy for your success," Reverend Anthony said. "You're a living testimony of what God can do."

Amanda suddenly slammed her fist into her plate. The table jumped. "Son of a—"

She covered her face with her hand, trying to breathe.

"Another spasm," she muttered. "Sorry."

"Amanda, are you alright?" the Reverend asked gently.

"Dad, maybe don't ask so many questions," Joshua added, nervously.

"I'm fine," Amanda replied, trying to steady herself. "Joshua . . . last time we talked, you were going back to school. How's that going?"

"Good—really good. I'm working on my Ph.D. Planning to take over for my dad."

Joshua smiled and nudged his father. "I'll be Doctor Joshua by the end of the year."

"That's wonderful," Amanda said.

Joshua's smile faded. "Thanks. But sometimes I feel old going back to school. Forty? Come on."

"It's never too late for an education. Especially for people like us. For our community. Education and technology—that's how we rise." Amanda's voice had conviction again.

Joshua nodded. "What I've always admired about you is that you *knew* what you wanted. You went after it. Me? I've changed careers five times. But you—you're a success."

Amanda's face hardened. "I've always wanted freedom," she said too quickly.

She clamped her hand over her mouth, but the words had already landed.

The men recoiled slightly at the raw emotion.

Tears welled in Amanda's eyes. "I didn't mean—"

"You didn't hurt me," Joshua said, softly.

Amanda wiped her face. "Being around you both reminds me of my childhood. That's all."

"If you don't want to talk, that's okay," Reverend Anthony said kindly. "We're here."

"No, you're not!" Amanda snapped, suddenly. She gritted her teeth, struggling for breath. "Sorry… it's just…" She took a deep breath. "It's the memories. From when I was locked up."

Joshua's expression twisted. "Amanda . . ."

"I was in a correctional facility. And you know what? No one got me out. Not fate. Not grace. Not prayer."

The wind picked up, scattering napkins and food scraps. The three of them held their plates steady.

"I got myself out," Amanda said. "I grew up in hell. And I had to *take* my freedom. People like me don't get grace. We take what we can or die trying."

Reverend Anthony tried to reach out. "Amanda—"

"You want to talk scripture?" Amanda interrupted, voice rising. "What about the story where God told a slave woman to go back to her master? Her *abuser*? To submit to torture? That was her fate. Either obey . . . or die in the desert."

She slammed the table and sent food flying. People nearby turned to stare.

"I'd rather die in the desert than return to bondage."

Amanda turned and stormed toward the food line. People moved aside, wordless, parting around her like the Red Sea. Her eyes were red, her body shaking. She grabbed some napkins, wiped her face, and glanced back. Joshua and Reverend Anthony sat motionless, stunned.

The ground felt like it shifted beneath her. Another fierce gust of Shiloh City wind tore through the block. Amanda covered her face, stumbling. As she tried to walk back to the bench, her knees buckled, her body swayed—and her eyes began to close.

Joshua jumped to his feet, rushing toward her.

CHAPTER 7

"AMANDA. AMANDA," a voice called. The irritation in the man's tone grew sharper. "Amanda, school is over. You need to go home—*now*."

Principal Huxley stood outside the girls' bathroom, arms crossed. Two janitors waited beside him, one gripping a mop, the other holding a bag of cleaning supplies.

"She just won't come out," the older janitor grumbled. "I gotta clean."

"Amanda, open this door," the principal ordered, knocking once. "Is there a problem?"

His annoyance bled through every word.

"Girl's nothing but trouble," the younger janitor muttered under his breath.

The sharp click-clack of high heels echoed down the hallway, catching everyone's attention. The men turned as a woman strode confidently toward them.

"Ms. Maverick," young Joshua called out, rushing beside her, his voice tight with concern. "She's been in there a long time."

"Lashana . . ." Principal Huxley started, clearly displeased.

"I'll handle it," she said, raising her hand to silence him. She pushed the bathroom door open and stepped inside without another word.

"Go home, Joshua," Principal Huxley said flatly, not even glancing at the boy.

Joshua hesitated, shifting his feet awkwardly.

"Joshua," the principal repeated, this time more firmly. "I said go *home*."

The boy sucked his teeth, clearly upset, but obeyed. Hands in his pockets, lips pouting, he dragged his feet as he walked away. Just before turning the corner, he looked back one more time, staring at the bathroom door.

Inside the cold, dimly lit restroom, Ms. Maverick's voice echoed gently.

"Amanda?"

The space was sterile—two stalls, two sinks. Pale fluorescent light flickered above, and a narrow window lined with metal bars let in a sliver of gray daylight. One faucet was still running, its rhythmic drip the only sound besides the creaking pipes.

A trail of damp paper towels led to the last stall.

"I'm almost finished," Amanda replied faintly.

Her voice was muffled, small—frightened.

Ms. Maverick crouched to see a pair of black school shoes peeking beneath the stall door.

"Is everything okay, sweetie?"

"I'm fine," Amanda said quickly. "I'm fine . . ."

Ms. Maverick stood and leaned gently against the stall. "Amanda . . . I think we need to talk."

Outside, the janitors were growing restless.

"Damn it, I need to clean that bathroom," the heavyset one grumbled. "What are they even doing in there? I swear, this middle school's nothing but hoodlums and future food stamp hoes."

Principal Huxley turned toward him, his expression hardening.

The janitor grunted, sloshing his mop in the bucket, then tugged at his sagging pants. He leaned on the wall, wheezing with age and exhaustion, still mumbling bitterly.

A thinner, younger janitor approached from the hallway, reeking of cigarettes. He slipped a lighter into his pocket as he walked up.

"They're still not done?" he scoffed.

"That teacher went in to get the girl out," the older janitor said. "No idea what's taking so long. Not like I'm getting paid overtime for this."

"You think the girl's got a shiv or something?" the younger one asked. "Last week, I saw a kid with a homemade blade. These kids are *wild*, man."

He nudged the older janitor, then gestured to his gut. "Hey, that pregnant girl—she looks like she's about to pop."

"Yeah?" the heavy janitor chuckled, a mean grin spreading across his face.

The younger one mimed a belly with his hands. "More little welfare queens on the way."

"Yup. This school is full of future ones." The old janitor laughed bitterly. "Just damn."

"Yessir, yessir," the younger one echoed, shaking his head like a preacher speaking passionate on stage at church.

Principal Huxley shot them both a sharp look. They ignored him.

"Yo, check this out," the thin janitor said. "I saw that kid—the one with the jacked-up cornrows."

"Yeah, yeah," the older janitor said. "His mama ain't got no business touching hair. Kid looks like a roach with antennas."

"That's the one," the thin one snorted. "Saw him swiping snacks from the cafeteria box. I asked how he got in—thing was locked. Kid just grinned, said, 'You want snacks? I got you. Chips? Cookies?' Like he's already running a hustle. Future dealer, man."

They both burst out laughing.

Principal Huxley's jaw tightened. He turned away from them, disgusted.

"Everything alright in there, Lashana?" he asked, knocking and pushing the door open slightly.

"Close the door!" Ms. Maverick snapped from inside.

Her voice echoed like a shot in the cold tile room.

Principal Huxley flinched and jerked his hand back, startled.

The three men froze, wide-eyed and silent for the first time.

The heavier janitor muttered a curse under his breath. "Man, I got things to do," he grumbled, barely disguising his irritation. He continued mumbling complaints to himself as he leaned on the mop handle like it was a crutch for his patience.

The bathroom door suddenly swung open. Ms. Maverick stepped out, holding it open behind her was Amanda who emerged slowly, her eyes downcast.

"Finally," one of the janitors muttered. Both pushed past the door, entering the restroom.

"Aw, *hell*—it stinks in here," the younger janitor coughed. "What the hell were they even—"

Their griping continued as they started cleaning, voices echoing inside the tiled walls.

Ms. Maverick turned without a word and nudged the door shut with her foot, sealing the janitors inside. The murmurs of their complaints muffled instantly.

Principal Huxley opened his mouth to speak, but Ms. Maverick lifted her hand—palm out—cutting him off.

"Amanda, go wait for me at the front entrance," she said gently.

Amanda nodded but hesitated, glancing back as she walked away. She caught the two adults leaning in, speaking in low tones. Their expressions were tight, unreadable, but Amanda felt the heat of being *talked about*.

"I'll call her uncle to pick her up," Principal Huxley said quietly.

Amanda crept back a few steps. "I can walk home…" she said, her voice barely above a whisper.

Ms. Maverick turned to her. "Sweetie, I think you should wait for your uncle."

"No . . . please . . ." Amanda replied, shaking her head. "I don't live far."

The two educators exchanged an uncertain glance.

"My uncle's at work. He can't come. I walk home all the time. I'll be okay," Amanda added, eyes glued to the floor.

Ms. Maverick crouched slightly, her tone softening. "I can take you home, honey. Just a quick drive."

Principal Huxley shot her a sharp look. "You *know* you can't do that. We don't give students rides—school policy." He muttered more under his breath, annoyance simmering behind his words.

Ms. Maverick exhaled hard, irritation flashing across her face.

"Alright," she said finally, standing tall. She looked Amanda in the eye. "Walk straight home, sweetie. Stay on the sidewalk by the street, okay?" Then, louder and slower, she added pointedly, "*Off* school grounds."

Amanda nodded, though she wasn't entirely sure what her teacher meant by that.

"You know it's against policy," Huxley repeated, his voice clipped.

Ms. Maverick didn't respond. She turned her back on him and walked away.

Amanda lingered a moment longer, then followed her teacher's quiet instructions, slipping out the front doors of the school and into the long shadows of Shiloh City.

Amanda pushed open the front doors of the school and began the slow walk home. Principal Huxley fell into step beside her, his arms folded tightly across his chest as he watched her retreat across the school grounds. Amanda clutched her stomach, each step heavier than the last. Her head spun with dizziness, her legs wobbling beneath her. Today, her backpack felt like it weighed a ton.

"Amanda!" Ms. Maverick called from her car across the street. She unlocked the passenger door and gestured for Amanda to hurry over. Without hesitation, Amanda dashed across and slid into the seat beside her.

"Today, you did a bit of growing up," Ms. Maverick said gently. "I think you could use a break."

Amanda's voice dropped to a near whisper, her eyes cast downward. "Are you going to get in trouble?"

Ms. Maverick laughed softly. "Maybe . . . but I've put my job on the line for my kids more than once."

Tears welled up in Amanda's eyes. She turned her face away so Ms. Maverick wouldn't see her crying. She swallowed hard, sniffing back the sobs as they drove.

"Well, come on," Ms. Maverick said playfully. "Show me where to go."

Amanda wiped her cheeks and gave directions. Ms. Maverick pulled up in front of a narrow townhome at the corner of the neighborhood. Three worn brown steps led up to the front door, which was attached to a row of similar townhouses. Cars were parked bumper to bumper along the sidewalks. Somewhere nearby, dogs barked and sirens wailed in the distance.

"Thank you!" Amanda said, jumping out of the car. Ms. Maverick called after her, but Amanda hurried toward the door, her hands trembling as she frantically searched for her keys in her backpack. She glanced nervously over her shoulder before finally finding them and unlocking the door.

Ms. Maverick turned off the car in the middle of the street and climbed the stairs to Amanda's door. She knocked once—no answer. Twice—still nothing. She knocked again, louder this time. The door suddenly slammed open.

"What you want?" a rough voice barked. A bald man with a long beard stood in the doorway, wearing faded jeans and a stained T-shirt. The blast of booming rap music nearly knocked Ms. Maverick off balance. The house smelled of mold mixed with cigar smoke and ash. Amid the noise, distant laughter and cheering echoed from inside.

"Hello, my name is Lashana Maverick. I'm Amanda's teacher—"

"What she do now?" the man interrupted, turning away. "Manda, get over here."

"No, sir, she's not in trouble," Ms. Maverick said firmly.

"Then what you want?" His tone was defensive, his eyes narrowing.

Amanda peeked cautiously over a partition inside the house, watching Ms. Maverick.

"What the hell you doing? Get over here now, damn it!" the man shouted.

"Yes, Uncle Fred," Amanda called, stepping forward slowly.

"Now!" Fred snapped, and Amanda hurried to him.

"Your teacher said she came to see if you were alright. You giving her trouble? You better behave."

"Really, sir. She's been a delight," Ms. Maverick said, spreading her hands in a calming gesture.

"I don't get it. Why you here then? Manda will see you at school if you ain't got nothing to say. Now, goodbye." Fred began to shut the door.

Ms. Maverick stepped back as the door closed between them. She returned to her car, parked in the middle of the street.

Inside, Amanda settled at the kitchen table. On one side of the house, men yelled and cheered, glued to a football game on the TV. On the other, a group of women chatted quietly, braiding and twisting each other's hair. One sat on the floor while another worked at her hair.

"The door again, Fred!" a woman shouted. "Fred!" She stood and walked toward the door. "Manda, your teacher's here."

She led Ms. Maverick into the room where Amanda sat.

"I thought you might need some help with your homework," Ms. Maverick said with a warm smile.

"What the—" Fred appeared in the doorway. "What you doing back here?"

"I figured since I was here, I could help Amanda with her homework. I won't be long, I promise."

"I got people here," Fred said, puffing out his chest and leaning forward to look bigger.

Ms. Maverick and Fred locked eyes. "Not a problem. I can take Amanda to the library, and we can work there."

"Nah, it's a school night. I don't want Manda running the streets."

Ms. Maverick straightened. "No problem. I'll work with Amanda right here. We shouldn't be long."

"I told you, I got people here," Fred growled, making a face like he might spit.

"Well, Amanda has homework to do. You wouldn't want her falling behind because her uncle's throwing a party, would you? If that happens, I'd have to report it to the school. You know how that can get messy. You know what I mean, Uncle Fred?" Ms. Maverick said, voice calm but firm.

The women braiding hair fell silent, watching Fred for his response. He licked his lips, eyes flicking to the woman beside him.

"You got half an hour," Fred finally said, pointing at Ms. Maverick. "But I better see some A's coming from her if she's getting *private lessons*."

"You won't have to worry," Ms. Maverick said confidently. Fred turned away.

"But I'll need you to turn down that music and the TV," she added. Fred clenched his fist.

"She'll need to concentrate," Ms. Maverick insisted. The women whispered among themselves, casting glances at Fred as if gossiping.

"Please," Ms. Maverick commanded. Fred gave her a dark look. "Like you said, I only have half an hour."

Fred stomped back into the other room, muttering under his breath. The women listened as he ordered his friends to turn down the volume.

"You do some kind of magic?" one woman joked. "Fred don't listen to nobody. He's the most stubborn man I know."

Ms. Maverick smiled. Amanda studied her teacher, impressed by her unusual strength in this place.

Leaning toward Amanda at the table, Ms. Maverick was interrupted by a young woman sitting on the floor, hair halfway braided.

"You're her teacher, right?" she asked.

"Yes," Ms. Maverick answered.

"You went to college and all that?"

"Yes," Ms. Maverick replied, exhaustion creeping into her voice.

"Was it worth it? I mean, it costs a lot," the young woman said, her voice tentative but curious. Her eyes darted nervously among the others, afraid of judgment.

"College opened my eyes to the world," Ms. Maverick said, passion returning to her voice. "It was a great experience. Education is key to moving up in life."

"You make more money going to college, right?" the young woman pressed, growing bolder.

"Girl, stop asking her questions," said an older woman braiding hair. "She's a teacher. You know she ain't rich. Plus we ain't got no money to send you anywhere."

Ms. Maverick squinted her eyes from the woman's statement. The young woman looked away, deflated. The sparkle of hope in her eyes dimmed, crushed by the older woman's bitterness.

"College is about more than money," Ms. Maverick said firmly, pride shining through. "It expands your worldview."

"You live in Shiloh Heights?" another young woman asked timidly from the couch.

Ms. Maverick shook her head. The young woman rolled her eyes now uninterested.

"I'm a teacher too," said another woman, settling near them. "So I know what she means."

Ms. Maverick's face lit up. "That's wonderful. What do you teach?"

"I teach Sunday School," the woman answered.

"Girl, you ain't no real teacher," another woman shouted from the couch.

"I'm a teacher for the Lord. Tell her, Manda." Amanda nodded but stayed silent.

"I'm her Auntie Rhonda," the woman said, holding out her hand for Ms. Maverick to shake.

"Rhonda!" Fred's voice boomed from the other room. "You got the drinks in there?"

"No, Fred!" Rhonda shouted back.

"Where are they then?"

"Check the box in the kitchen."

Their voices escalated, bouncing off the walls as neither seemed to hear the other. Everyone winced at the growing volume.

"It's really nice to meet you, but I need to help Amanda. Is there another room where we can work in private?" Ms. Maverick asked, trying to smooth the irritation from her face.

Just then, a young boy burst into the room, tears streaming. He crashed into Amanda's chest. "Amanda, they pushed me down." His sobs broke free.

"Boy, stop being such a little sissy," Rhonda barked, then glanced at Ms. Maverick. "They're just playing around. Mikey, go play with the boys. Get!"

Two older boys shuffled in, teasing Mikey in Amanda's arms.

"Stop bothering him," Amanda growled, gritting her teeth and raising a fist.

"Amanda, leave them alone. You know they're just teasing. Mikey, go. Manda's got her teacher here." Rhonda's stern stare sent Mikey following the older boys out. Moments later, the boys' laughter was cut short by a thud and Mikey's soft sobs.

Ms. Maverick watched Amanda clutch her pencil, frustration and tears threatening to spill. Suddenly, the pencil snapped in her grip.

"Girl, don't cry for no reason. They're just playing. Go get your teacher a seat," Rhonda ordered, pointing toward the door. Amanda slumped out.

"Is she like this at school? That girl's got some anger problems. I tell her she can't let the sun go down on her anger. She's always trying to fight my boys. Girls can't be hitting boys now," Rhonda said.

Ms. Maverick looked at her, confused.

"My boys gotta toughen up little Mikey. Amanda won't always be there. Can't have him growing up to be no sissy," Rhonda added with a proud smile.

"Do you all live here?" Ms. Maverick asked, scanning the cramped room.

Rhonda's face stiffened. "We come and go."

"Does Amanda have her own room? She's at that age—she needs her own space."

"Fred and I are going to the courthouse next month. He'll move in with me. I got some space," Rhonda said.

"I thought you were Amanda's aunt?" Ms. Maverick pressed.

"Well, I will be," Rhonda said, hand on her chest, passion coloring her voice. "I was best friends with Amanda's mother. She had her at sixteen. We've been raising her and Mikey. He's what, seven?" She glanced at another woman for confirmation. "Amanda comes to me for everything. I'm like her mother. Between you and me, Amanda's mother wanted to put her up for adoption as a baby. Didn't think she could handle it. But the Lord spoke to Fred and me, and we took her in."

From the other room, the men erupted in cheers for their team. The television volume spiked. Fred and another man began arguing, their voices rising until they tackled each other. Others rushed in to break it up.

"Excuse me," Rhonda said, her face flushing with embarrassment. She strode over and berated the men, pushing Fred away from the scuffle. Fred spun toward her, shouting in her face. Rhonda tried to shove him back, one hand raised defensively to shield herself. They paused, suddenly aware of the outsider watching.

Ms. Maverick turned at the sound of something dragging behind her. Amanda stood frozen in the corner, clutching a chair like a shield.

Rhonda returned and sank onto the couch beside the other woman, her eyes glossy and breath uneven.

The women fell silent while the men's voices swelled again with excitement from the game.

"Has Fred . . . behaved like this when Amanda is around?" Ms. Maverick asked cautiously.

Rhonda's eyes sharpened, shoulders stiffening. Concern flickered across her face. "Fred took them in when they had no one. Fred's not abusive. Don't come in here thinking you can accuse him."

"I'm not accusing anyone," Ms. Maverick said, her posture stiffening, ready to stand her ground.

"Then mind your business. Amanda owes everything to Fred. Don't come in here with accusations."

"I'm concerned about his behavior—"

"Maybe you had some bougie daddy who could pay for college, but we don't have that. Plus, teacher," Rhonda mocked, hands on hips, "if Fred loses his temper sometimes, who cares?" Ms. Maverick's eyes widened in shock.

"What's left for her, huh? Manda better be grateful to Fred. If she leaves, she's got nothing but foster care—where they'll beat her up and move her from home to home. At least she's got family here. You don't leave where you've been planted. That servant couldn't leave her job. God told her to return to Abraham. Heck, she was a runaway slave, mistreated. But all she had left was to die in the desert or return to work. Sometimes that's all we get."

Amanda peered over the chair, fists tightening around it. "No," she said quietly—but loud enough for the women to hear.

The women burst into simultaneous chatter about Fred and Rhonda's relationship. Rhonda scowled, snapping back at them. Their bickering almost matched the noise coming from the men's side.

Ms. Maverick turned back to Amanda, pushing the chair fully into the room. She placed her hands over Amanda's and lowered herself to the girl's level.

"I'd rather die in the desert than return to bondage," she said softly.

CHAPTER 8

"HER BLOOD PRESSURE was just high," Cassandra said, showing Joshua the small machine's panel in her hand. Amanda leaned heavily on the bench, exhausted. Her eyelids fluttered as she took in the faces of her loved ones around her. The fierce winds of Shiloh City had finally subsided, and a single ray of sunlight broke through, casting a soft glow on downtown.

"I guess you need to cut back on the soul food, Amanda," Malcolm teased, bumping her shoulder playfully.

Amanda squinted, groaning at his joke.

"Should we take her to the hospital?" Joshua asked, watching Cassandra pack up her medical equipment.

"Only if she wants to. But I think Ms. Amanda will be fine," Cassandra replied. She leaned down toward Amanda on the bench. "Here, Ms. Amanda. Drink some water."

Amanda's hand moved slowly toward the bottle.

"You're very handy with this equipment, young lady," Reverend Anthony remarked, eyeing the suitcase of medical supplies laid out on the bench.

"Thank you, sir," Cassandra said, glancing up at him while still tending to Amanda.

"What happened?" Amanda asked sluggishly.

"You fell over and didn't answer me for a while," Joshua answered, leaning in close and nearly bumping Cassandra. "You handed me your phone. You said, 'Call Cass. Call Cass.'"

"I don't know why I'm not your emergency contact," Malcolm teased. "But once we got the call, we rushed right back."

Amanda shot him a tired look. "Show me how to use any of that equipment, and I'll change it in my phone." Her voice was still weak but carried a flicker of life.

"Good to see you coming back around. Nothing can stop you, Mandy," Malcolm said with a grin.

"I can take you home. I think you just need some rest," Joshua offered, standing from his spot below her.

Malcolm leaned close to Amanda and whispered, "I see his game." He wiggled his eyebrows. Joshua shot him a sharp glare.

"Malcolm," Amanda sighed, exasperated. She pushed herself up slightly on the bench and looked at the father-son duo. "I apologize . . . "

Reverend Anthony placed a gentle hand on Amanda's shoulder. "Don't worry about anything. Just get some rest." He gave her a reassuring smile.

"Your phone," Joshua said, pointing.

"It's Mikey," Amanda replied, weariness thick in her voice.

"I was so worried, I called everybody," Joshua explained.

"Let's give her a minute, folks," Reverend Anthony said, motioning for the group to give Amanda space.

"You okay?" Malcolm asked, noticing Cassandra's intense focus elsewhere.

"That truck's circled the area at least ten times," she answered, eyes fixed on the street.

"You think—" Malcolm started, but his phone suddenly rang. Both he and Cassandra jumped. Malcolm fumbled into his jacket pocket and answered. The frantic voice on the other end twisted Malcolm's expression from confusion to annoyance.

Cassandra glanced back at the street. "I'm going to check something out." She tried to catch Malcolm's attention, but he just nodded, still engaged on the phone.

Without hesitation, Cassandra bolted toward the street, weaving through the line of people waiting for food. The quiet soldier kept a cautious distance as a white van turned the corner and slipped into a parking garage. Cassandra reached for the gun tucked in her belt, moving slowly toward the driver's side.

The parking garage was eerily empty, the loneliness pressing in. Her footsteps echoed as men's voices from the truck bounced off the concrete walls.

"We'll circle back in fifteen minutes," one man said.

"This is the stupidest mission the bossy lady in the mask has given us yet," another complained.

"Show some respect. She's the elder. And don't worry, she knows what she's doing. *Nightmare* will show himself. We just have to keep watching his allies. He's a demon—a snake that's bitten every member of Psalms Society."

"My bad . . . but is it true? They say Nightmare burned down Psalms Society eighteen years ago. He . . . he tortured the elders, ravaged our land," the man asked, speaking through a mouthful of food.

"He's always been our enemy. Now he's stolen the psalms necklace from us—a transgression we won't forgive," the man's voice was thick with both anger and devotion.

"Necklace?" The food-mouthed man blinked, confused.

"Yeah. You haven't been paying attention in class, have you? It's our sacred symbol. It promotes unity, freedom, and prosperity. The one who wears the psalms necklace leads Psalms Society. We follow that person without question," the devoted psalmist explained.

"So . . . if Nightmare puts on the necklace, does that make him the leader?" the man asked, chewing.

"No. It's more than that. The previous leader must gift it to a new leader. That's how it works. The psalms necklace symbolizes a great, charismatic gift bestowed upon a leader—someone who will usher in a new age of freedom and enlightenment." His voice cracked slightly, emotion rising. "We are the psalmists. The sword of the Psalms Society. We will get our sacred necklace back from that wicked creature."

"I see . . ." The food-mouthed man paused thoughtfully. "But I heard that bossy lady in the mask told the squad leader we're here to find out if Nightmare's son contacted him. They're working together to take us down."

"Well, you're mistaken. We're here for the psalms necklace," the devoted psalmist insisted.

"No, we're here for Nightmare's son," the other corrected.

"No, you're wrong," the devoted psalmist shot back. The two began to bicker heatedly.

Cassandra took a breath and quickly raised her gun toward the driver's seat. The men squealed in fright. They wore psalmist attire but no masks. Cassandra's expression held a flicker of surprise—as if she had expected more.

"Please . . ." the man with food in his mouth stammered, dropping the burger he held. Cassandra noticed fast-food wrappers and bags scattered between them inside the van. Confusion flickered across her face.

"Get out of the van. Now." She ordered sharply, gun steady. "Hands where I can see them."

The men hesitated, then slowly opened the doors and stepped out.

"You, front of the car. No funny business," she said to the psalmist emerging from the passenger side.

Both men trembled, raising their hands above their heads.

"We are the psalmists. The spirit of change. The anointed. We proclaim good news to the poor and freedom to prisoners. We restore sight to the blind and set the oppressed free." The devoted psalmist met Cassandra's gaze with steady seriousness, unafraid of the gun pointed at him.

His partner slumped, tears spilling down his cheeks. "Please . . ." he begged. "I just joined. I haven't been promoted to official psalmist. I haven't even been in the Blue Room."

Cassandra kept her gun trained on them. "Once we find out where Nightmare's son has gone, we'll be out of your hair. I promise."

"No, we're here for the psalms necklace," the devoted psalmist argued.

"No, I'm telling you—it's Nightmare's son," the other insisted.

"Guys," Cassandra snapped, seeing them lose focus.

"When I joined Psalms Society, I thought it'd be enlightening. Stress-free," the man with food blurted, slumping against the pavement. "Now I'm about to get mugged by a woman."

The psalmists began to argue again, voices rising, as the quiet soldier struggled to get their attention.

Cassandra fired a warning shot high into the air. Both flinched. "Okay, let's start again. What is your mission here?"

They spoke at once, each trying to be heard.

"You're free to join the Psalms Society too, young lady," the devoted psalmist offered, arms open as if inviting a hug. "Free from society's madness and suffering. Psalms Society rejects classism. We are people—not of race or gender, but of freedom and prosperity. Above all, we wish you health and that your soul prospers. We are just that—souls."

"Don't fall for his sales pitch," the other said. "I've been with them three months, and I'm thinking about quitting. It's just too much. Look." He pulled down his shirt collar, revealing a deep wound on his chest. "Nightmare did that to me the night we attacked you guys in the limo."

"You want to go back to suffering? This is the way to freedom and prosperity," the devoted psalmist insisted, placing a hand on his partner's chest. "We extend an invitation to you, miss. Nightmare and his family were once with us."

"No thanks." Cassandra gestured with her gun. "We're going to Mr. Rob. He'll know what to do."

"Please, no! Don't take us to Nightmare. Please, kind lady," the wounded psalmist cried, grabbing her leg.

"Enough."

They turned to see the psalmist leader and more members behind him.

"Drop the gun," the leader ordered.

Cassandra didn't flinch but held her gaze steady.

"Drop it," he repeated.

"Squad leader, we were just—" the devoted psalmist began.

"Silence," another member barked, pointing at them. "You call yourselves psalmists? We are the warriors—the blade of our society. We protect and defend our home and prosperity." He pointed at Cassandra. "Let death seize our enemies; let them go down alive into hell."

The psalmists began chanting in unison: "Let death seize our enemies; let them go down alive into hell."

The leader raised his hand, and the chanting ceased.

"Put the gun down . . . Rob's protector."

Cassandra held firm.

"The offer stands. You're free to join us. Let the psalms of our prosperity elevate you." The leader reached out his hand toward her.

"Thanks, but I think I'll pass. Not interested in your crazy cult," Cassandra teased.

"We are not a cult. We are a way of life. Revolutionaries. Activists. Freedom."

"You're spiraling. You're not even sure what your mission here is, huh?" Cassandra said.

The leader squinted.

The members behind Cassandra began arguing among themselves about their mission.

"We follow orders . . . even if they change," the leader said, walking slowly toward Cassandra. She nervously shifted her gun closer to the wounded psalmist, who flinched.

"You fight well. You'd be a great member," the leader complimented.

"I said no thanks. Stop moving, or I'll shoot."

"You're not Rob. You're not a monster." His steps echoed through the garage. "You protect gangsters—pestilences that make Shiloh City filthy. But there's another option . . . we can prosper your soul."

He reached out his hand again. "Please… prosperity awaits."

"You . . . you call him Rob?" Cassandra motioned her gun up and down. "They call him *Nightmare*. Are you…"

"Am I what?"

"Ezra?"

"Who? You think I'm associated with Rob?" The leader laughed.

"Yes. I do. I think you have your own agenda."

The leader swiftly drew a dagger from his chest pocket.

"If you're so bold, let me see what's under that mask. Let them see." Cassandra nodded toward the members behind her.

"Have you seen what he looks like under the mask?" she asked them. They shook their heads.

"You're not devoted to this cause. You're after Mr. Rob for yourself."

"You're trying to break our resolve, but we refuse to accept." The leader grabbed Cassandra's arm and twisted the gun from her hand.

"Shoot me," Cassandra dared, opening her jacket to taunt him.

He raised the gun at her.

The members shouted protests— "Squad leader, elder spoke to you—we don't use guns!"

Voices echoed chaotically.

"Stop . . . shut up . . . I can't . . . I don't want to go into the Blue Room..." The leader winced, clutching his head, losing focus.

He lowered the gun and stepped back.

Cassandra elbowed him hard, making him drop the weapon.

He shook his head, trying to snap out of it, reaching for the gun again despite the psalmists shouting.

Cassandra punched him hard, and he crumpled to the floor on his back.

She jumped on his chest and tried to remove his mask. He fought back fiercely.

The others slowly closed in, daggers drawn, ready to strike.

He shoved her off, but in the struggle, Cassandra slipped off the mask. It fell to the ground.

She stared, expecting to see his face.

But the leader pulled his hood tighter, hiding his features. He turned away, searching the floor for the mask.

The psalmists circled Cassandra, daggers raised, poised to attack.

Suddenly, a gunshot cracked through the air.

Everyone jolted.

Malcolm stood nearby, gun aimed at the circle. He fired, hitting one member. The man collapsed, clutching his leg.

Malcolm fired again, hitting another.

Like swarming ants, the psalmists scattered, fleeing the parking garage in all directions.

Cassandra squinted through the chaos, locking eyes on the leader's concealed face.

Malcolm kept firing until he emptied his gun, then helped Cassandra to her feet.

"Thanks . . . but how'd you know I was here?" Cassandra gave Malcolm a suspicious look. "Mr. Malcolm, are you even supposed to have a gun?"

Malcolm smiled brightly. "Cassie, by now you should know—men in my tax bracket have our own rules." He pulled out his phone from his jacket pocket. "Told you that tracker I clipped to your belt would come in handy."

She looked down, feeling around her belt. "You didn't *tell* me anything about a tracker." Her glare sharpened, and Malcolm's smile faltered, a blush rising to his cheeks.

"Oh . . . didn't I?" He gave an awkward chuckle, then held his phone out to her. "Look. You're here. Amanda's here. Now I just need to figure out how to get Rob to wear one."

Cassandra shot him another dirty look.

Malcolm laughed uneasily but quickly turned serious, staring down at his phone. "Come on, Cassie—we have to go." He patted her arm and started toward the parking garage exit. "You can tell me what happened on the way."

"You okay? What's going on?" Cassandra asked, noticing the shift in his tone.

"It's Daisy," Malcolm muttered.

Click. Flash. Click.

Camera flashes went off in rapid bursts as Malcolm and Cassandra walked a long carpet that snaked through a crowded studio. Photographers barked directions; models struck perfect poses. The rhythmic flickering of lights made Cassandra's head spin.

Malcolm, all business, charged ahead—but noticed she was falling behind. He turned and saw her mesmerized by a group of shirtless male models posing under artificial rain.

Water streamed down their muscular frames, cascading over defined abs and chiseled arms. One model, drenched and glistening, struck a pose as droplets rolled down his torso like they were following the steps of a stone fountain. Cassandra's jaw slackened. Her eyes locked on the sensual curve of his torso and the perfect symmetry of his tan, toned body.

The model noticed her ogling and gave her a charming wink.

Cassandra let out a girlish giggle, fanning herself with one hand, the other covering her mouth in a futile attempt to hide her smile.

Malcolm groaned, annoyed. He grabbed her arm and pulled her forward.

She followed, still grinning, stealing one last glance over her shoulder.

Daisy posed confidently under the lights, the thin silk dress hugging her lean frame and flowing with the gusts from nearby fans. Her cheekbones stood out under perfectly applied makeup, and the camera loved every inch of her elegance.

She shifted gracefully to the floor, her long legs stretching out, her arms posed upward. The blond wig framed her face like a halo.

"Ready for the next set?" a photographer called.

Daisy nodded and disappeared behind a curtain. Moments later, she returned—this time in a tight, shimmering two-piece bikini.

Cameras flashed again as Daisy took center stage, commanding attention with each movement. She dropped to the floor for the final pose, beaming confidently at the lens.

"Excellent, Daisy. Take five," a photographer said, lowering his camera.

Jessie stepped onto the set to help her up, sneaking a quick kiss.

"Hey, lover boy! Don't mess up her makeup!" a photographer warned.

The couple chuckled.

"Not every guy gets to say he's dating a model," Jessie teased.

"You like?" Daisy teased, flipping her blond hair over her shoulder. "Maybe I'll keep this wig on tonight."

Jessie laughed. "No thanks, babe. My passion is justice. Yours is art."

She playfully pouted. "Mikey's doing it. I could have them dress you in a cute little cop outfit. Maybe even go shirtless . . ."

She kissed him again.

"Daisy!" the photographer called out. "Makeup!"

"Sorry!" she laughed, arms still around Jessie's neck.

At the studio's entrance, a large man in a suit blocked Malcolm and Cassandra from going any farther.

"Let me in there," Malcolm demanded, pointing past the man. "That's my daughter."

"Sir, don't make me throw you out," the guard said flatly, unmoved.

Malcolm leaned toward Cassandra. "If you beat him up, I'll give you a raise."

Cassandra gave him a deadpan look.

"Fine," Malcolm grumbled. He pulled out his wallet and began counting. "I've got five hundred dollars. All yours if you let me in."

The guard didn't flinch.

"I'm so mad I left my gun in the car," Malcolm muttered.

Just then, a voice called from behind them. "Malcolm?"

They turned to see Mikey approaching—shirtless, muscles flexing with every step. Cassandra's eyes widened as she took in the sight of his sculpted torso.

Mikey grinned, enjoying the attention. He strutted up to them, bouncing his pecs in Cassandra's direction.

Cassandra giggled, covering her mouth with one hand. "Oh . . . wow." She reached out and traced a finger down his abs.

"Cassandra, get a grip!" Malcolm groaned.

"Mikey, tell this guy to let me in."

"Malcolm, I don't know if Daisy—"

"Now!" Malcolm snapped, face reddening with frustration.

Mikey sighed and nodded to the guard, who finally stepped aside.

Malcolm pushed through the door without hesitation.

On set, the photographer admired Daisy from behind his camera. "Take another break, girl. You're a goddess among ants—we're not worthy."

Compliments flew from the crew. Daisy had impressed them all with her passion and professionalism.

Exhausted, she made her way to Jessie, who was busy working on his laptop.

He looked up as her footsteps approached, quickly pulling out a chair. "Here—sit."

"Thanks, but I'm good," Daisy said, stretching. "I don't want to sit down and fall asleep."

"You've been working hard," Jessie said, eyes shifting back to his screen.

"I love what I do. My mom was working her way into modeling before she met my dad. Probably the only reason he married her. He's a real sexist pig."

"I don't doubt that," Jessie said with a chuckle, still typing.

Daisy crossed her arms, her voice growing more earnest. "I'm confident in all *this*"—she gestured to her body—"and I want other girls to be, too. Our bodies aren't here for men's pleasure. They're ours to own, to express. One day, I want to run something of my own—not just help manage a set. I want to build something creative and empowering. But neither of my parents have ever seen me as a leader."

"You helped organize this whole shoot," Jessie said, scribbling notes on a pad as he glanced at his laptop.

"My leadership and initiative have always been spat on by both my parents. They've never seen me for who I really am."

"Yup," Jessie mumbled, his focus still buried in his notepad.

Daisy raised an eyebrow. "Are you even listening? I'm pouring my heart out here."

"Sorry . . . babe," Jessie replied, scribbling furiously.

She closed his laptop with a soft click and gave him a warm smile. "Maybe that's why I like you. You're passionate about justice. I'm passionate about leadership."

"Justice means everything to me . . ." Jessie said, finally looking up. He noticed the change in her expression—she was serious now. He set his notepad and pencil aside.

"My dad . . . he was all about justice too. Kind, driven. He loved upholding the law and loved this country. He pushed me to follow in his footsteps. I never thought I'd have a personal life—just the job—until I met you."

Daisy's look softened.

"They said he was captured in combat," Jessie continued, his voice growing quieter. "At least, that's the official story. But I've found evidence . . . there's a group out there, something underground. They're capturing injured soldiers—taking them and . . . reprogramming them. Like mind control or psychological warfare. I know my father was taken."

Jessie's voice rose suddenly, and Daisy instinctively pulled back.

"Sorry," he said, catching himself.

She walked around the desk and gently cradled his head in her hands.

"Last year, I was deployed overseas. We were ambushed . . . by someone in a mask. Took out most of my unit. I was lucky to survive. But when we finally brought him down, I had to know who he was. I pulled off his mask… and I recognized him. He was in my dad's platoon. His best friend. Someone I knew. And he didn't even recognize me."

Jessie paused, eyes distant. "It was like he'd been erased. Like someone rewired his brain. He wasn't a traitor—he was a victim."

"I'm so sorry," Daisy whispered, massaging his scalp gently. "You're working so hard. I know you'll solve this." She kissed him on the forehead, then turned his face to hers. "Wait… I thought you were a cop?"

Jessie smirked. "I never actually said that, did I?"

Daisy pouted playfully.

"I work for the CIA," he admitted. "I'm undercover right now. I wanted an overseas assignment—anything that could lead me to my dad—but instead, they stuck me here. We always had our suspicions about Shiloh City . . . but your dad, Amanda, and Rob confirmed things in ways I wasn't ready for."

"Oh, so you're just using me to get to my dad?" Daisy teased. "Maybe I should set up a lunch date for you two."

Jessie chuckled and took her hand, kissing it. "No. My love for you is real. I feel like a prince who finally found his princess."

He leaned in for a kiss, but Daisy pushed him back, laughing. "The moment's over. You made it weird."

They both laughed.

Then Jessie's expression sobered. "But your dad…"

"What? That he's a sexist pig and a drama king?" Daisy shrugged. "He's definitely not a terrorist."

"He might not be," Jessie said, "but he's a gangster. All of them are. No wonder the police hate them."

Daisy frowned. "What are you talking about?"

Jessie reopened his laptop and turned the screen toward her. "From what I've gathered, your dad, Rob, and Amanda run Shiloh City like their personal empire. Your dad buys up businesses downtown. When owners refuse to sell? Rob pays them a visit. He's the enforcer. The muscle. The bully."

He pulled up a younger photo of Amanda. "She went to prison. Probably something Mikey doesn't even know. Looks like she shot someone. And she came out more dangerous than when she went in."

He clicked again. Another photo appeared: Amanda on stage receiving an award.

"'Shiloh City's First Black Female Millionaire,'" Jessie read sarcastically. "My ass."

A new image popped up—Amanda and Mikey on stage together. "I like Mikey. He's a good guy. But Amanda? She never went to business school. Never went to college. And yet they're swimming in wealth. Doesn't add up."

Jessie showed another image—Mikey leaping off a stage into a cheering crowd.

"She runs his entire brand. His speaking engagements. The thing is, they're operating as a religious nonprofit."

"So?" Daisy asked, frowning.

"There's nothing religious about those shows," Jessie said firmly. "Amanda's using loopholes, using Mikey as her puppet. On top of that, she runs a girls' home or foster facility. She shouldn't even legally be allowed to. No way someone with her record could pass a background check. From what I've read, even in prison, she ran the place like a mob boss."

"I know her. She's sweet."

"Sure, to your face. But behind the scenes…"

He pulled up a file on Rob. "Now him? He's got a long history—assault, intimidation, even got dishonorably discharged. But he's never done real time. Your dad's lawyers, probably."

Daisy leaned in closer, curiosity now replacing her skepticism.

"Is he really your uncle?" Jessie asked. "I mean, how does a disgraced soldier end up doing business with a tech mogul like your dad? Only common ground I see is their temper."

"Rob used to work security for my dad after the military. He was in love with my Aunt Phoebe. Only time I've ever seen him smile."

Jessie lowered his voice, leaning in.

"Not to scare you… but I think he was a contract killer. An assassin. One of my sources—some loudmouth named Dunkin—let it slip to my boss. Something's off about that guy too…"

He paused, wiping his forehead.

"Rob is bad news. He's worked for—and *against*—America. I'd arrest him right now if I had the proof. He's dangerous. Unstable. And worse? He's been all over—from Japan, the Caribbean, the Middle East—and everywhere he goes, this follows."

Jessie pulled up a grainy photo.

The figure in it wore strange, battle-worn gear: a gray armored chest plate, black sash down to his boots, metal bracers on both arms, a sleek sword at his hip, and a thin, ominous-looking gun. His face was hidden behind a metallic demon mask with glowing red eyes.

"People who have seen this thing call it *Nightmare,*" Jessie said. "Some think it's just a legend. Everyone at the agency believes it used to be Rob. Maybe he wore this as part of some covert ops unit. Or maybe he's just insane. But the profile matches—military-grade killer hiding behind a mask."

Daisy stared at the photo, chills creeping up her arms.

Jessie typed again. "Reports say others wearing similar gear have appeared in Shiloh City recently."

"You think Uncle Rob's behind your dad's disappearance?" she asked, still unsettled.

"I don't know," Jessie said, rising to his feet. "But I *do* know he's at the center of something dangerous. And your dad and Amanda are in it as well."

"What does this terrorist group want with Uncle Rob?"

"I haven't figured that part out yet. But if he—or whoever he's working with—has anything to do with my dad's disappearance, I swear I'll take them down."

Daisy stepped beside him and placed a hand on his shoulder. "I believe you. You're too driven not to find the truth."

Jessie's eyes welled up. "If he's even still alive..."

"Hey." Daisy pulled him close, curling into his chest. "Don't think like that. Stay positive. My dad taught me something in business—never surrender to doubt. Doubt is weakness."

"You're the strongest woman I know," Jessie said, tilting her chin up. Their lips met in a deep, passionate kiss—

"Hey!" Malcolm's voice cut through the moment like a blade.

Daisy and Jessie jumped as Malcolm stormed toward them.

"Daisy, what the hell? You moved out!" He smacked the desk with his palm. "The maids said all your stuff's gone. Get up. Get up!"

He rushed forward too quickly and slammed into the desk, gritting his teeth as he fought off the pain.

Then he stared his daughter down. "How do you keep getting past my security system?"

Daisy only gave him a smug, charming smile.

"Malcolm—" Jessie began.

"You!" Malcolm pointed a finger an inch from his nose. "Since the day you got here, you've been nothing but a pain in my ass."

"Dad, stop." Daisy stood tall. "You can't control me. Cut me off—go ahead. I don't need your money."

"You think your mother is going to give it? You can't live without your shopping sprees, your facials . . . your influencer lifestyle. You won't last five minutes in the real world."

"Neither would you," Daisy blurted back.

"You have no idea. No idea," Malcolm said, shaking his head.

"Don't act like you bootstrapped your way here. Grandpa Dave gave you Armory."

Malcolm yanked Daisy away from Jessie, gripping her arm. The sudden motion sent Jessie tumbling from his chair. As Malcolm pulled her back, Daisy turned Jessie's laptop toward herself.

"Your grandfather didn't do a damn thing for me," Malcolm growled. "Not for me, not for your Aunt Phoebe. *I* turned Armory into a profitable company—*me* and your aunt. Don't spit on her name." Soft tears slid down his cheeks. "Don't you dare spit on her sacrifice."

"Malcolm, take your hands off her," Jessie said, rising to his feet.

Malcolm chuckled darkly. "You. I've got something for you."

"What, gonna sic Uncle Rob on him?" Daisy snapped, pulling her arm free.

"Daisy—" Jessie warned.

"What?" Malcolm turned to her, eyes sharp with confusion and alarm.

Daisy's eyes flicked past him—Cassandra and Mikey had just entered the room behind Malcolm.

"Do you know?" she asked, locking eyes with Cassandra.

"Daisy—" Jessie said again, voice urgent.

"Uncle Rob is an assassin," Daisy blurted out.

Mikey stared at her. Shock crossed his face—followed by the flicker of a realization, as if pieces were falling into place.

"He's a thug," Daisy went on. "A weapon my dad and Amanda use to threaten business competitors. And when he gets charged—which he *has*—Dad's lawyers sweep it all under the rug."

"I *knew* something was off about him," Mikey muttered. "He's insane. I mean, I took his car once and—"

"He's lying to you," Malcolm interrupted, eyes blazing. "You're being fed spy stories from this clown."

"I *knew* you were some kind of agent," he hissed at Jessie. "CIA? FBI? You people sniff around until something breaks."

"If Rob is who you say he is," Jessie said, stepping forward, "then maybe you should be worried."

Malcolm laughed grimly. "They all say that—before the nightmares start."

"You be careful working for that man," Mikey said quietly to Cassandra, touching her arm. "I always thought his relationship with Amanda was . . . weird. He's a demon. I hate him. More than I hate my own dad—and I *don't even know* my dad's name."

Cassandra stared at him, startled by the calm rage in his voice.

"Rob tortured me," Mikey said. "All because I stole his car when I was a stupid teenager. One bad decision. But he's . . . something evil. A demon from hell."

Malcolm's voice cut through the tension again, louder now, overwhelming Mikey's confession. He and Daisy locked into another shouting match, their words sharp, raw, charged.

As they argued, Cassandra and Mikey turned toward Jessie's laptop. The blurred photo of a masked figure—Rob in his suspected assassin gear—was still on screen.

"Damn . . ." Mikey muttered. "A real assassin. I can't even say I'm surprised. Now if he *ever* mouths off to me again . . ." Mikey rubbed his hands together slowly, still staring at the laptop. "I've got something on him now. Revenge is sweet."

Cassandra moved closer, peering at the image in silence.

"Come on, Malcolm," Mikey said gently, placing a hand on his shoulder. "Let's not make a scene."

Malcolm shook him off violently. "Daisy, *please.* Everything I do is to protect you."

"From terrorists?" Daisy asked, voice dripping with disbelief.

Malcolm and Cassandra froze. Cassandra instinctively stepped back from the laptop.

"I know, Dad," Daisy said. "I know everything. You and Amanda . . . I never thought—never imagined."

"Daisy, this man—" Malcolm pointed at Jessie.

"—has only ever told me the truth," she cut in. "Something you've never done. You never told me why you and Mom really split. You've always been cold, and I get it—Mom left, Aunt Phoebe died—but that doesn't give you the right to smother me. I'm not your prisoner."

"I'm not trying to control you," Malcolm said, his voice breaking. "I'm trying to *keep you safe.* Those people out there—they're insane."

"You know what Mom always said?" Daisy's voice softened, but the words cut deeper. "We never needed you to take care of us. You never *have.*"

Malcolm stepped back like he'd been hit. One hand clutched at his chest. His eyes filled with panic.

"The only reason me and Mikey are in danger is because of your connection to Rob," Daisy continued. "But I'm not going to stop living my life because of him. Or because of you."

Jessie's expression shifted—pride flickered in his eyes as he moved beside her and placed his arm gently around her.

Malcolm stood trembling, his fists clenched tight. Tears streamed down his cheeks as he stared at the floor.

"Everyone leaves you, Dad," Daisy said softly. "Now I am too. Cut me off. I'll make it on my own."

She patted Jessie's chest and motioned for him to grab his things. Together, they turned toward the door.

"I'll see you at your show, Mikey," Daisy added, her voice calm. "We've got a lot to talk about."

Jessie nodded respectfully at Mikey and followed Daisy out.

"I just wanted to protect her," Malcolm whispered, barely audible.

"Mr. Malcolm," Cassandra said gently, motioning toward a chair. "Please. Sit."

But Malcolm didn't move. He stood there like stone.

Mikey pulled the chair out and brought it around, but Malcolm still wouldn't budge.

"She's the only thing I have left . . ." he whispered. "Fate's taken everything else from me."

"Malcolm, man," Mikey said softly. "It'll be okay. She just needs time to cool off."

"Fate always spits on people like me," Malcolm muttered, dazed. His eyes had gone vacant.

Cassandra and Mikey exchanged a glance.

Then Mikey's phone buzzed.

"Hey, I've got a meeting," he said to Cassandra. "You got this?"

"I think so. Go ahead," she said.

He started to leave, then turned back.

"Look, I know things are . . . wild right now. But I'd really like it if you came to my show. Got a backstage ticket with your name on it."

"I'll be there," Cassandra replied.

He handed her the ticket and left.

Malcolm drove fast, his hands tight on the wheel, his eyes red and puffy. The engine roared and the tires squealed as the car took sharp turns along the winding road.

"Mr. Malcolm—" Cassandra moaned, gripping her seatbelt in the back.

"I *know,* Cassie," Malcolm snapped.

"Please, you're going too fast. Let me drive. Just pull over—"

"I'm fine!" he barked. "I *need* to drive. Trust me—you don't want me not behind the wheel right now."

"Mr. Malcolm, you almost hit—"

"Cassie, don't. I said I'm fine!" he shouted. "I'm used to fate shaking up my world, taking everything from me."

He looked up, catching her worried gaze in the rear-view mirror. "Forget it," he muttered.

He rolled the window down all the way. The wind blasted in, whipping through the car like a storm.

"I need to cool down," Malcolm said, his voice low, almost to himself.

The cold air rushed over him as he drove, dragging his mind back into the shadows of memory.

CHAPTER 9

“SHE WON’T STOP crying,” Malcolm wailed, cradling the baby in his arms as he held the door open. The veins in his eyes were bloodshot, and he swayed from side to side like a drunk.

A young woman in camouflage fatigues and heavy brown boots stepped through the door. She pulled off her military cap, revealing a messy ponytail, and opened her arms instinctively.

Her presence brought a brightness into the dim, stale apartment—and with it, a flicker of life to Malcolm’s weary expression.

“Pheebz, she just won’t stop crying,” Malcolm groaned.

Phoebe took the baby, gently patting her back. “It’s okay, Daisy. It’s alright. Aunt Phoebe’s here.” She gave Malcolm a quick glance. “Actually, scratch that. I changed my mind. I don’t want her calling me Aunt Pheebz anymore. It’s *Sergeant Phoebe* now.” Her proud smile didn’t mask her concern.

“That’s great,” Malcolm said softly, wrapping her in a tired hug.

"Thanks." Phoebe looked around the cluttered space. "Malcolm . . . she's probably crying because this place is a disaster."

"You army types love things clean and proper," Malcolm said, flopping onto the couch—half-buried under a pile of laundry.

Baby Daisy's cries finally quieted as Phoebe held her.

Phoebe paced with Daisy in her arms, soothing her with a steady rub on the back. The apartment was small and chaotic—laundry everywhere, the smell of mildew clinging to the air. The carpet felt stiff and crunchy under her boots, as if it had been soaked and dried wrong.

"This is insane," Phoebe said. "You and Lola should just move back into the manor."

"Dad kicked me out. Cut me off," Malcolm replied, his voice trailing off like he was already falling asleep.

"You can't live like this, Mal."

He shoved a heap of clothes off the armchair. "Sit."

"I'll stand," she replied firmly. Her tone wasn't a suggestion—it was judgment dressed in restraint.

"It's not that dirty. Don't be such a priss," Malcolm said, trying to joke.

"I'm worried about you." Her voice softened. "We need to fix things with Dad."

"No." Malcolm's voice spiked. "He doesn't approve of Daisy. Doesn't approve of Lola. So forget it."

"Mal, I know how he is—but in his own warped way, he *is* worried about your future. You were supposed to go to Yale. Now you're here changing diapers." She glanced around. "Do you even have a clock in this place? What time is it?"

Malcolm shrugged.

Phoebe's eyes narrowed. "Where's Lola?"

"She's at a gig. I said I'd watch Daisy. She's chasing her modeling dream," he added, wiggling his eyebrows.

Phoebe gave him a skeptical look. "How long has she been gone?"

"All day."

She pressed her lips into a tight line. "Get in the shower. Change your clothes. We're going to talk to Dad."

Malcolm groaned. "You think you're the boss of me now?"

He leaned down and kissed Daisy. "My big sister never stops nagging."

"Do you want me to beat you up in front of your baby?" Phoebe asked, holding Daisy where she could see her face. "I used to beat up your dad. You're eighteen, and I can *still* kick your butt."

Malcolm chuckled as he shuffled toward the bathroom.

"There he is . . ." Malcolm muttered, spotting their father at the bar inside the family-owned club. He was hunched over, nursing the dregs of a drink, staring at nothing.

"The Devil himself," Malcolm said, gripping Daisy's carrier tightly.

"Stop," Phoebe warned, and exhaled. "Just follow me."

They moved past the small crowd toward the bar. Another man sat beside their father, sliding a paper across the counter.

"Dave, got another offer this morning. If we sell—"

"Not now, Tony," Dave said, waving him off and raising his glass like a king on a crumbling throne.

"What's this about selling?" Phoebe asked sharply.

Both men turned to see her in uniform.

"Great, you're back," Tony said with thin sarcasm. "Camouflage suits you."

Phoebe rolled her eyes.

"Women belong in the kitchen, not on the battlefield," Tony sneered with a smile, clearly trying to provoke her.

Phoebe pointed at him. "Try me."

"What I do with my company is none of your business," Dave said, without so much as a glance at Malcolm. "What's *he* doing here, Phoebe?"

Everyone knew who he meant.

"I'll tell him what he told me once," Dave continued, downing the last of his drink. "He can stay the hell out of my life."

Malcolm stiffened. Quietly, he set Daisy's carrier on the bar.

Phoebe leaned in, her voice calm but firm. "Dad, this has to stop."

Tony cut in again, but Phoebe silenced him with a glare.

Daisy started crying again. As Phoebe argued with Dave, Malcolm pulled a bottle and wipes from the diaper bag and began organizing them on the bar.

"What the hell?" the bartender snapped, slamming a glass down. "Get that baby out of here. All that damn crying is bothering my customers."

Malcolm flinched, hands hovering over the carrier, eyes brimming with exhaustion and shame.

"This is *our* club," Phoebe shot back. "You don't speak to us like that."

Dave snorted. "There's the fire I needed from Malcolm. Not some weak, boot-licking punk. If Junior were still alive—"

"He's *not*, Dad. Dave died," Phoebe said bluntly.

"He was *captured*," Dave bellowed. "The son who carried my name. The one who made me proud. They're still searching for him. That's what fate does. It *takes*. Just like it's trying to take my company now."

He lifted his glass again, but it was empty. He stared at it like it had betrayed him.

"Let me remind you—Armory is *my* company. Mine!"

Tony nodded quickly and slid the paper back toward Dave.

"Tony, get the hell out of here," Phoebe ordered.

"Don't talk to me like—"

"Or *what*?" She stepped into his space, chin high, unwavering. "My dad is drunk. And you're trying to take advantage of him. Get."

She shoved him once—he stumbled.

She shoved him again. He staggered farther back, face red with humiliation.

The room was silent. Eyes from nearby tables watched with anticipation.

"What are you going to do?" Phoebe taunted. "Everyone's watching. Get this straight—Malcolm and I own more shares than you. You're not selling our family's legacy."

Tony breathed hard, then reached for the paper. Phoebe slapped her finger on it. "We're *not* selling."

Tony glared, but backed down and stormed out.

Malcolm watched Phoebe. She stood firm, throat tight, fighting tears with everything she had. He could see the strain on her face, the pressure she was swallowing just to hold everything together.

He felt a wave of awe crash over him.

"Dad," Phoebe said, turning to Dave. "Pull it together. Malcolm is *eighteen.* He's figuring out adulthood. He had a baby—so what? That's no reason to disown him."

Dave stared into his empty glass.

"You're not Zoey. You're not your mother," he muttered. "She was my life. You just . . . suck it all away."

Phoebe's eyes narrowed, but she didn't flinch. Malcolm stood behind her, silent, still holding Daisy's carrier—watching his sister hold a family on the edge of collapse.

"Dad, you married Mom out of necessity. Please don't start," Phoebe warned, her voice clipped with restraint.

"Isn't that what marriage is?" Dave smirked, leaning in closer. "I told your slow brother his *giraffe broad* is only after his money. *My* money. She knows exactly how business works in Shiloh Heights."

Phoebe exhaled sharply. Calmly, she took the glass from her father's hand and set it on the opposite end of the bar. Then she turned to the bartender.

"He's finished," she said flatly. She wrapped an arm around her father and helped him up. As she guided him away, she glanced back at the bartender. Her tone turned cold. "If you ever speak to my brother like that again, you'll be out on the street. And I'll make sure the only job you can get is selling your body for cash."

Malcolm's tired, humiliated expression flickered with something close to hope at his sister's defense. The bartender rolled his eyes and collected Dave's glass. Phoebe pointed at him—a warning.

"Gangster lady," Malcolm muttered with a crooked grin as he followed. "You order troops around like this in the army?"

Phoebe didn't respond. She only tightened her arm around their father as they walked toward the exit.

The sunlight in Shiloh Heights was warm and unapologetically golden, draping the hilltop enclave in a soft, luxurious glow. Perched high above the rest of Shiloh City, the neighborhood basked in wealth and separation. The elite didn't just live here—they ruled from it, casting disdainful shadows over the middle and downtown districts. Shiloh Heights held its chin high, nose in the air, proudly ignoring the rest of the city below.

Outside their father's office, Phoebe sat stiffly, frustration leaking through her composed posture. Malcolm sat beside her, quietly rocking baby Daisy's stroller back and forth.

"Dad is falling apart," she muttered. "He's crazy if he thinks he's going to sell the company."

Malcolm stayed silent, his eyes on Daisy as she reached her tiny fingers toward him, cooing softly.

Phoebe went on, unaware or uncaring of his silence. "He always wanted *you* to run the company, Malcolm. He told me that himself."

Malcolm sighed, still watching his daughter. The briefcase under his arm began to slide. He caught it quickly and rested it on his lap, holding it tightly. His expression dimmed. Eyes shut. Shoulders tense.

"He wanted you and Dave to run it together. But after all the loss in our family, he's breaking. Doubting himself. And doubt—"

"Is weakness," Malcolm finished in a whisper.

"Exactly." Phoebe suddenly turned to him, jabbing his shoulder. "So why aren't you stepping up? What the hell is wrong with you?"

"Let Armory die for all I care," Malcolm snapped.

Phoebe blinked. "We grew up there. Armory *is* our family. You want to lose that too?"

"Yes." Malcolm's voice was hard. "Everything else has already been taken from us. Why not this?"

"Because this is *something* we can fight for. We still have control, Malcolm. Don't lose sight of that."

"Nothing matters," he murmured, his voice breaking.

"Stow that talk!"

"Pheebz, I'm not one of your soldiers. You can't just bark orders at me."

"You're my brother," she said quietly. "You're all I have left. You . . . and Armory."

Malcolm looked at her. Despite her weary eyes, there was still a fire beneath her expression—fierce, unrelenting.

He shifted uncomfortably, clutching his briefcase. Phoebe noticed. Even his oversized baby bag sat several feet away, but the briefcase never left his grip.

"What's in there?" she asked, her tone sharper now.

Malcolm didn't answer.

Phoebe grabbed it.

"Hey—"

Too late. She yanked it from under him, shoved him gently aside, and flipped it open. Her eyes scanned the thick stack of papers.

"Wow . . . and here I thought this would be full of half-naked pictures of Lola. But this?" She shuffled through the documents. "You've been researching."

Malcolm squinted, disappointment clouding his face.

"Why the look?" she asked. "This is incredible. Malcolm, you're the smartest person in this company. Eighteen, and your tech skills are miles beyond anyone else here."

"No. I think *you* are," Malcolm said softly. "I was working with R&D—developing advanced bulletproof vests, embedded tracking systems, other enhancements for military gear. We have prototypes downstairs. The potential is huge. But—"

"But what? That sounds like quitter talk."

"Daisy happened." His voice cracked slightly. "Dad says it's too expensive, but I ran the numbers. I spoke with Finance, Accounting—even Tony likes the concept. I know I'm young and dropped out of school, but I know our soldiers. You and Dave fought for this country. We could help soldiers returning with trauma. PTSD support. Gear that protects better. Not just . . . useless little trinkets." He rubbed Daisy's belly, his voice lowering. "Dad always said I'd take over Armory. But he never believed in me. He spat on my ideas. On my leadership. He wanted me to *abandon* Daisy. I swear he did."

Phoebe placed a hand on his shoulder.

"He only cares about optics. Dave was a star—just like you. A war hero. Me? I couldn't even enlist. I doubt I have a future. My ideas . . . they're not good enough," Malcolm said.

"Never say that. Never. Doubt is weakness."

She shoved him back against the chair.

The room went quiet. A few employees looked over.

"Dad's right about one thing," Phoebe said, her voice rising. "It's time for you to grow the hell up."

Malcolm stared at her, stunned.

"You're a father now. Get it together. Stop doubting yourself. Be strong—because you *are* strong. Don't let Dad or anyone else tell you otherwise." She grabbed his face. "Do you understand me?"

He nodded.

"Good." She slapped his cheek—lightly, but firm. "If you'd given me some wiseass answer, I'd have knocked you flat in front of everyone."

They both laughed softly, tension dissolving.

"Your father will see you now," a woman said, walking over.

"Thank you, Sarah," Phoebe said with a grateful smile.

As Sarah led them toward the office, Phoebe waved to several employees along the way. Malcolm, pushing Daisy's carriage, pulled a face that screamed *Seriously?* Phoebe ignored him.

"You don't have to schmooze with everyone," Malcolm muttered, irritation laced with sarcasm.

Without breaking stride, Phoebe reached over and twisted his nipple.

"Ow—damn!" Malcolm yelped, wincing from the pain.

Phoebe gave a sweet, unbothered smile, then dropped her voice into something firmer. "One day you'll understand the power of networking. You have to know how to work with people, Malcolm."

He rubbed his chest and shot her a sour look as Sarah opened the office door.

Inside, several men in sharp, expensive suits clustered in conversation. Phoebe walked in confidently, weaving between them, shaking hands like she belonged there—because she did.

"What the hell?" Dave hissed, appearing behind her with a forced smile for the man she was speaking to. He placed a firm hand on her back and gently steered her aside. "You said Malcolm's giraffe broad was watching the baby."

He gestured toward the back of the room, where Malcolm was awkwardly maneuvering the baby carriage between chairs. Daisy let out a soft grunt, drawing curious stares from several board members.

"She had another gig, apparently," Phoebe said, her sarcasm dry. "And let's not forget Malcolm isn't allowed at the manor, remember? Who else was going to take her?"

"Damn it," Dave muttered as he brushed past her. "Malcolm—tell that woman who answers the phones to watch the kid until this is over."

"Her name's Sarah. She's worked here for three years—" Phoebe began, but Dave cut her off.

"I don't need her resume, Pheebz. I just need her to babysit."

Phoebe took a deep breath and reached for the stroller. "If you'd just let Malcolm back into the manor—"

"Don't start nagging now. Not here." Dave cut her off again, eyes scanning the room. He noticed several board members watching the whispered exchange with raised brows. He gave them a tight-lipped smile and a casual wave, trying to smooth it over.

Phoebe composed herself and stepped forward. "The meeting will begin shortly. Please, everyone, take your seats," she announced. Her hands rubbed together—nerves peeking through her poised exterior.

"Pheebz, you don't run anything here. Get it straight," Dave hissed behind her, voice low and sharp.

She turned calmly to Malcolm and took the stroller from him. "When I have to leave my post to clean up after our drunk father and help my lost little brother off the street, *then* you can tell me who runs this place."

"Pheebz, don't start," Dave warned.

"Someone has to take charge. And it won't be either of you unless you get your acts together." She handed Malcolm his briefcase. Her tone dropped with intensity. "It's time to stand up."

Malcolm met her eyes, hesitant but holding on.

Phoebe turned and walked out of the room with baby Daisy. Dave shook his head as the board members took their seats.

"Damn, girl does nothing but nag. You pitched me on the asinine idea about having Malcolm here as a united front to the board and I'm already regretting it." he muttered under his breath.

He crossed the room to a security guard near the door. "Make sure no one disturbs this meeting. Nobody else comes in."

The man nodded.

Dave turned back to the room and clapped his hands together with artificial cheer. "Alright, gentlemen. Time to get started. We should've hosted this at the Men's Club, huh?" he joked. The board members chuckled politely.

He draped an arm over Malcolm's shoulder and leaned in, smiling for the room but whispering through gritted teeth: "Don't embarrass me."

They walked toward the only two unoccupied chairs at the far end of the long conference table. The weight of eyes followed them.

"Don't speak unless spoken to," Dave murmured as they approached the seats. "And don't let your loudmouth sister fill your head with foolish ideas."

Malcolm clutched his briefcase tightly. His fingers twitched around the handle as he took in the sea of polished faces staring at him—expecting something bold. Something new. Something different.

CHAPTER 10

MALCOLM PULLED UP to his estate in Shiloh Heights, the automated gates swinging open as he approached. He drove around back, where the garage door lifted in anticipation. Inside, the cavernous space gleamed with sleek, high-end vehicles and scattered cutting-edge tech.

Still on the phone with Amanda, Malcolm's voice echoed through the garage, loud and commanding. Several maids looked up as he and Cassandra entered the grand hallway of the mansion, heading toward the main room.

As they stepped inside, Cassandra immediately noticed Rob sitting across from Malcolm's desk, fiddling with a laptop, shifting it around as though it personally offended him.

"Amanda, just because they're influencers doesn't mean they're safe," Malcolm said sharply into the phone as he ascended the staircase.

Cassandra exhaled quietly and walked over to Rob. She dragged a chair to sit across from him. He looked up, visibly annoyed by her movement but said nothing.

"Can I help you, Mr. Rob?" she asked evenly.

Rob grunted, clearly frustrated, and handed her the laptop. "I . . . I need to speak to General Samuel, but the damn computer won't cooperate."

"Here you go," Cassandra said after quickly resetting the device and placing it back in front of him. She eyed him, hesitant. There was tension in her posture, unease behind her steady tone.

"Thanks . . ." Rob muttered, then caught her expression. "What's wrong? Did someone die?"

"I wanted to ask about Ezra," Cassandra said, her voice tentative.

Rob stiffened and gave a low growl.

"And . . . about Nightmare," she added, wincing at her own words.

Rob shot up from his seat. "Did Malcolm show you that room? He can't help himself—loves showing off." He pointed toward a door tucked behind Malcolm's desk, his agitation rising.

"No, Mr. Rob, he didn't take me anywhere. I just..." she hesitated. "I wanted to know why you think Ezra is still alive. I . . . saw the Psalmist leader's face and—"

"Because I didn't see a body," Rob snapped, cutting her off. He leaned in close, his voice intense. "You always have to see the body. Don't trust them. They lie."

"Who are you talking about? I don't understand," Cassandra said, trying to remain calm. Her hand went to her forehead in frustration. Then, softly: "Are you really an assassin?"

Rob smirked. "And what if I am?"

Cassandra's discomfort showed on her face just as a voice chimed in from the laptop.

"Don't be too hard on the old man," the voice said.

"Sir," Cassandra greeted quickly.

"It's good to see you again, Cassandra. I hope Rob's not driving you too crazy," General Samuel's voice teased.

Rob rolled his eyes.

"You and Rob are cut from the same cloth," Samuel continued. "Born fighters."

Rob turned the laptop away from Cassandra, his face growing solemn. "That cult has come back into my life."

"I thought you burned their commune to the ground," Samuel said.

"Apparently, that wasn't enough to send the message," Rob muttered.

"I didn't know you and General Samuel knew each other," Cassandra said, surprised.

"I recommended your service to Rob," Samuel replied. "He was there when . . . you had to leave the military."

"She was tired of the hypocrisy," Rob growled. "Just like I was. She saw something had to be done—and she did it. Your government bosses, they clean up their messes with silence. People like Cassandra and me? We take action."

Samuel chuckled. "You two really are alike." Rob and Cassandra avoided each other's gaze. "Malcolm says it's always entertaining watching Rob get worked up."

Rob scowled at the screen.

Samuel turned to Cassandra. "How are you doing, soldier? Rob dragged you into one of his adventures, didn't he? He does that with everyone. Me, Ezra . . . He's a real hoot."

"This isn't a game, Samuel," Rob muttered, rubbing his temples as if trying to stave off a migraine.

"You okay, buddy? Seriously, I hope you're seeing someone."

"I'm fine," Rob replied, but his tone betrayed the truth.

"You still having those nightmares?"

Rob didn't respond. He looked away.

"I'll take that as a yes. There's no shame in asking for help. You've saved my life more times than I can count. You even dragged me out from behind enemy lines, remember?"

"Still with that story . . ." Rob grumbled.

Samuel chuckled again. "Let me see the body!" he said in a mocking version of Rob's gruff voice.

"You could've been taken. Trafficked. Brainwashed. Don't joke about that," Rob muttered.

"Mal, Mal!" Samuel suddenly called as Malcolm passed behind them, still talking to Amanda on his phone.

Malcolm gave a wave and a cheerful smile before walking out again, still mid-conversation.

Cassandra turned back to the screen. "What . . . What do you mean?"

"Rob and I were in special ops together," Samuel said. "He saved my ass more times than I can count. He's got the instincts of a ghost and the mind of a chess master. We were deployed overseas for a deep-cover reconnaissance op. A few of our guys went missing. Intel said they were taken."

"Rob told us to hold back," Samuel continued. "Said we needed to gather intel, watch patterns, learn who was moving in and out of the village. But command got impatient. They ordered us to engage or pull out."

Rob cut in bitterly. "I told them to wait. Just one more week. I was mapping their entire rotation. But they wouldn't listen. They *never* listen."

"Eventually, the unit fractured," Samuel said. "Some of the team went rogue and launched early. They were captured. We stayed back—alone. Another month passed. Rob's intel finally paid off. We found our entry point."

"But then we were ambushed," Samuel said, his voice lowering. "They fought like zealots—masks, robes, swords. Not even modern. We couldn't tell who they were. Until we pulled one of the masks off . . ."

"It was one of ours," Rob finished. "Turned. Brainwashed. Like he was possessed."

"That was our cue to retreat. But they followed us home. They attacked again—relentless. I got hit. Next thing I knew, I woke up in an American hospital."

"They told us he'd died," Rob said darkly. "But I knew something was off. A doctor from our own base was treating injured soldiers—patching them up just to ship them off to those maniacs overseas. Using our own men against us."

"Did you report this?" Cassandra asked.

"Report it?" Rob scoffed, his voice rising. "To who?"

Samuel scratched his chin awkwardly. "We *might've* had more evidence . . . if Rob hadn't killed the doctor."

"Don't twist it. I saved your life," Rob snapped. "And I know they're doing the same thing to Ezra. I *know* it."

"That's actually what I wanted to talk about," Cassandra tried again.

"The Psalms Society," Rob cut in, ignoring her. "That cult targeting us? They're a spinoff from that same group. No one believes us. But we know the truth."

A long silence followed. Rob finally quieted, the intensity draining from his face.

Samuel sighed. "Buddy . . . You know I loved Ezra. But this—this is different."

Rob's voice rose again. "It's *exactly* the same."

"Please—" Cassandra said sharply. "I got a good look at the Psalmist—the leader. I want to know more about Ezra. What happened to him?"

"You . . . you saw him?" Rob asked, locking eyes with her.

"Not clearly. But if I saw a photo of Ezra, maybe I could compare."

"I think I have one on my phone . . ." Rob patted his pockets. "Damn. Where—" He started searching the desk with growing frustration.

Cassandra let out an irritated sigh.

"Malcolm sent me this," General Samuel said, pulling up an image on the laptop screen. It showed Amanda, Malcolm, Rob, and a young man with tan skin and a bright, effortless smile. He had his arms wrapped around the group as they huddled together for the picture.

"And look—Rob's actually smiling," Samuel added with a grin. "A rare photo of Nightmare himself cracking a smile."

Rob stared at the screen, falling silent as the image pulled him into memory.

"Well?" General Samuel asked, watching Cassandra study the picture. "Was that the guy?"

"I . . . I don't think so. Sorry. When I pulled off the mask, it was just a glimpse. The man I saw had a scar on his face. Ezra doesn't."

"He was taken from me . . ." Rob's voice dropped low.

Cassandra and Samuel turned to him.

"Ezra was a soldier, like you, Cassandra," General Samuel said. "He, Rob, and I were part of the same team. And we were damn good. The kid had real promise. But he left the military to care for his mother. Couldn't find steady work. Around that time, Rob had been discharged—retired from his . . . contractual work. Rob helped him get a job in security with Malcolm, same as he did."

Cassandra looked at Rob, who gave a slow nod.

"Ezra was the kindest kid you'd meet," Samuel continued. "Never questioned orders. Always showed up. He was nothing like Rob." He smiled faintly. "But they became like father and son."

"Until the legal trouble started," Rob muttered.

"That's Malcolm's version," he snapped, anticipating their reactions. "See, there was this dirty pirate lawyer—don't give me that look, he was a dirty pirate. Always coming at me with assault charges. I was in court so much I should've paid rent. We found out he was working with

Dunkin, getting those thugs off every time. And when he couldn't dig up anything on me, he threatened to come after Malcolm and Amanda. Said he'd tear down their businesses piece by piece."

Rob rubbed his chin, his eyes drifting toward the staircase. A couple of maids passed by. He immediately went quiet, watching them disappear into another wing of the house. When they were gone, he leaned closer to the laptop and Cassandra, his voice lowered like he was revealing classified intel.

"I would've handled that lawyer myself," he growled, "but Ezra . . ." Rob stopped, his breath catching. His fingers drummed anxiously on the table. "I told that boy to stay away from Daisy." He rubbed his temple. "Anyway, things got complicated. Ezra got hurt. Malcolm and Amanda rushed him to the hospital. Said he died. They never let me see the body. Not even Ezra's mother. Something was off. I know it. They took him. They took him!"

He slapped his cheek gently, trying to force down the rising emotion. "Three years. It's been three years. I haven't stopped looking. Not once. Even when Malcolm and Amanda gave up."

Silence fell over the room again. Only the quiet sounds of the kitchen staff working and cleaning echoed faintly through the mansion.

After a long pause, General Samuel finally asked, "How are you going to take them down, Rob?"

Rob turned slowly, as if waking from a trance.

"What's your plan?" Samuel asked. "How can I help?"

Rob didn't answer right away. He stared at the floor, his mind clearly racing.

"Is Nightmare going to make a comeback?" Samuel asked, grinning slyly.

Rob grimaced, then glanced at Cassandra, who was studying him with a mix of caution and curiosity.

"No . . . " he muttered, almost embarrassed. "My defensive tactics haven't worked."

He looked up, a sharper edge in his eyes.

"Now it's time to go on the offensive."

The early morning sun kissed Malcolm's manor with golden light. The dawn broke gently over the manicured lawns and the sprawling estate nestled in Shiloh Heights. Sunlight filtered through Malcolm's bedroom window, softly urging the day to begin.

He stepped out of his room, the polished floors cool beneath his feet as he passed the many closed doors lining the long hallway.

"Mr. Malcolm," one of the maids called softly. Her voice trembled, and she looked visibly shaken.

"He did it again?" Malcolm asked, already tired.

He slid open a nearby door, revealing a room in disarray—shattered glass, overturned furniture, scattered electronics. Malcolm sighed. "Let me grab my tablet. I'll check where he is on the grounds."

"He's downstairs," the maid answered. "In your study."

Malcolm descended the grand staircase, the sound of his slippers quiet on the steps. In the study, he found Rob hunched over a laptop, typing with obsessive focus. His face was pale, his eyes puffy and sunken from exhaustion.

"Rob, buddy," Malcolm called gently.

No response.

"Rob!" he said louder, moving in and waving a hand in front of the laptop screen. "Your nightmares are getting worse."

"I'm not sleeping much," Rob muttered, barely audible. "So I've decided not to sleep at all."

"You need rest, man."

Rob turned slightly but didn't answer.

"I've got the day off. Why don't you try to nap on the couch? I'll stay right here."

Rob looked up, relief slowly spreading across the couch like a tired child. "I . . . I have some things to finish," he yawned. "But maybe just an hour. Wake me in an hour. I mean it."

Malcolm raised an eyebrow. "Sure."

"And don't leave the house," Rob added, settling onto the couch. "Your staff doesn't like being alone with me."

Malcolm chuckled. "Gee, I can't imagine why. It's not like a certain someone keeps destroying rooms and yelling at shadows all night."

As he spoke, a maid entered quietly and handed Malcolm a cup of coffee. Rob shot her a scowl as she retreated.

"See?" he said. "They're terrified."

"You don't need coffee," Malcolm replied, laughing. "You need sleep."

"Just promise you'll stay. Don't sneak off while I'm out." Rob was already reclining, his voice growing softer.

"Rob, I told Mikey I'd come to the show."

Rob bolted upright. "You're going to watch that crap? His self-help, inspirational drivel? It's nothing but emotional manipulation. Witchcraft in a nice suit. Giving people false hope—it's idiotic."

Malcolm sipped his coffee, unimpressed.

"Or maybe you're going to see Daisy," Rob added bitterly. "Amanda's right. Give her space."

"That new officer might be there," Malcolm said. "Maybe you could beat him up for me. Maybe Nightmare could make an appearance."

Rob grumbled. "I am not going to that ridiculous thing. I'm not a sap like his audience."

"Well, I'm not staying here all day. Cassandra will be there, so you're out of luck either way. Come with me, or hang out here with the maids."

"I told you—they hate me," Rob groaned.

"Then I guess you're coming," Malcolm said, turning his back.

Rob muttered curses under his breath, but his resistance faded as his eyes drifted closed. Malcolm watched as the tension in his friend's body finally released.

"Just . . . don't leave me," Rob murmured, almost too softly to hear.

Malcolm paused, turning back.

"Don't leave me, Mara . . . please, just don't leave."

The words struck Malcolm like a slap. Rob's voice had gone thin and childlike, worn with fear and memory. A tear traced its way down Rob's cheek as he slipped into sleep.

Malcolm stood still for a moment, the quiet ticking of the study clock the only sound. He lowered himself into a chair across the room, watching over his friend, just as he'd promised.

CHAPTER 11

UPBEAT MUSIC BLASTED through the arena in Shiloh Heights. The parking lot overflowed with cars as eager attendees poured in, buzzing with anticipation for what was promised to be a life-changing show. Inside, the crowd roared, the energy palpable. Stage lights pulsed, and thick smoke billowed from vents in the ceiling.

Suddenly, the music cut. Silence fell like a curtain, amplifying the tension. Smoke continued to drift across the stage as the crowd waited, breath held.

"Who's ready for change?" boomed Mikey's voice, echoing across the arena.

The audience erupted into chants and cheers.

"Who's ready to be elevated?" he called again.

The cheers intensified.

"I can't hear you!" Mikey shouted.

The crowd's response was deafening, fans craning their necks, scanning the stage. But he wasn't there. His voice came from all around them, piped through hidden speakers.

"This is your year," Mikey continued, his voice rising with conviction. "Your year to be transformed into a new you. Elevated to be the best . . ."

The voice stopped.

A spotlight swept across the audience, searching, until it halted on a lone figure in a dark robe standing in a middle section. The robed figure dramatically threw off the garment—Mikey.

"Elevated to be the best *you*!" he cried, racing through the crowd, slapping high-fives as fans reached out to touch him.

He vanished briefly into the smoke, only to reappear on stage, leaping through the haze to thunderous applause.

"You guys are amazing," he said, grinning. "I want to bring you into a new way of living. A higher way. People from all over have sent in stories about how these messages have transformed their lives."

He gave a subtle finger cue, and a video began playing on the massive screens. A young couple appeared, giving a heartfelt testimony about how Mikey's teachings saved their marriage and gave them a fresh start. Another video followed—a man who had once been addicted to drugs, now clean and thriving, crediting Mikey's show for the turnaround.

"And tonight," Mikey continued, "we have a special guest in the building." He paused, letting the crowd buzz. "The fashion icon herself. Daughter of Malcolm—the tech mogul of Shiloh Heights—please welcome Daisy!"

The crowd erupted as Daisy stepped onto the stage, radiant and poised. She kissed Mikey on the cheek and gave him a warm hug. Leaning in, she whispered, "I wish you'd left out the part about my dad."

Mikey whispered back, "You have to use the brand, baby. Capitalize on his fame. It's time we step out on our own—leave the hypocrites behind. Fate's in our hands now."

The side-stage screens zoomed in on them, capturing their smiles and playful energy. Mikey gestured toward the audience.

"Follow Daisy—check the screen to connect with this badass woman warrior!"

He and Daisy did a playful dance before she exited the stage, where Jessie waited behind the curtain to greet her.

Mikey returned to the front, soaking in the applause.

"You've all been asking for more—more guests, more voices, more elevation. Well tonight, another influencer joins us."

Backstage, Amanda walked briskly toward a crew member holding a clipboard and headset.

"This isn't on the schedule. What's Mikey doing?" she demanded.

"He updated the plan last minute. Said you were fine with it," the crew member replied, flustered.

She didn't respond. She moved closer to the wings, trying to see what Mikey was about to pull.

"I want you all to give a massive welcome to someone who literally flew in tonight," Mikey announced. "The one and only—Cassius!"

Gasps swept through the audience. The spotlight locked onto a man high above the stage, cloaked in a robe, precariously balanced.

"What is Mikey doing?" Amanda muttered. She turned sharply. "Stop the show. Get him down—now."

But before anyone could act, the figure leapt.

Cassius descended like a feather—until his heavy boots slammed onto the stage floor with a thunderous crack that echoed through the arena. The crowd screamed in amazement as Cassius removed his harness and stood tall, larger than life.

"Ladies and gentlemen," Mikey said, motioning dramatically, "I call him the Gifted Giant. Look at that entrance!"

Cassius raised one arm and grabbed Mikey's in solidarity. The crowd went wild.

"For those of you who don't know me," Cassius said, his voice low and powerful, "that little catchphrase—'let's be enlightened together'—that's mine. It's more than a mantra. It's my mission. Three years ago, I hit rock bottom. Then I found Mikey's work, and it changed everything."

He turned to Mikey, towering over him.

"I was inspired by this man. Now I run a retreat for people searching for purpose. We started with ten members. Now we've grown to ten thousand."

The crowd roared.

"Thank you, brother," Cassius said. "Thank you for giving me this platform."

"No problem, brother," Mikey replied, pulling him into a hug. "You said you wanted to partner, and I knew—we're gonna change lives."

Cassius exited the stage as Mikey returned to the center.

"It's time for you all to break free from tired routines. You were *not* made just to struggle and pay bills. You were *created* to pursue dreams. Fate is here to help you build the life you never thought possible."

He paused, lowering his voice.

"But where are you putting your energy? Where are your thoughts? Channel them into something uplifting. Something powerful. My voice will help."

The crowd laughed, many nodding along.

Amanda, arms crossed backstage, didn't laugh. Her glare fixed on Mikey, a storm building behind her eyes.

Outside the arena, Cassandra's car rolled into the VIP lot. A security guard waved her toward a designated spot, but the bickering in the backseat drew her attention.

Rob and Malcolm argued endlessly.

"Look how late we are," Malcolm groaned, flashing his watch at Rob.

"We didn't miss much," Rob muttered, folding his arms.

Cassandra and Malcolm stepped out of the car. Malcolm turned, annoyed.

"Rob," he called.

Rob grumbled, slowly emerging from the car, hobbling as he followed. His expression was sour, his mood even worse.

Mikey walked backstage, stretching his arms as the adrenaline from the show still hummed in his veins.

"You're doing a great job, Mikey," a staffer called out as he passed.

Mikey gave a casual wave of thanks and continued walking until he reached a small crowd gathered in a corner.

Cassius lounged across one of the ornate couches backstage, speaking with a group of staff members who hung on his every word.

"Greatness is already inside you," Cassius said, locking eyes with a young crew member beside him. He took the man's hand and pressed it to his chest. "Feel that?"

The man nodded.

"That's my heart. It's still beating—yours too. And as long as that's true, we have the power to bring about change. As long as this heart beats, we don't surrender to darkness."

Mikey stood behind the crowd, observing. Cassius caught his eye and gave a knowing smile.

"Mikey!" Amanda's voice rang out backstage. "Where is he?" she asked another passing crew member.

"Not sure, ma'am," the staffer replied nervously.

Frustrated, Amanda kept moving through the busy backstage area, searching.

Cassius stood and motioned for Mikey to take his place on the couch. "Come on, man. You need rest. You've got another round out there soon. Recharge."

The others murmured in agreement, urging Mikey to sit. He gave in and sank into the cushion. Cassius placed a firm hand on his shoulder.

"I'm proud of you, young man. You've been given a rare gift—charisma and leadership."

"That means a lot, Cassius," Mikey said, touching his arm. "You and your camp are the only ones who've ever really invested in me."

"There he is," Amanda muttered, spotting him at last.

"Amanda!" a voice called behind her. She turned to see Joshua and Reverend Anthony weaving their way through crew members.

Joshua pulled her into a half-hug while she kept her eyes locked on Mikey.

"How are you holding up?" Reverend Anthony asked gently, placing a hand on her arm.

"I'm fine. Thank you," Amanda said, distracted. "Glad you both came."

"I know it's Mikey's event, but you're the one holding everything together," Joshua added, pulling a bouquet of flowers from behind his back. "These are for you."

"Thanks . . ." Amanda said, taking them while still watching Mikey rise from his seat.

"Is Mr. Malcolm here? Josh was wondering in the car," Reverend Anthony teased.

"Dad . . ." Joshua groaned.

Amanda shook her head. "No, I haven't seen him."

Reverend Anthony stepped closer. "If I ever said something to upset you, Amanda, I'm sorry. I want to be someone you can talk to. About anything."

She handed him the flowers. "Could you hold these? Sorry. I'll be right back."

Before they could respond, she slipped past them and intercepted Mikey.

He stopped cold, eyes widening slightly at her furious expression.

"What the hell, Mikey? Did you seriously change the schedule without telling me? And who the hell is that man?"

"Chill, Manda—"

"Don't tell me to chill!" she hissed, shoving him in the shoulder. Mikey stumbled back a step. Around them, staff, performers—even Cassius—went quiet, watching.

"What is wrong with you?" Mikey demanded, puffing his chest, locking eyes with her.

"What's wrong with me?" she snapped. "If that man had fallen, we'd be looking at lawsuits, liability—maybe even charges. We might *already* be in trouble."

Mikey sneered. "Well, you could always send your assassin to clean it up for you."

Amanda's eyes narrowed. Her mouth tightened. She didn't reply right away.

Mikey smirked. "Jessie told me everything. You and Malcolm. You've never forgiven me for what happened when I was a kid."

"Mikey, now is not the time—"

"You blame me for going to jail. I *see* it in your eyes every time you look at me."

Amanda closed her eyes, fists clenched tight.

"You let Rob bully me. I thought you'd always have my back, Amanda. But you let your personal thug, your so-called enforcer, treat me like garbage."

Her hand lifted halfway—like she might hit him—but she stopped herself, trembling.

"Don't play the victim," Mikey said through her teeth. "We *both* survived Uncle Fred. Or maybe this is the real you now—Shiloh City's gangster."

Mikey raised his voice, drawing stares from everyone backstage. "Well, guess what? Me and Daisy don't need you or Malcolm. We can stand on our own. And if you want to sic Rob on us again, go ahead."

Amanda's voice dropped, shaky but controlled. "Everything I've done—every step—has been to *protect* you."

"Don't make me laugh," Mikey spat. "Shiloh City's first Black female millionaire. You don't care about protecting me. You've just been using me. Me and Daisy? We're cutting the strings."

Joshua rushed over, alarmed. "Hey, come on—cool it," he said, grabbing Mikey's arm.

"Back off, boy," Mikey growled, yanking his arm away. "Maybe try getting a life instead of chasing my sister. She doesn't want you."

"Hey!" Joshua snapped, stepping in front of Amanda. "You better watch your mouth when you talk to your sister."

"You don't even really know her. The people she hangs out with. If you *did* know her, you'd run straight back to church, choir boy."

Joshua's fist clenched. He launched it toward Mikey——but before it landed, his father's hand caught it mid-air.

The Reverend gripped his son's arm firmly and shook his head, eyes heavy with disappointment.

"Crawl back to daddy," Mikey taunted.

"Okay, that's enough," Reverend Anthony said, stepping forward. "Let's all take a breath and calm down."

"There's nothing to calm down about, Reverend. Don't act so righteous. When Amanda needed help, you were nowhere to be found."

The Reverend looked at Amanda. Pain erupted across her face. Her fists clenched at her sides, and her breath came fast and heavy like she was moments away from launching at someone.

"Matter of fact, all of you can get the hell out," Mikey barked. "Let me call security."

"Mikey, I'm the boss. I built this company. Stop acting like a fool and get back on stage—" Amanda snapped.

"Or what? You'll sic Rob on me?" Mikey cut in, sneering. "I'm done taking orders from you. Fire me. Do whatever you want. I'm done—with *you*."

Amanda's eyes widened in shock. A tear broke free, trailing down her cheek. Her body trembled as she fought to keep her fury contained.

Suddenly, heavy footsteps echoed nearby.

Cassius approached and placed a firm hand on Mikey's chest. "Let's take a breather," he said calmly. "Come on, man. You've got another show coming up. Don't let all this cloud your mind. Just head over there." He pointed to the far end of the stage.

Mikey scowled, glaring at Amanda, then turned and stormed off toward Jessie and Daisy, who had been silently watching the scene unfold.

Amanda turned away from the confrontation.

"Let's give her some space," Cassius said, spreading his arms and gently guiding the others—Joshua and Reverend Anthony—away. Joshua lingered, concerned, watching Amanda hold herself together.

Amanda breathed deeply, wiping at her tears. She moved toward the edge of the room, overlooking the crowd settling back into their seats after intermission.

Cassius approached and handed her a small tissue box.

"They're starting to come back in. You guys did a great job—huge turnout."

"Thanks," Amanda murmured, dabbing her eyes.

Cassius leaned on a nearby bar, his massive frame stretching out across the counter.

"I'm sorry about the skydiving thing. Mikey never told me you weren't okay with it."

"It's fine," she sniffed, trying to collect herself.

"He's a remarkable young man. Charismatic. A real leader. Must run in the family," Cassius added, handing her another tissue.

"He'd make a great Psalmist."

Amanda froze.

Cassius reached into his jacket and pulled out a necklace with hanging pen and paper shaped icons. He dangled it in front of her. Amanda's face paled.

Cassius grinned, confidence oozing from him.

"You heard me right." He leaned in, whispering, "I thought it was time I came in person. See, I run Psalms Society." He looked her dead in the eyes.

"I'm their leader."

From a distance, Joshua watched Cassius whisper in Amanda's ear, noting the fear spreading across her face. A group of Psalmist members approached from behind.

Cassius stepped back and calmly took Amanda's hand.

"Now, please, Amanda," he said with that same unsettling smile. "Where is *Nightmare*?"

Mikey screamed, slamming his fist into the wall. Jessie and Daisy stood behind him, stunned.

"Your next show's about to start," Jessie said softly, placing a hand on his back.

"I can't. I just can't. She's been lying to me this whole time," Mikey muttered.

"Cut her off," Daisy said. "That's what I did. You're better off. You've got the talent. You don't need her."

Mikey looked at her, seeing the sincerity in her eyes.

"The backstage door's down the hall and to your right," a voice called from the shadows.

Malcolm appeared, flanked by Cassandra and Rob. Seeing his daughter, Malcolm's expression grew stern. He walked past her and the others in silence. Rob gave Mikey a cold, menacing glare.

"Why is that killer here? He wasn't invited," Mikey snapped.

"Mikey—" Jessie whispered, trying to stop him.

Rob stopped, turned, and marched toward them. "You've got some nerve talking to me like that. You stole my car."

"If I wasn't Amanda's brother, you'd probably have killed me. That's what you do, right? Kill boys and girls. You're a psycho—a costume-wearing, murder-crazed psycho," Mikey fired back, stepping in Rob's face.

"Careful," Rob growled. "You go back on stage with fewer teeth if you keep talking."

"Don't talk to him like that," Daisy said, stepping beside Mikey.

"If Aunt Phoebe had known who you really were, she would've never loved you."

The words landed like a punch to Rob's chest. He took a step back.

"Daisy, that's enough," Malcolm said sharply.

"Or what? You'll cut me off?" she challenged.

"You and Amanda have lied so much, it's given Mikey and me *PTSD*—"

"What do you know about any of that?" Rob barked. "Little Dantley Daisy. People like you have no clue. You don't know what it's like to relive something… to feel the same pain over and over. The lashes. The blood. The screams. It's all here." He tapped his head. "It never leaves. You're stuck in the moment—forever. You don't know what it's like to kill a man. To feel his spirit leave his body… and part of it cling to you. It sits on your soul. Every time. You keep feeling it." Rob's hand trembled as his voice faded to a whisper.

"You would know a lot about killing, wouldn't you?" Jessie said.

Mikey and Daisy turned in surprise at his sudden outburst.

"Get him! Get him!" Mikey laughed.

"You three mutts with your innocent, wagging tongues," Rob growled, pointing at them. "If you weren't Malcolm's daughter—"

"He's not my father," Daisy interrupted, glaring at Malcolm. "He's just a man who thought he could control me. But I won't be controlled."

"What?" Rob roared. "You stupid little girl. Do you even know—"

"Rob, let's just go," Malcolm cut in, trying to de-escalate.

"No," Rob snapped. "She thinks she's so big and bad? Fine! She needs to hear the damn truth." Daisy met his rage with a cold, confident smile and crossed her arms. Jessie tensed beside her.

Rob stepped closer. "Do you know your vain, witch of a mother *cheated* on your dad?"

Daisy's expression sharpened.

"Yeah, that little divorce you like to parade around? Your mom cheated. And she didn't care who knew. Took Malcolm for half of everything—everything he worked for. Broke him. And guess what, princess? She didn't even want you."

Daisy's eyes welled with tears.

"She's off gallivanting around the world, living her best life—without a child to weigh her down. That's the truth. So keep running that damn privileged little mouth of yours. My mom died when I was nine. I had to leave my drunk father and live with Alex. So don't you dare act like you're better than anyone. You're not a mighty oak. You're a shrub."

"Hey!" Jessie shoved Rob back as Daisy began to cry.

"Daisy—" Malcolm reached out, voice heavy with emotion.

She covered her face and ran. Jessie swore under his breath, bumping Rob with his shoulder as he stormed past.

Rob turned in disbelief, his pride stung.

As Jessie passed, Rob slammed him into the wall. "You better watch yourself. I'm not taking what you're dishing out. I never did with fate, and I won't with you."

Jessie stared him down. Rob's eyes blazed. Jessie brushed Rob's hand off and walked away, following Daisy.

Malcolm sobbed, hiding his face—but the sound of his pain filled the hall. Cassandra placed a hand on his back, trying to comfort him.

Rob then turned his fury on Mikey.

"You think you're a tough guy now, huh? Officer Pretty Boy feed you some stories about me and Amanda? Well, here's the one: they're all true." He stepped toward Mikey, who instinctively backed away. "Not so brave without your sister, are you?" Rob sneered. He touched Mikey's cheek. "Without Amanda, you're nothing. And deep down you know it. She built this—*not* you. You're just the mouth. *She's* the brains. And the heart. Two things you don't have."

"Rob, stop," Cassandra demanded, stepping in. "That's enough. Go cool off." She gently touched Mikey's trembling shoulder.

Rob muttered a curse and stormed off down the hall.

"You're up," Cassandra reminded Mikey softly. "Take a breath . . . And I'm sorry." She led him toward the backstage door.

"He gets everyone around him killed. Ask them about Ezra," Mikey muttered. "Quit while you're still ahead."

Cassandra glanced down the hallway—Rob was gone. She turned back to see Malcolm collapsing to the floor in sobs. She rushed to help the broken man to his feet.

Rob kicked over a trash can as he entered the arena's underground garage. His breath came in heavy snarls. Hands shoved deep into his pockets, he paced—then stopped. Took two steps. Paused again.

"You can come out now," he said.

Psalmist members stepped from the shadows. Their leader walked forward. Rob squared up, ready for a fight.

"Wait." A voice echoed from the far end of the garage.

The elder psalmist stepped forward, flanked by several others. "You've already failed to capture Nightmare."

"We have him now," the psalmist leader insisted.

"I don't want a repeat of last time," the elder snapped. "I'm not leaving this to chance."

The members behind her surged forward.

"Stop!" she commanded. They froze. "*I* will handle this."

She pulled back her brown robe and drew a dagger.

Rob smirked. "You? Handle *me*? Alone?"

"Think I can't defeat you because I'm a woman?" she said coolly, circling him.

"Leaders like you don't get your hands dirty."

"Oh, you'll find mine are *plenty* dirty."

She lunged. Rob easily grabbed her arm and knocked the dagger aside. But she kicked his leg hard, and he yelped in pain.

"You shouldn't underestimate your opponent," she taunted.

He swung at her—she dodged and landed a swift kick to his gut, forcing him back. As she charged, he elbowed her mask and shoved her to the ground.

Rob stood, breathing hard. The elder laughed—as if enjoying herself. Her members looked on, sensing her strange vigor.

She reached into her robe and pulled out a small canister. With a flick of her wrist, she dropped it—blue smoke exploded into the air.

"Dammit," Rob growled. He felt a sharp sting—his arm bled. Another scrape on his back. He whirled, searching through the smoke.

Rob heard her footsteps. He tripped her, but she vanished. Suddenly, she reappeared, striking him with an open palm to the chest. He hit the ground hard.

Wind surged through the garage, clearing the smoke. The elder stood over him. Rob gritted his teeth.

From her robe, she drew a small pistol. Rob's eyes widened.

"Elder, we don't use guns," one of the psalmists called out.

She fired a tranquilizer dart into Rob's chest. He flinched but surged to his feet—she shot him again. He stumbled toward her—another shot. He collapsed at her feet.

"Load him up," she ordered.

Several psalmists moved to carry Rob. As the leader tried to follow, she held out her arm.

"That's how you complete a mission," she said coldly. "Make sure there are no more loose ends."

She pointed toward a hallway—Cassandra was sprinting toward them.

The elder followed her members as they placed Rob into a white van. Cassandra neared, but the psalmist leader blocked her path.

"Drive," the elder commanded.

Cassandra watched helplessly as the van pulled away—Rob inside, gone.

CHAPTER 12

A JOLT OF disbelief and disappointment surged through Cassandra as she watched the van carrying Rob speed off. The garage was quiet—eerily so—until the remaining Psalmist members began to close in around her.

She gripped her gun tightly, eyes scanning the encroaching figures as they crept closer.

Her weapon snapped toward the Psalmist leader, who stood boldly in front of her.

"We really have to stop meeting like this," he said with a smirk.

"Too bad you can't take me on your own," Cassandra shot back. "I beat you last time, remember?"

The Psalmist leader exhaled slowly, unfazed. "What do you take me for?" He stepped toward her with calm intent, extending his hand. "There's still a place for someone like you. Join us."

As Cassandra aimed the gun higher, he gently pushed the barrel aside. "You're special."

She hesitated—just for a second—and slowly reached for his outstretched hand. Around them, the Psalmist members lowered their daggers, watching.

"A new and enlightening life awaits," he whispered, gripping her hand and beginning to lead her away.

"I don't think so."

In one swift motion, Cassandra twisted behind him and locked him in a headlock, pressing the gun firmly against his temple.

"Back off," she barked at the others, "or I'll decorate your crazy costumes with his brains."

The Psalmist members halted, uncertain.

"Blow my head off then," the leader growled, straining against her hold. "What are you waiting for?" He turned his head slightly. "Come!" he shouted. "She won't shoot!"

The others shifted nervously, unsure whether to obey.

As they struggled, Cassandra noticed a strange burgundy smoke beginning to seep from the seams of his mask.

Suddenly, he broke free, shoving her off. A dagger flashed in his hand.

Cassandra raised her gun.

The two stood locked in a deadly standoff.

Cassius stood tall before Amanda, holding her hand with an unsettling grin stretched across his face. He was clearly waiting for a response. Amanda quickly yanked her hand away from the giant man.

"You're a smart woman, Amanda. I promise—we'll leave you and Mikey alone," Cassius said smoothly. But the devious glint in his eye told a different story. "Just tell me where Nightmare is."

"Amanda!" Joshua called out, alarmed by the way the Psalmist members had surrounded her, with Cassius looming over her like a predator.

"He has the face of a concerned lover," Cassius mocked, nudging Amanda with his elbow.

"Leave now, Joshua," Amanda said without turning to him.

"What's going on?" Joshua asked, approaching cautiously.

"Let him through," Cassius said with a smile. He motioned to the circle of Psalmists. "Move. Let him in."

The Psalmists stepped aside.

"Joshua, I've got this under control. Please . . . just go," Amanda said through gritted teeth.

"No, let him stay," Cassius said, placing a heavy hand on Amanda's shoulder. "I was just telling her how lovely she is."

Amanda shoved his arm off, but Cassius only laughed. Slowly, he moved his massive hand up her back and rested it on the nape of her neck. She froze, her body tensing under his chilling touch.

"Amanda!" Joshua rushed toward her.

One of the Psalmist members intercepted him with a quick jab to the stomach. Joshua collapsed hard to the ground.

"You're strong," Cassius said, stepping away from Amanda. His heavy footsteps thundered across the floor as he approached Joshua. "But I doubt he is."

He turned back to Amanda and extended his hand. A Psalmist member placed a dagger in it.

"You know . . . Nightmare's not the only one who's good at torture."

"If you hurt him—" Amanda began, but Cassius cut her off.

"I follow through on my threats. But no one has to get hurt . . . except Nightmare."

He crouched beside Joshua, then touched his earpiece. A faint voice could be heard on the other end.

"They got him," Cassius announced. He stood and looked at Amanda. "It was nice working with your brother. Really. The kid has a gift."

He gave Joshua a condescending pat on the cheek, then turned and walked off, motioning to his followers.

Amanda rushed to Joshua's side as the Psalmists hurried away. He began asking questions, but her eyes stayed locked on the retreating cultists.

Outside the arena, most of the Psalmists dispersed quickly. But Cassius lingered. He paused at a hallway screen, watching live footage of Mikey.

"Sir?" one of the cultists called to him.

"Go on ahead. I'll meet you there," Cassius replied, absently twirling the Psalmist pendant around his neck.

The Psalmist members moved slowly, tightening their circle around Cassandra. Daggers drawn, they watched as she and the Psalmist leader stalked each other in the middle of the garage.

"Maybe I'll fight you myself," the leader said, his tone oddly calm. "Maybe then you'll understand—we mean what we say. We want to enlighten the world. We're only here for Rob."

"Squad leader, we need to leave. Security could show up any second," one of the cultists called out.

"No," the leader snapped. "She'll go after Rob. But if we convert her now, she stops being a threat. The elders would be proud."

"Let's just take her," another member muttered, stepping closer to Cassandra.

She turned sharply, aiming her gun at him.

"She fights like a soldier," the cultist added. "Let's take her to the camp."

"By force?" the squad leader asked.

The Psalmist member didn't respond, continuing to move forward. Cassandra fired a warning shot at his feet. He jumped back.

"That's what they do," she spat, turning back to the leader. "They take soldiers and brainwash them. You sure you are who you say you are?"

"Silence!" the leader shouted. He lunged, wrestling the gun from her hands. Cassandra shoved him backward and darted behind a nearby car.

Gunshots rang out—shattering glass and echoing in the garage—as the leader fired wildly at her hiding spot.

"We don't use guns," one of the psalmists said, grabbing the leader's arm. "You know this. Put it down."

The squad leader yanked his arm free, eyes darting.

"Are you giving the orders now?" he snapped.

Behind the car, Cassandra crouched, listening. The tension in the garage thickened.

"You've lost it," the psalmists said. "When we get back, I hope the elders and Cassius tear into you. You never belonged in this position."

The squad leader turned Cassandra's gun on him.

The psalmists raised his hands, backing away. "Come on, man. Stop," he pleaded. "Are you one of them… or one of us?"

A shot cracked through the air.

Cassandra flinched.

A bucket of cold water splashed over Rob, slowly waking him. He gasped and blinked through the blur, taking in his surroundings. He was inside Dunkin's warehouse, deep in the heart of Shiloh City. His arms and legs were tightly bound to a metal chair.

Two Psalmist members exited the room as Rob stirred, no longer needing to monitor him. Beside him, the elder Psalmist silently arranged tools on a table—cold steel catching the light.

"Mara . . ." Rob rasped, squinting at the figure. "Mara, don't mess around. I know it's you under there."

The elder said nothing.

"Mara!" Rob snapped.

The figure took a slow breath and removed her mask, letting long dark hair cascade over her shoulders.

"I should've known you'd figure it out," she said evenly.

"Don't act so proud," Rob growled. "You hit me on my wounded leg. Of all the enemies I've faced, you're the only one who would hit me and hold *nothing* back."

"That's all you have to say to me after eighteen years?" Mara asked, almost amused.

"Say to you?" Rob's voice hardened. "You left me. Ran off to join this cult—and I can see you're doing *great* at it." He rocked violently in the chair, trying to lunge toward her with his teeth. "Where's Lucas? Where's our son? Did you drag him into this madness?"

Mara slapped him hard across the face.

She glanced over her shoulder to make sure no other Psalmists were watching.

"You got your wish," she said bitterly. "Lucas became a gun for hire. Just like you always wanted."

Rob's expression cracked. He stammered, "I never wanted him in this life. I wanted him to be strong—to fight fate and flip it the finger."

"Well, now he's our enemy," Mara said, her voice tightening with sorrow.

"*Yours*, not mine. *You* left me. You took Lucas. You joined this wicked cult."

"You act like it wasn't your fault. You loved being Nightmare more than you loved your family."

"No. No—it was your damn hippie sister. She brought this cult's poison into your head."

Mara shook her head slowly, disappointed. "Even now, you can't admit when you were wrong."

"Where is Lucas, Mara?" Rob demanded, rocking his chair again. "Get me the hell out of here."

Mara ignored him, calmly placing knives and torture tools in a precise line across the table.

"I need you to do me a favor," she said at last, still not looking at him.

Rob snorted. "The only favor I'd do for you—"

"After you burned the camp to the ground, new leadership was needed," Mara said quietly. "I was sure—*sure*—that one day, I would be made leader. After everything I've done . . . and still, I'm passed over."

She paused, eyes distant, caught in bitter reflection. Rob glared at her with open disgust.

"Cassius was put in charge," she continued. "I pretend to follow his leadership, but deep down . . . I know I'm the one who belongs in control."

"You want me to kill him?" Rob scoffed. "How much are your rates these days?"

Mara gave a faint, mocking smile. "How much are *yours*?"

Rob's tone turned desperate. "Mara, don't play with me. Where is Lucas? Just . . . just tell me he's safe."

She said nothing. Instead, she kept polishing the knives and tools laid out in front of her, methodically, as if his question hadn't reached her at all.

"Mara!" Rob shouted, struggling violently against the restraints. The chair creaked beneath him, but wouldn't give.

She finally spoke, her voice quiet but resolute. "Lucas and I . . . he broke from the Psalms Society. Formed his own following. Decided to fight against us." Her eyes met his. "And he's followed in your footsteps perfectly."

Rob's voice cracked. "What did this twisted cult do to him? Did you not protect our *son*?"

"I did the best I could," she said, almost defensively. "You, as his father, can't say the same. Nightmare always came first for you."

She stepped closer and lifted his chin, forcing him to meet her eyes. "Tell me honestly—has Lucas contacted you in any way?"

Rob yanked his face from her grip, jaw clenched.

"You don't want Cassius torturing you for that information," Mara warned, her voice low. "He's a monster."

Rob's eyes burned. "Takes a monster to recognize one."

She let out a bitter sigh. "You always make things difficult."

"Lucas is in trouble, Rob. He needs both of us."

Rob's laugh was empty. "Looks like his father abandoned him, and his mother's forsaken him. What the hell does he need *us* for?"

"Rob, please..." Mara touched his chest gently. "One thing we can agree on is that we love Lucas. But he's changed. He's become the worst parts of both of us. He needs help."

Rob looked into her eyes, searching for sincerity. Just as he opened his mouth to respond, the clatter of footsteps echoed through the warehouse. Cassius stepped into the light with Mikey close behind.

Cassius laughed, pointing. "Nightmare in the flesh. I knew you wouldn't fail me, my love."

A scowl twisted Rob's face the moment he saw Mikey.

"See? I told you I had a good surprise," Cassius said, nudging Mikey with his elbow.

Mikey nodded uneasily, eyes fixed on Rob, who was still bound to the chair.

Cassius leaned in close, nearly nose-to-nose with Rob. The stale stench of coffee clung to his breath. "The great Nightmare. I'm a fan of the stories," he said.

Rob spat in his face.

Cassius calmly leaned back and wiped his cheek. "Feisty. You and she made Lucas together. I see the resemblance," he said, glancing at Mara but keeping his focus on Rob.

"He told me he hasn't heard from Lucas," Mara interjected.

"Of course not. He's Nightmare—a cold killer," Cassius said, turning and casually sitting on Rob's lap like a throne. Rob struggled to breathe under his weight.

"When my little brother told me some cranky old man was roughing him up, I didn't think much of it. Then I put two and two together. Rob is Nightmare."

"Who the hell is your brother?" Rob grunted, straining beneath him.

Cassius stood and smirked. "Really? You don't see the resemblance? Dunkin." He paused, waiting for the revelation to sink in. Rob remained unfazed. "Yeah, we're twins. Identical. Both tall. Both bald. It's not ringing any bells?"

He sighed when no one reacted.

"I told Dunkin to skip town and relax while I clean up his city."

"This is *my* city," Rob snarled. "Dunkin's a worm. Just like you."

"You go around bullying people with Amanda and Malcolm. You three think you're the real gangsters of Shiloh City, huh?"

"Cassius, he said Lucas never contacted him," Mara reminded.

"Mara, don't pretend to care. You hate him more than anyone. He left you. Abandoned you and Lucas. *We* gave you a family. A purpose. He only brings death."

Cassius began unbuttoning Rob's shirt.

"I *know* Lucas and his little coalition haven't contacted you. He probably hates you more than he hates us. But what I want is the Nightmare armor. Malcolm upgraded it, didn't he? Why don't you hand it over like a good wounded soldier?"

Rob smirked and leaned forward. "I'd rather watch you, Mikey, and Mara drown—gasping for air. And I'll be laughing from my boat."

Cassius chuckled. "So dark, my friend. But this is the fun part."

With a grunt, he tore Rob's shirt open, revealing scarred, battered skin. Mikey moved closer to Mara as they both recoiled at the sight—deep wounds, crude stitch jobs, and signs of long-forgotten battles.

"Mara," Cassius teased, "you want to do the pants? For old times' sake?"

She rolled her eyes and scoffed. Then her gaze fell on Mikey—he was wearing the Psalmist necklace.

"Take that off," she snapped, reaching toward his neck.

"Oh, that?" Cassius said, still unbuckling Rob's belt. "I *want* him to wear it."

Mara turned her glare to Cassius. Her eyes burned with rage.

"I'll become protector of the Psalms Society. We need a new face—someone young. Someone with charisma. Leadership."

"I have that," Mara said, voice sharp. "You'd give it to some outsider you barely know?"

"I know Mikey plenty," Cassius replied, winking at him.

"I don't know if I'm ready for all this," Mikey said, fingering the necklace nervously.

"You *will* be," Cassius assured, pulling off Rob's pants. "Mara, should I keep the underwear?" He grinned. "Yeah . . . I'll keep it." He patted Rob's face mockingly.

"I've fought my whole life for leadership," Mara said, her voice rising.

"You clawed your way into our ranks, sure," Cassius replied. "But you're like me. Like Mikey. You don't believe in this Psalmist nonsense. Motivational fluff. Affirmations. It's all garbage. People eat it up—but the human heart? The human mind? Weak. Manipulatable."

He stepped closer to Rob and grabbed his neck, squeezing as he spoke. "And you, Rob—you know it too."

He turned to Mara again. "Besides . . . you could never handle a war with your son."

"I don't *want* a war," Mikey blurted out.

"But you *want* power. And you *deserve* it." Cassius smiled. "I can see it in your eyes."

Mikey's face flushed with pride.

"I take the armor. You lead the Psalmists. They'll follow because of the necklace. You've got the look. The voice. Fate has smiled on you." Cassius said removing his meaty hands from Rob's neck. He loomed over Mikey, placing a massive hand on his shoulder. Mikey stood a bit taller, clutching the necklace. Cassius beamed, while Mara stood still, stunned—forgotten.

"You'll never be Nightmare," Rob growled. "Never. I am Nightmare. I'd rather die than tell you where the armor is."

Cassius smiled and dragged a chair in front of him.

"I know," he said calmly, sitting down to begin the next phase.

Rob let out a bloodcurdling scream. Cassius turned to Mikey with a twisted grin, as if showing off his work. Mara, however, clenched her fists. She raised a trembling hand to her mouth and shifted slightly where she stood. Her eyes darted across the room until they landed on Mikey—and the necklace hanging from his neck.

She began to drift into thought.

Mara's moment of self-reflection was abruptly shattered by another scream from Rob. The echoes swallowed her thoughts and blurred her memories, but her gaze remained fixed on the necklace. Mikey winced as Rob cried out again, louder this time.

Then, a sudden gust of wind burst through the warehouse's open window. It blew Mara's hair sideways, but she didn't flinch. Her eyes stayed locked forward. The necklace swayed around Mikey's neck in the breeze, and as it did, something deeper stirred inside her—something more important than fear or loyalty.

Another gust followed, stronger than the last, briefly masking Rob's agony. When the wind passed, Rob was left panting—gasping like an old dog trying to catch its breath. In that stillness, he and Mara locked eyes.

No words were spoken. But in that moment, they knew. Despite the dreams they'd chased, despite the betrayals and buried pain, despite the wounds they'd given and received—something else lingered between them. Their eyes held. In silence. In understanding. Two broken souls, drifting into the same thought. The one thing that still mattered most to them both.

CHAPTER 13

THERE WAS AN ominous weight in the car, as if something wasn't right. Mara gripped the wheel, her gut twisting. She kept checking the rearview mirror, watching her young son. His face was tense, his gaze locked on the car floor.

"Your father will probably be off on another assignment when we get home, sweetie," Mara said gently. But the closer they got to the house, the more anxious Lucas looked.

He didn't answer—just nodded and stared out the window.

"Mom . . ." he finally said, voice barely above a whisper, eyes still turned away.

They turned onto the gravel driveway. Their house appeared up ahead, flanked by farmland and a weathered barn out back.

"Mom . . ." Lucas repeated.

"What is it, Lucas?" Mara asked, glancing at him in the mirror.

"Dad is going to be really mad."

"Sweetie, just tell him what happened. He'll understand."

Lucas didn't look convinced. Mara reached back and patted his leg with a forced smile. She gently turned his face toward her, revealing a swollen lip. Her eyes lingered on the bruise—despite trying not to look. She smiled again, weaker this time, pretending everything was fine.

Lucas pulled his face away and went back to staring out the window.

Mara sighed and opened the car door.

"Mom . . ." he said again, his voice soft, almost cracking.

She turned to him once more.

"Dad's going to be mad . . . because I didn't fight back."

"Sweetie . . ." she touched his leg, reassuring him.

"He's going to say he was right. That I should be homeschooled. That I need to train harder." Lucas shook his head, his voice trembling. "I didn't want to hurt him. I just didn't want to fight."

"Lucas . . ." She reached over and held his hand. "Everything's going to be okay. I promise." Her smile returned—this time warmer, more real.

They carried grocery bags into the house. As Mara opened the front door, a burst of gunfire cracked through the air. She paused, placed the bags gently on the counter, and looked out the kitchen window.

In the distance, Rob was shooting at targets, wiping sweat from his brow before heading toward the house.

"Go wash up," she said to Lucas. "I'll talk to your dad."

Lucas nodded and disappeared down the hall. Mara began prepping dinner.

A few minutes later, the front door creaked open. Rob stepped inside, smiling.

"Something smells good," he said, leaning over to kiss her head.

Mara leaned back and pointed at him. "Don't."

"What? What did I do now?" he mumbled, placing his rifle against the counter.

"Don't leave that there," she said without turning around.

"It's just for a second. Let me wash my hands."

"Rob. Not today."

"What kind of mood are you in now?" he muttered. "I just got home. I want to see my son and make love to my wife. Is that a crime?"

Mara rolled her eyes. "The fact that you don't see it—that's the problem."

She scrubbed carrots at the sink, frustration mounting.

Rob moved closer, trying to explain. "What do you expect me to do, Mara? Fate never gave me a real job. But we've got no money problems. No missed bills."

"You're missing the important moments in Lucas' life," she said, still not facing him.

"I love that boy more than anything. He knows that."

Mara didn't respond. She pulled a pepper from the bag and washed it under the sink.

"Maybe spend less time away and more time with him," she finally said, placing the pepper aside.

"When I'm home, I spend all my time with him."

"Training him."

"That's our thing. He's meant for more."

Mara turned and stared at him. "You want him to grow up like you? A killer? A gun for hire?"

Rob stiffened. Her words hit harder than a bullet. "Mara, don't start. I do what I have to—for this family. Lucas can be anything he wants. But I'll be damned if he's ever someone's slave. Especially fate's."

"Everyone's slave but yours," she snapped.

Rob was silent. Her words stuck in his throat. He opened his mouth but said nothing.

"Damn," he finally muttered, wiping his face. "I don't know what's gotten into you."

He turned toward the hallway. "Lucas. Lucas!"

"He's sleeping," Mara said quickly.

Rob eyed her with suspicion.

"He had exams. He's exhausted. I was up with him all night studying," she added.

Their eyes locked again—one final cold stare—before Rob grabbed his rifle and stormed off.

He opened a door in the living room wall and descended into the basement. Mara turned—and there was Lucas, hiding behind the wall.

The bruise on his face seemed darker now.

In the basement, Rob sat on the floor, cleaning a thin sword as the sun dipped below the horizon. He stared out a long horizontal window at the farmland beyond.

"Dad . . ." Lucas whispered from the stairwell.

Rob looked up, his face lighting up. "Lucas!"

He stood quickly, sword in hand, and walked toward his son.

"Your mom said you were asleep—I didn't want to wake you. I heard about school. I'm proud of you. Honestly, I wanted to homeschool you like I was, but you've proven me wrong."

He placed the sword on a nearby shelf. The basement was filled with trinkets from around the world—blades, artifacts, relics of another life. One wall was lined with knives and swords. Another displayed a glass cabinet, half open, stocked with guns and ammunition.

Lucas's eyes drifted toward the far wall—toward the armor.

A full suit of brushed steel: chest plate, arm guards, leg plates, and a knight-like helmet.

It stared back at him.

The red lenses in the eyes seemed to glow . . . watching.

"Lucas?" Rob said.

Lucas snapped out of his trance. "Mom said dinner's ready," he muttered, head lowered.

Rob wrapped his arm around his son's shoulder.

"I love you, my boy," he said as they walked up the stairs.

Lucas kept his head down, hiding his bruised face.

"I got you something from my last assignment," Rob said, hopeful. He glanced at his son, waiting for even a flicker of excitement, but Lucas didn't look up.

As they climbed the stairs, Mara shot Rob a sharp glare. She placed the dinner plates on the table just as father and son approached.

"Maybe I'll get a kiss from Mom tonight," Rob said, nudging Lucas with a grin.

He turned toward Mara—when the lights abruptly shut off.

All three froze.

"Maybe it's a power outage?" Rob offered, inching toward the window. He paused, tense. "No . . . wait." He held out a protective hand toward his wife and son. "Someone's here."

Mara and Lucas stiffened. They knew Rob well enough to know—he didn't joke about things like this.

"Mara, go downstairs with Lucas. Now. Grab your gun. Don't let anyone through—"

Rob cut off, eyes locked on blue smoke seeping into the room. From within the haze, two glowing red eyes emerged.

He charged without hesitation, slamming the figure into the dinner table. Plates crashed to the floor. Mara grabbed Lucas and rushed into the kitchen.

The red-eyed intruder kicked Rob away, then leapt onto the chandelier. Using it as a swing, she launched herself forward, knocking Rob hard across the room. He crashed into the living room, rolled under the couch, and retrieved a long knife stashed beneath it.

He returned to the kitchen, weapon gripped tight.

The figure laughed—soft and unsettling. Her voice echoed.

"Hold on. Hold on," she said, lifting a hand, then removing her mask with the other. A cascade of red hair spilled past her shoulders.

Rob froze, lowering his knife. "Charlotte," he muttered, wiping his face with one hand.

She grinned. "Still in fighting shape, huh?"

"You think this is funny? You scared the hell out of us. I could've killed you." He raised the knife again. "Maybe I should."

"Relax, in-law," Charlotte teased.

"Mara, it's your damn hippie sister," Rob called out.

Mara and Lucas cautiously stepped into the room. Charlotte used the red lenses from her mask to light her face in the dark.

"Woooooo," she moaned, playfully. Rob rolled his eyes and left, muttering curses under his breath.

Lucas moved through the darkness, trying to find his aunt. Just then, the lights flickered back on.

"What the hell, Charlotte?" Mara shouted. "What are you even wearing?" She pinched the odd fabric of Charlotte's outfit. "Did you dye your hair?"

"You like it?" Charlotte twirled proudly. "I've got a lot to tell you."

"You fight—You fight like that?" Rob stammered, still stunned.

"I've joined an enlightened group. I'm their top soldier," Charlotte said, revealing a necklace shaped like a pen and paper.

"Aunty Charlotte!" Lucas ran up and hugged her.

Rob turned to Mara, whispering, "Your damn hippie sister has joined some kind of cult. A dangerous one."

He stormed off toward the basement. "There's no money for you, Charlotte. None!"

"Don't need any, in-law," she called after him.

Charlotte knelt down and handed Lucas a small dagger inscribed with strange markings. "Got this for you, buddy."

"Thanks," Lucas mumbled, not quite sure what to make of it.

"Charlotte, help me clean up," Mara said, sighing.

The moon hung high over the house as the chaos of the evening faded. Mara and Charlotte sat across from each other at the dining table.

"He's a sweet kid. My favorite nephew," Charlotte said, placing her mask on the table.

Mara folded her arms. "Charlotte, what kind of trouble have you gotten yourself into this time?"

"No trouble, big sister. I've come to share some incredible news. Life-changing stuff," Charlotte beamed.

"Oh God. You're pregnant," Mara groaned, rubbing her face.

"Very funny," Charlotte replied, making a face. She hesitated. Mara noticed the shift in her sister's demeanor.

"You're twenty-five, Charlotte. Whatever this is, it's not for you. You could do so much more—"

"You're judging me already?" Charlotte cut in, voice suddenly more serious.

"Charlotte . . ."

"I met people who changed my life—and they can change yours too. I was meant for something greater. So are you. I know you don't want to just wash Rob's underwear and wait by the phone, hoping he's not dead. I know you worry. He's not going to stop."

Mara looked away. She didn't respond, but her silence spoke volumes.

"You're only five years older than me," Charlotte pressed. "It's not too late. I met people who taught me how to bend fate to my will."

Mara eyed the strange outfit again. "They taught you to fight like that? I've never seen Rob that shaken."

"They taught me so much more. I'm the first female leader of the Psalmists. My troops call me Squad Leader." She dangled the necklace in front of Mara. "Sorry . . . it's called the Psalms Society. We're an enlightened community working to build a better world. We have our own land, schools, businesses—"

"Charlotte, it sounds like a cult," Mara interrupted.

"People say that, but it's not. I swear. Come see it for yourself. I want to invite you. Rob, Lucas—they'd love it too."

Mara gave her a skeptical look.

"Think about it. A fresh start. A better life. For all of you." Charlotte pulled open her backpack and poured brochures across the table. "Here's the address. You can live there for free. They'll give you your own home. Rob's military background would be perfect. There are other kids—Lucas would fit right in."

"Charlotte," Mara said, voice rising slightly. She calmed herself. "This is too much. You've gotten yourself into something again."

"Gotten myself into something?" Charlotte snapped. "I've always been the 'wandering sister,' the flake. But at least I live. At least I try. Can you say the same? You take care of Rob, day in and day out, but for what? I see the fear in your eyes, Mara."

Mara spun a pamphlet in her hand, not looking up.

"I'm a mother," she said quietly.

"A mother. And what else?" Charlotte asked. "You were meant for more."

The night dragged on, and Mara lay awake in bed, her mind spinning with her sister's words. She turned to Rob as he began to stir.

"Rob," she whispered, wrapping her arms around him.

"That's your 'I want something' voice," he said without opening his eyes. "What is it?"

"Do you ever get tired of . . . your job?"

Rob chuckled softly, but didn't answer.

Mara's expression shifted to annoyance, though she kept her voice calm.

"Do you ever wish you could spend more time with Lucas . . . and me?"

Rob leaned up from the bed, already on the defensive.

"I heard your hippie sister last night. She made sure the entire house did. We are *not* joining any cult. Your sister will be out of that nonsense in a month. That's what she's good at—quitting." He paused. "The only thing I *don't* understand is her combat ability. She was trained. Really well trained."

"Maybe we could go check it out. Just to see if Charlotte's safe," Mara suggested gently.

"Charlotte's an adult. She can take care of herself. Don't let your flaky sister get in your head."

"Maybe . . . maybe we just need a different environment. A fresh atmosphere for Lucas might do him good."

Rob stared at her.

"What? You begged me to put him in that school, and now you want to move?"

"It's just—"

"Mara, don't start with the bitter act again." Rob waved her off. "Charlotte's been like this since she was a kid. I didn't grow up with whatever drama you two did. You and your sister aren't the same."

Her face darkened.

"You don't have a clue what goes on here. You're not around enough to know anything about Lucas or me."

Their voices grew louder, echoing from the basement. Upstairs, Charlotte stirred on the couch, blinking herself awake. Lucas entered the room quietly.

"They fight a lot, huh, buddy?" Charlotte asked, yawning.

"Mom misses my dad when he's gone," Lucas replied.

"Come here, kid." She pulled him into a hug. "What are you now—sixteen? You can drive, right? Take me to the store, buy me some wine? I'll drink it in your car, Officer Lucas." She tickled him.

Lucas burst into laughter. "I'm twelve, Aunty Charlotte."

Charlotte grinned but suddenly stopped, noticing his swollen lip. She gently touched it with her thumb.

"What the hell happened?" Rob's voice thundered as he stormed into the room. Charlotte and Lucas both flinched. He knelt beside his son, inspecting the injury.

"Sorry, Lucas," Mara said, entering. She closed her eyes, embarrassed. "I let it slip."

"You can't keep secrets from *Night*—" Rob froze mid-sentence, glancing at Charlotte.

"Dad, really, I'm fine," Lucas muttered, pulling away.

"You're not fine." Rob's tone sharpened. "What did the school do?" He turned to Mara. "Never mind." He bolted downstairs.

Lucas covered his face, eyes brimming with tears. Moments later, Rob returned, sword in one hand, a demonic-looking mask in the other.

"Nice mask, in-law. Mine's better," Charlotte quipped.

Rob ignored her. He slipped the mask over his face. "Where's the boy? Tell me his name."

Mara and Charlotte began arguing with him, their voices climbing over each other.

"Dad, please—I don't want anyone to get hurt," Lucas pleaded, his voice rising above the chaos.

"I'm not going to *hurt* him," Rob said. "Just shake him up a little. Or maybe I'll fight his father. He's a minor—his dad will do."

"Dad . . ." Lucas said more firmly.

"Oh, you're standing up to me now?" Rob snapped. "Where was this when that kid hit you? I taught you to be strong. This—this is weakness." He looked to Mara. "I trained you to fight too. And you did *nothing*?"

"Normal people don't go around scaring children in masks," Charlotte said dryly.

Rob and Mara rolled their eyes at her, unamused.

"I didn't raise a coward," Rob growled, locking eyes with Lucas. "Fate will beat you down, son. It'll crush you without mercy. You need to be stronger than the world around you."

"Blah, blah, fate, mercy," Charlotte mocked. "You take yourself way too seriously."

Rob turned on her, smirking. "Says the woman bouncing from commune to commune. You'll never find a man that way. 'Single by choice'? Yeah, right."

"Say what you want about me, Rob. But not about Psalms Society. That place is *life*—"

"Blah, blah, blah." Rob mimicked her. "How much weed do you and your enlightened friends smoke to believe in that metaphysical garbage?"

Their argument escalated as Mara led Lucas to his room.

"Mom . . . do you love Dad?" Lucas asked, his voice trembling with need.

Mara blinked, surprised. "Yes, sweetie. He might not show it the way we want, but he loves you. And he loves me."

"I'm tired of all the fighting . . . I'm tired of Nightmare," Lucas whispered.

"Me too, son." She wrapped her arms around him and pulled him close. "Me too."

But Lucas didn't hug her back.

Outside, a car pulled up. Men stepped out, dressed in the same Psalms Society uniforms Charlotte had worn—

only their faces were bare. Charlotte met them at the curb, speaking in hushed tones. Mara watched from the window.

"She's leaving," Mara said softly.

"I give it a month before she quits," Rob muttered, sharpening his sword on the floor.

"She's gone," Mara replied, still watching the vehicle pull away.

"She'll be back. I'm surprised she didn't ask for money this time."

"She did," Mara admitted.

Rob growled and nicked his finger with the blade. "Damn it!" He shoved his finger in his mouth. "How much?"

"She said it was a donation to Psalms Society."

"We're funding a cult now. Fantastic." He stood. "Lucas! Lucas!" No response. "What the hell is he doing?" He moved toward the boy's room.

From the window, Mara heard glass shatter.

She rushed to the room and found Rob standing by the broken window, fists clenched.

"One of Charlotte's damn cult friends took him. I saw them put Lucas in the car." He stormed past her, searching frantically, panic overtaking him. Then, as if regaining control, he slapped his own face, steadying himself. Grabbing his sword, he turned toward the door.

"Rob, wait!" Mara called out.

"I'm going to send those cult bastards straight to hell—and I'm going to make Charlotte *watch.*"

"I'm coming with you."

"No. You'll only slow me down," Rob growled.

Mara caught his arm. Her grip surprised him—it was firm, unmoving.

"He is *our* son," she said.

Rob stared at her. In her eyes, he saw a strength he'd forgotten she had. Mara stepped ahead of him and opened the front door.

CHAPTER 14

CASSANDRA JUMPED at the sound of a gunshot, her breath catching as she clutched her chest. Her heart pounded louder with every faint noise echoing through the arena's dimly lit garage.

"Drop your weapon!" a man's voice shouted.

Cassandra peeked around the vehicle she was hiding behind. A squad of men in security uniforms were closing in, surrounding a group of Psalmist members. The air crackled with tension as both sides shouted over one another—commands like *"Get on the floor!"* and *"Drop your weapons!"* rang out.

The Psalmist leader slowly backed away as the security team moved closer. Then another wave of pressure came from the opposite direction—police officers converging, boxing the Psalmists in on both sides.

Some of the Psalmists turned, now facing the newly arrived officers.

"What the hell are they supposed to be?" Officer Dan muttered, eyeing the group's strange clothing and demeanor.

The officers beside him didn't answer. They stood still, watching the eerie calm of the Psalmist line.

"Trouble," Jessie said grimly, stepping up beside Dan. As he scanned the area, his eyes locked on Cassandra, crouched behind a car.

"Drop your knives, freaks. You're surrounded," Dan barked, amplifying his voice with cupped hands. "Don't do anything stupid. One move and someone gets hurt. Let's all calm down."

Then, as if on cue, the Psalmist members began chanting in unison. "Let death seize our enemies . . . let them go down alive into hell."

The words, spoken in eerie synchronization, chilled the air.

Dan scowled. "Move in slowly. Don't fire unless absolutely necessary," he ordered.

The officers on his side advanced cautiously, mirrored by the approaching security team behind the Psalmists.

The cult members swayed slightly, murmuring their chant like a ritual. Their leader's gaze drifted across the garage—locking eyes with Cassandra still hiding behind the car.

Jessie moved fast, crossing the space and crouching beside her.

"You okay?" he asked, offering his hand.

"Yeah . . . thanks. I'm fine," Cassandra said, gripping his hand and pulling herself to her feet.

"These freaks again are after Rob, aren't they?" Jessie asked, scanning the situation. "Where is he? Did they take him?"

Cassandra hesitated, her eyes giving away what her silence confirmed.

Jessie nodded grimly. "Got it. Come on. Let's get you out of here—they've got this handled." He placed a steadying hand on her back, guiding her toward a safer exit.

"Stop!" the Psalmist leader shouted suddenly, spotting them. He raised his gun, aiming it directly at Cassandra and Jessie.

"You fire, and we're all dead," one of his own followers hissed, leaning in close to the leader.

The Psalmist leader's eyes locked onto Cassandra. Jessie and Cassandra froze as he slowly raised Cassandra's gun and aimed it at them.

"Drop it! Drop it!" Officer Dan shouted, raising his weapon. Other officers quickly followed suit, targeting the leader.

Several Psalmists raised their hands in surrender, their daggers clattering to the concrete floor. The leader glanced at his fellow members giving up, then reluctantly began to lower the gun. His gaze remained fixed on Cassandra and Jessie as they cautiously backed away.

"No funny stuff. Put the damn gun all the way down!" another officer shouted.

The Squad leader finally placed the weapon on the ground. He straightened slowly, hands lifted in surrender. Police and security personnel surged forward, moving in to apprehend the Psalmists.

Then a loud detonation echoed through the garage—blue smoke flooded the air.

Jessie and Cassandra turned in alarm. Out of the haze, the Psalmist leader leapt forward, grabbing Cassandra's gun again and charging straight toward them.

"Move!" Jessie shouted, yanking Cassandra's hand as they sprinted out of the garage.

Outside, Daisy leaned on Jessie's car, startled by the approaching pair.

"Daisy, run!" Jessie called.

Before she could react, the Psalmist leader vaulted onto the hood of her car. She screamed, shrinking back as he loomed over her.

"Daisy!" Jessie cried out, still running.

The leader reached toward her, his motion slow and uncertain.

"What's your name?" he asked, voice distorted beneath the mask.

"Go to hell!" Daisy snarled. She yanked his arm hard, sending him crashing to the pavement.

He hit the ground, rolled, and sprang back up, gun in hand.

"Get down, Daisy!" Malcolm shouted from across the lot. He aimed a compact pistol-shaped device and fired. Daisy dropped instantly as a burst of rubber bullets pelted the Psalmist leader. The man grunted, staggering from the impact, clutching his gut and mask before scrambling away.

"He'll be back," Malcolm muttered, approaching with Amanda at his side. "That was one of Armory's latest non-lethal prototypes. Rubber rounds only." His tone held pride, but Amanda didn't share his enthusiasm. They hurried to Daisy, and Malcolm helped her to her feet.

"Thanks . . . Dad," Daisy said, breathless, still clinging to Jessie.

"I'll always protect you," Malcolm replied, then fixed his eyes on Jessie. "Get her out of here. Keep her safe."

Jessie nodded.

"Go," Malcolm ordered. Jessie and Daisy jumped into his car and sped away.

"Malcolm!" Amanda called sharply.

"I'm coming," he replied, but his face remained tense, his eyes lingering on the direction his daughter had gone.

"Jessie, stop," Daisy said suddenly, as several pedestrians crossed the road ahead. Jessie tapped impatiently on the steering wheel, waiting for them to pass. Once the way was clear, he resumed driving.

"Take me to my house," Daisy said firmly.

"Daisy . . ." Jessie began, his tone weary.

"This terrorist group is the closest link you have to your father. You can't miss this chance," Daisy said, voice calm but resolute.

"I need to get you somewhere safe."

"Are we in this together or not?" she asked.

Jessie exhaled, defeated.

"All we have to do is see what my dad's doing. If we follow them, maybe we can find out more. This is what you've been waiting for," Daisy said, placing a hand gently on his arm.

Jessie hesitated.

"Babe," she added, kissing his cheek.

He met her eyes—he knew she was right. He shifted gears again just as more people crossed the street, causing another delay.

"I don't know what I'd do if something happened to you," Jessie murmured. "I've got no one left, except you."

"That's why we're in this together," Daisy said, squeezing his arm. "What happens to you, happens to me."

Suddenly, the car's rear window shattered.

The Psalmist leader swung the door open, gun in hand—Cassandra's gun.

"Drive," he ordered coldly.

Jessie gripped the wheel, heart pounding.

"Drive, or be shot," the leader warned, now aiming the gun at Daisy.

Jessie looked at him through the rearview mirror. "Where are we going?"

"Malcolm's house." The leader leaned forward, eyeing Daisy. "You know how to disable the security system."

She hesitated, then gave a small nod.

"Daisy, it's going to be okay," Jessie said, though the fear in his voice betrayed the words. Both of them sat trembling as Jessie obeyed and drove.

Malcolm burst through the manor's doors like a soldier charging the front lines. He rushed to his desk and snatched up a tablet, typing furiously. The device pinged and a location appeared on the screen.

"He's at Dunkin's warehouse," Malcolm muttered.

"I'll call my boys downtown and see if—" Amanda stopped as she saw him heading toward a hidden door behind his office. "Malcolm, don't!" she called.

Cassandra paused, curiosity drawing her closer. A maid peeked in from the hallway, dust rag in hand.

"I didn't even know that door opened," she whispered to Cassandra. "We always thought Rob hid dead bodies in there." She laughed and patted Cassandra's arm before strolling away.

Cassandra cautiously stepped through the door.

The secret room was a time capsule. Yellowed newspapers lined the walls—headlines of an armored figure wreaking havoc across the Middle East. Photos were everywhere: Malcolm, Rob, Daisy, and a woman who must have been family. In one photo, the woman pressed an ice cream cone to Rob's nose as he grimaced, sticky dessert dripping down his face.

Other frames showed Malcolm and Amanda dressed for a gala, smiling for the camera. The largest portrait displayed a younger Daisy with Malcolm and a beautiful woman. But the woman's face had been doodled on with a mustache and glasses—someone's idea of a joke.

Another photo caught Cassandra's eye—a stern-looking man in a military uniform, chest heavy with medals. The plaque beneath read a date and a name.

"Malcolm, I know what you're thinking," Amanda said softly behind her.

Cassandra moved deeper into the room—and stopped.

In the center stood a tall display case. Inside, a full set of brushed steel armor rested on a mannequin: two chest plates, two leg guards, a black sash, and a knight-style mask. A hood draped over the head.

"Is this . . ." Cassandra reached out and touched the glass.

Amanda and Malcolm both turned toward her.

"I'm putting on the armor," Malcolm said. "I'm going to save Rob."

"Malcolm, that's insane. You'll get yourself killed."

"It's bulletproof. Lightweight—so even I can handle it. I've upgraded the weapon system since the last version," Malcolm said, typing rapidly on his phone while Amanda argued with him. His voice grew louder, edged with anxiety. "Who else is going to save Rob? The police?"

He pressed a concealed button on the wall, and the display case hissed open.

"Malcolm, no," Amanda warned, stepping forward as he removed one of the arm plates and began strapping it on.

Suddenly, a siren blared through the room.

Malcolm snatched his tablet off the desk and stared at the screen. His face paled.

"It's Daisy . . ." he said. "She says she's in trouble."

Amanda and Cassandra moved toward him, alarmed.

"She's on the manor grounds—with a guy holding a gun," Malcolm continued, eyes wide.

"Are you sure?" Cassandra asked, her voice tight.

"She just bypassed my security protocols," Malcolm said, tapping on the screen. "Only someone who knows the system could've done that." He turned the tablet toward them, showing a live feed: Jessie's car pulling onto the property.

Cassandra turned to the open armor case. Her fingers brushed the edge of the glass, cold against her skin. Her eyes flicked between the display, Malcolm, and Amanda—uncertainty hardening into something else. Resolve.

"Get out," the psalmist leader ordered.

Without a word, Jessie and Daisy opened their doors and stepped out.

"Put in the code," he said, motioning toward the manor's front entrance.

Daisy hesitated, confused. "How does he even know there's a code?" she muttered to herself.

"Put in the code," the psalmist leader snapped again, more forcefully.

Jessie moved in front of her protectively. "Daisy, it's going to be okay," he said, his voice steady but low.

"Stop wasting time," the leader barked, his tone tightening.

"Daisy!" Malcolm's voice rang out as he approached with determined steps. He held one arm behind his back, the other aimed directly at the psalmist leader with a pistol.

"Drop your gun or I'll shoot," the psalmist leader countered, raising Cassandra's weapon.

"No, you won't," came Amanda's voice. She stepped out from the other side, sword in hand, the gleam of steel catching the light. Her other arm was also held behind her back.

The psalmist leader suddenly fired a shot into the air, making everyone flinch.

"I said drop your weapons! Now!" he shouted.

"Who are you?" Amanda demanded. "What do you want? Rob's not here. The psalmist necklace isn't here. What is it that you're after?"

The psalmist leader remained silent, eyes darting between Amanda and Malcolm as they began to corner him.

"Leave now," Amanda ordered. "Or we'll put you down."

Still, the man said nothing. His gaze finally settled on Daisy, who stood trembling in Jessie's arms. Then, slowly, he began to lower his weapon and crouched toward the ground.

Without warning, he fired directly at Jessie.

Cassandra threw herself in front of the shot, a metallic thud echoing as the bullet ricocheted off the metal chest plate she wore and fell harmlessly to the ground.

"You like?" Malcolm said, taunting the psalmist leader. "Shock absorbent. No ricochets. No friendly fire."

"Malcolm, not now," Amanda hissed.

The psalmist leader took a step toward Daisy and Jessie.

Malcolm raised his gun, smirking. "Don't get any ideas. This isn't a prototype—it's fully loaded. Amanda may avoid guns, but I'll light you up."

"Malcolm," Amanda groaned, exasperated.

The psalmist leader suddenly rolled and fired at Malcolm, who ducked just in time. A metallic clang rang out as the bullet hit his armored forearm. Malcolm pressed a button, and a volley of miniature shurikens blasted out of the gauntlet.

The psalmist leader dodged, but the shurikens shredded Jessie's car, glass exploding from the windows.

"I'll pay for that," Malcolm muttered, already tapping a new sequence into his wrist controls.

"Get behind the car!" Cassandra shouted, waving Jessie and Daisy back.

Amanda charged with her sword, slashing at the psalmist leader as he dove into the bushes. He hurled his dagger at her, forcing her to dive to the ground.

Cassandra intercepted him before he could reach Malcolm, slamming into him with her armored chest. He stumbled, and she stomped on his hand, kicking the gun away. As he tried to rise, she pinned him with her knee and tore off his mask.

A burst of thick burgundy smoke exploded from within the mask, sending Cassandra stumbling back.

The smoke began to swell and spread, swirling until the winds of Shiloh City stirred and carried it away.

As the haze lifted, the psalmist leader's face was revealed.

From behind the car, Daisy peeked out, wide-eyed.

The psalmist leader stared silently at Malcolm and Amanda. The wind moved gently across the scene, brushing the mask where it lay, untouched on the ground. Amanda and Malcolm stood frozen, eyes locked on the man before them.

The psalmist leader's expression mirrored theirs—stunned, tense, haunted.

None of them spoke.

They simply stared, unmoving, caught in the quiet storm of recognition as the winds of Shiloh City drifted between them.

CHAPTER 15

ROB BURST through the courtroom doors with a loud grunt, his boots slamming against the polished floor. He swore under his breath and stomped down the corridor like a toddler denied his favorite toy. Following closely behind was a nervous man in an expensive suit, beads of sweat gathering at his brow. A weary security guard trailed them, clearly frustrated and more than a little concerned by Rob's erratic behavior.

Malcolm sat calmly on a bench outside the courtroom, next to a young man with tan skin and a calming presence. As Rob stormed toward them, Malcolm quickly stood.

"That damn dirty pirate lawyer! That damn dirty pirate lawyer!" Rob shouted, throwing his arms in the air.

"I take it the hearing didn't go well," Malcolm said with a dry chuckle.

"Malcolm, your lawyers are garbage." Rob spun around to face the man in the suit. "I want my money back. You think you'll get away with this?"

The lawyer shrank back instinctively.

"Sir, I'm going to have to ask you to leave the courthouse," the security guard said, his voice tense with exhaustion.

"Throw me out, then!" Rob bellowed. "Throw me to the street and let the dogs lick my bones clean!"

The guard stiffened and reached for his nightstick.

Rob turned back to Malcolm and the lawyer. "These lawyers of yours are useless!" he growled, shoving the attorney aside.

Malcolm gently pulled the man away, offering quiet apologies as Rob continued to rant.

"Malcolm . . ." Rob said, lowering his voice. Malcolm sighed.

"What does 'being held in contempt' mean? Can you talk to the judge for me?"

"Oh, Rob . . ." Malcolm said, rubbing his temple.

"Don't 'Oh, Rob' me. That sleazy lawyer and the judge were in cahoots. Your guy barely said a word, so I had to speak up for myself!"

"Let's get some air," the young man beside Malcolm said, motioning toward the exit. He could feel the tension rising. The security guard was now glaring, clearly at the end of his rope.

"Ezra, don't you start," Rob snapped. "You nearly made me late for my own lynching. They grabbed me by the groin, lifted me up like some trophy, and dropped me hard. He did it!" Rob jabbed a finger at the flustered lawyer.

The lawyer looked helplessly to Malcolm. "He, uh… he has to pay some substantial damages. But that's far better than jail. Honestly, I think he got off easy."

"Easy? I'm paying damages *and* paying you!" Rob shouted, throwing up his hands.

"Rob, you did assault the man," the lawyer added meekly, half-hiding behind Malcolm.

Rob shot him a vicious glare, fists clenched, trembling with restrained fury. He was just about to lunge forward when the courtroom doors opened again.

A young man stepped out—thick beard, short wavy hair, and a designer white sweater jacket that looked out of place among the suits. He commanded two older men who followed his instructions wordlessly, peeling off down another hallway. Three silver earrings dangled from one of his ears, glinting under the fluorescent lights. Both his hands were adorned with chunky rings and leather wristbands.

He locked eyes with Rob and Malcolm, gave them a wink, and held the door open for Dunkin—who shuffled out slowly on crutches, his neck in a brace. The behemoth loomed over the younger man like a shadow.

"You're faking that injury, and you know it!" Rob barked.

Dunkin smirked and gave his body a dramatic wiggle. The young man whispered something in his ear, and both chuckled. For once, Dunkin said nothing.

"Time to leave," the security guard snapped, stepping forward and motioning toward the exit.

Rob shoved past him and stormed toward the young man and Dunkin.

"You're barking up the wrong tree, Rob," the young man said, stepping protectively in front of Dunkin. "You must really love coming back to court. Over. And over. And over . . . I could keep going."

Dunkin leaned down and whispered again. More snickering. Rob's body tensed. His breathing grew shallow.

Ezra jumped in front of him, arms spread. "Rob, not here. Not in the courthouse, man."

Rob locked eyes with the young man, who stood unfazed, daring him to make a move.

"Rob, please. You're already in deep. Don't make it worse," Ezra begged, holding onto his arm.

Rob snarled but didn't budge. Malcolm stepped in too, placing a hand on Rob's shoulder. "Come on, buddy. Let it go."

Rob let out a guttural growl and shoved both of them aside, storming away.

"That's a good boy," the young man taunted with a smug grin.

Malcolm exhaled heavily, shaking his head.

Rob turned back suddenly, charging at the man with a roar. "You damn dirty pirate lawyer!"

Ezra jumped in, pushing Rob just in time. Rob stumbled back in surprise, then shoved Ezra in the chest, hard enough to make him stumble.

Rob advanced again.

Ezra grabbed his arm, spun him around, and forced him onto a bench.

Rob shot back to his feet, teeth clenched. "Move."

"You taught me everything," Ezra said calmly. "When my dad died, you were the one who stepped in. You're like a father to me. I can't lose another one."

Rob hesitated, breathing heavy. Slowly, his shoulders dropped. The storm in his chest calmed.

Malcolm stepped beside him. "Come on," he said quietly.

Just then, two more security guards entered the hallway, alert.

"Is there a problem, sir?" one asked, directing the question to the smug young man.

"Is there, Rob?" the young lawyer said, flashing his teeth.

Rob glanced between his friends and the guards, then turned and walked away without a word.

"You should walk out on all fours," the young lawyer called after him, then let out a mocking bark.

"Hey—shut up," Malcolm snapped, following Rob.

"I hear Armory stock's down again," the young man said. Malcolm froze. "I also heard a few Armory factories might not be up to code. Maybe I should take a closer look."

Malcolm stepped forward, fists clenched, but Ezra placed a hand on his chest, giving him a firm nod. Malcolm took a breath and followed Rob down the stairs.

"Damn that punk," Malcolm muttered. "Dad dies, leaves him a fortune. No manners. Doesn't even wear a suit to court."

As they exited the courthouse, the wind of Shiloh City whistled around them. Rob trudged ahead, hunched and brooding like an old dog nursing invisible wounds.

"That's Henry," Malcolm muttered to Ezra. "Spoiled brat. His rich parents paid his way through law school. Now he's got it out for Rob."

"I've seen Rob angry before," Ezra said, "but that guy really knows how to push his buttons."

"He's going to be a problem," Malcolm said as he opened the car door for Rob.

Rob muttered and grumbled as he slid into the back seat.

Ezra climbed into the driver's side.

"Good form, son," Rob said suddenly. "You fought me on a psychological level. Got in my head. That's how strategy begins."

Ezra smiled faintly. "I fought you with love . . . and the truth."

Rob growled something incoherent about lawsuits and slumped deeper into his seat.

"Nightmare should pay him a visit. Yeah, Nightmare should pay him a visit," he whispered to himself. "That damn dirty pirate lawyer won't know what hit him."

As Ezra backed out of the parking space, he and Malcolm both caught sight of Henry standing atop the courthouse steps. He was on the phone, but his eyes were locked on their car. A smug grin crept across his face as they pulled away.

Just as their vehicle disappeared down the street, a large truck rolled up to the courthouse, music thundering from its speakers. The windows were tinted black, hiding whoever sat inside. Without missing a beat, Henry ended his call, opened the passenger door, and helped Dunkin climb in. Moments later, both men vanished into the vehicle, the bass-heavy music echoing behind them.

Rob stormed through the mansion, passing Amanda and Daisy on the couch. Amanda was rattling off computer terminology, pointing to diagrams on her laptop. Daisy leaned in, focused and engaged, her brow furrowed in determination. Both women glanced up as Rob passed by without a word, his heavy steps echoing through the room.

"Didn't go well," Ezra said, stepping in behind him. He flashed a soft smile at Daisy, and the two exchanged a quiet laugh. "Hey, Ms. Amanda. How are you?" He leaned down, hugging her and planting a quick kiss on her cheek. "Why don't I get assigned to guard you more often? I love hanging with the girls at the home."

"They love you too, Ezra," Amanda replied with a bright smile.

"Ezra and I were down at the home Monday, and one of the girls—" Daisy began.

"You two were at the home last Monday?" Amanda cut in, her voice slightly more curious. "Ezra, Rob said you couldn't help him because you were with your mom all day."

Ezra's expression tensed. "Oh, yeah—she changed her mind. You know how she is," he said with a nervous laugh, scratching the side of his face.

Daisy opened her mouth to speak again, but was interrupted by a loud, guttural growl from another room. The maids paused, startled by the sound of something slamming or falling. They exchanged anxious glances before slowly approaching the hallway.

Malcolm entered the room quickly, his face calm but focused. Without saying a word, he motioned for the maids to stand down and headed toward the noise.

"Is Uncle Rob okay? He's been going to court a lot lately," Daisy asked, watching Amanda and Ezra carefully for any reaction.

"Rob's getting forgetful," Amanda said with a teasing tone. "Half the time, he's not even present when he drives. We might have to start thinking about putting him in a home."

Daisy laughed. "You sound just like my dad." But her smile faltered, her instincts sensing there was more they weren't saying.

"He can live with me," Ezra offered. "Two ex-soldiers, living the bachelor life."

Daisy chuckled again, but Amanda shot her a look. The laughter quickly faded.

"Ezra . . ." Rob's voice came from the hallway. He leaned into the room, looking uncharacteristically quiet. "We still cooking that meal we had on tour?"

Ezra grinned. "I'm coming." He started toward the kitchen, but Amanda blocked his path with a raised arm.

"After dinner, can I have a word with you?"

Ezra slid past her, smiling. "Anytime, second mama." He darted into the kitchen.

"Wait . . ." Daisy said, turning to Amanda. "Didn't Uncle Rob go to court for assault?"

Amanda avoided eye contact, smiling awkwardly. "That's . . . complicated."

The scent of food filled the air—rich, seasoned, and savory. Ezra and Rob had been busy in the kitchen, plating dishes for Amanda, Malcolm, and Daisy.

Malcolm eyed his plate. "I was expecting caviar and T-bones."

"Cooks probably feel blessed not having to cater to your pampered taste buds," Rob joked, taking a seat next to Ezra.

Soon the table fell silent—only the clatter of silverware and chewing broke the quiet.

Amanda's phone rang. She stood and stepped out of the room.

"That hit the spot," Rob said, patting his belly. "After the day I've had, I needed this. Feels like fate's just spitting in my face lately."

"You're welcome," Ezra said. "Reminds me of the old days—me, you, and General Samuel. I owe everything to you, Malcolm, and Amanda for what you did for me and my mom."

"You're very welcome, son," Rob said softly, gazing at his empty plate.

"Ezra, are you sure you can't come to the club tonight?" Daisy asked.

"Yeah, I have to help my mom with some things," Ezra replied.

"Like what?" Rob asked, leaning back in his chair, suspicious.

"Well, she needs me to—"

"What, that's tonight?" Malcolm interrupted. "Daisy, I thought we were going to watch a movie."

"Dad, I told you this morning," Daisy replied with clear irritation. She glared at him, knowing he was trying to dig for answers he already had.

"Yeah, but . . ." Malcolm fumbled with his words. "I just thought maybe we could do something—special."

"Malcolm," Amanda said, re-entering the room. "Can I speak with you for a moment?" Her tone had shifted. Malcolm saw the look on his daughter's face, then reluctantly wiped his hands and followed Amanda out.

Rob leaned toward Ezra. "There better not be any funny business."

Ezra leaned back, grinning.

"I will kill," Rob said. "Or better yet, Malcolm will."

"Rob, we're just friends. Good friends," Ezra said.

"Stay away, if you know what's good for you," Rob muttered, noticing Daisy watching them whisper.

"Rob . . ." Amanda called. He turned to her. "Don't get angry."

"Why would you say that? Now I'm angry," Rob snapped.

"Some of Dunkin's guys were spotted at the club," Amanda said carefully. "My downtown contacts say they were starting trouble. They think Dunkin's stirring something up . . . with us."

"Dunkin's not even allowed at the club," Rob growled, pacing. "He's taunting me. That damn giant and his dirty pirate lawyer."

Daisy glanced around the table, confused but clearly sensing something was off.

"Dunkin's just a thug from downtown, sweetheart," Amanda said quickly, trying to defuse the tension. "He's been trying to stir trouble with your father and Rob."

Rob scoffed at Amanda's attempt to minimize the situation. He opened his mouth to argue, but Amanda cut him off.

"My associates handled it. Dunkin's men are gone. Malcolm, the club is secure." She paused before adding, "But . . . the club is being sued. The lawyer mentioned overcrowding, a fire hazard—something about too many people on the premises."

"What?" Rob shot to his feet. "It's that damn pirate lawyer. He's coming for all of us!"

"Rob, we'll handle it. Don't get worked up," Amanda said, trying to steady him. But Rob was already storming toward the front of the mansion.

"Rob! Rob…" she called after him.

"Buddy, remember you wanted to meet with General Sam?" Malcolm said, jogging to catch up. "I was going to set up the video call in a bit."

Rob paused at the bottom of the staircase. "If I talk to him, I can't go after Dunkin today," he muttered. "He needs to be punished." His tone had shifted—more to himself than to them.

Amanda and Malcolm exchanged a look, unsettled by the way Rob seemed to drift into his own world.

"He's helping me look into something," Rob added under his breath, catching their stares. "I'll find them. I will." He turned and started up the stairs.

"On that note," Malcolm said, stepping back into the kitchen, "Daisy, I don't think it's safe for you to go to the club tonight."

"Dad, Amanda said the bad guys are gone. Her *associates* handled it," Daisy replied, her voice tinged with sarcasm. She looked to Amanda for confirmation.

Amanda scratched the side of her face, clearly avoiding the question. She turned and walked toward Ezra at the table.

Daisy, frustrated, launched into a list of reasons why she should be allowed to go. Her voice rose, and soon she and Malcolm were locked in a heated argument.

Meanwhile, Amanda leaned down to Ezra and whispered, "I think we all should start heading home. And more importantly—we should all *stay* home tonight." Her tone left no room for interpretation.

"Yes, Mommy," Ezra replied playfully, leaning back in his chair. But Amanda studied his face, sensing he might not follow her advice.

"I just got the little guy down for a nap, so now the adults can play," Malcolm said, walking into the living room where Amanda was seated, typing away at her laptop surrounded by coding and computer science books.

Amanda raised an eyebrow. "What do you mean?"

Malcolm grinned. "Rob's upstairs, chatting with General Sam. Some secret project they're working on."

"You think it's another mission for Nightmare?" she asked.

"No," Malcolm said, shaking his head. "I think he's chasing someone. Maybe stalking a *woman* he met overseas." He tapped the door behind his desk. "But when he's ready . . ."

Amanda frowned. "It's not good for him. He loses himself when he puts that thing on."

"I've made it safer. Or tried to," Malcolm said, sounding hopeful. Then something caught his eye. "Hey… there's some kind of glitch on the system."

Amanda walked over as he typed into the laptop. Onscreen, they saw live footage of Daisy climbing out of a second-story window.

"Is she—?" Amanda began.

"She's climbing down!" Malcolm exclaimed.

A second camera feed showed Daisy sprinting toward a car parked by the gate.

"That's Ezra's car!"

"Malcolm," Amanda said, trying to keep him calm.

"DAISY!" he shouted, bolting out of the room and up the stairs.

"Oh, she left hours ago," a maid said casually as Malcolm passed.

"What!" he shouted, spinning around.

"I thought it was okay. Mr. Ezra comes late all the time and—"

"What!" Malcolm bellowed, racing down the stairs and grabbing his keys.

In another room, Rob glared toward the hallway. "Hey, can you guys shut up?" he barked. He sat at a desk, mid-call with General Samuel on his laptop. He slammed the door shut.

"She's at the club. I know it," Malcolm muttered, storming toward the garage.

"Malcolm," Amanda called, catching his arm. "I know you want to protect her. But she's not a child anymore."

Malcolm froze. The fear in his face was clear—but underneath it, a flicker of understanding. Still, he pulled away and ran toward the car.

Amanda rushed after him.

The club pulsed with music so loud it shook the walls. Lights flickered. Partygoers jumped, danced, and screamed, bodies drenched in sweat and energy. Glittering outfits caught the strobe lights as the crowd surged.

Daisy stood near the bar, laughing with her friends. "Two, please," she told the bartender, handing one drink to Ezra. "Why won't you dance?" she yelled over the music.

"I *don't* dance!" Ezra shouted back, leaning close to be heard.

Suddenly, a man bumped into Daisy—hard. Ezra shot to his feet, fists clenched, staring the man down.

The man glanced back as if daring Ezra to make a move.

Daisy put a hand on Ezra's chest, calming him. She smiled and kissed him on the cheek, then motioned to the bartender for another drink.

She tugged Ezra's sleeve, encouraging him to follow her into the dancing crowd. He shook his head with a smile.

Daisy disappeared into the crush of people, dancing wildly. She turned and gestured again for Ezra to join her. Again, he declined. She rolled her eyes and kept dancing with her friends.

After a few songs, Daisy headed toward the bathroom with her group. Several men stood outside the door, watching them with leering eyes.

One man opened his mouth to speak, but Daisy was faster—she flashed a can of pepper spray from her purse, glaring at him.

"Too much scum from downtown here tonight," she said loudly to her friends, making sure the men heard as they stepped into the bathroom.

Ezra, growing uneasy, scanned the crowd. The music surged again.

"Daisy? Daisy?" he called, pushing through people toward the back hallway.

He bumped into someone.

"Sorry—" he began, then froze.

Standing in front of him was Henry. He smiled coolly.

"Rob's little buddy. Ezra, right?" Henry said.

Behind him stood several familiar faces—men from the courthouse. The same ones who'd opened the truck door for Dunkin.

Ezra tried to move past Henry without saying a word.

"Hold on a second," Henry said, extending an arm. "Is Malcolm here?"

"No," Ezra muttered, pushing by.

"How's Rob? Did he finally find a tree to go piss under?" Henry said, lifting one leg and leaning against the wall like a dog. His crew burst into laughter.

Ezra rolled his eyes and kept walking, scanning the crowd for Daisy.

"Speak of the devil," Henry said as Daisy emerged from the bathroom with her friends. "Malcolm's daughter herself!" he called out, loud enough for her to hear. He opened his arms, inviting a hug.

Daisy eyed him warily, hand slipping into her purse, fingers brushing her pepper spray.

Henry extended a hand. "I'm Henry. Your father and his buddies have a not-so-flattering nickname for me—*the pirate lawyer.* Probably jealous of my rugged beard." He stroked his chin theatrically. His three earrings jingled as he moved. "And maybe it's the rum."

Daisy chuckled. "I'm sorry—how do you know my dad?"

"This guy was in that big case on the news," one of her friends whispered to her.

Henry gave a showy spin. "Guilty. I'm famous."

"You're, like, super rich, right?" her friend asked, eyes gleaming.

"Thirsty much?" Daisy teased, drawing laughter from the group. Her friend didn't seem amused.

"Yeah, my dad died and left me everything," Henry said, his voice dropping. The cocky air momentarily faded.

"I'm sorry to hear that," Daisy said, softening.

"That's why I'm here, maybe. Trying to drink the grief away. A dance from a damn fine sexy woman might help me forget my sorrows." he teased, flashing a grin and offering his arm to Daisy.

"Pirate boy, you really know how to charm a girl," Daisy replied playfully.

From around the corner, Ezra watched, his jaw tightening as he saw Daisy follow Henry back into the club. His blood simmered. Eyes hard, he slipped into the crowd.

He pushed through dancers as the music pounded, bodies jumping in sync. Ezra stood alone, scanning the crowd, a statue among chaos.

At the bar, Henry and Daisy shared a laugh.

"You got any rum?" Henry asked the bartender.

"Stop," Daisy laughed, pulling out some cash. "Two, please," she said, pointing at a bottle.

"Daisy, you don't have to."

"It's my treat. Relax."

They clinked glasses and took a sip.

"Daisy," Ezra called out, approaching. He shot a hard look at Henry, who responded with a smug grin.

Ezra's expression shifted—uncertain, then distant. He saw something between Daisy and Henry. Something natural. Effortless. Something he and Daisy might never have.

"Hey," Daisy said. "I've been looking for you! I want you to meet—"

"We've met," Ezra cut in.

Daisy glanced at Henry, who nodded. "Yeah, I've seen him around with Rob. And your dad."

"He keeps showing up, harassing Rob," Ezra added, voice sharp.

"No," Henry said, winking. "I defend the people Rob harasses."

"My uncle curses about you all the time," Daisy laughed.

"Uncle?" Henry raised an eyebrow. "Robbie's your uncle?"

"It's . . . complicated," Ezra said before Daisy could explain.

Henry tilted his head, watching Ezra breathe heavier. "So . . . you two a thing?"

Neither of them answered.

"What do you do, Ezra?" Henry asked, leaning back on the bar with his drink. "You're Rob's chauffeur, right?"

"Not exactly," Ezra said, visibly deflating.

"Ezra used to be in the military," Daisy said, chin lifted proudly. "We both come from military families."

"Oh," Henry said with a dry chuckle. "Well, thank you for your service."

Ezra stiffened at the tone.

Henry's phone buzzed on the bar.

"Well, I'm glad you found something else that fulfills you," Henry said, standing and patting Ezra's shoulder. "Excuse me. Pirate lawyer duties," he joked, flashing a smile at Daisy, who laughed again.

Ezra caught the flicker of concern on Henry's face as he turned away—then noticed how quickly he exited, like a man chasing a departing bus.

"Daisy, he wants to sue your dad," Ezra said, watching Henry disappear.

"What are *we*?" Daisy asked suddenly.

"Don't change the subject," Ezra replied just as fast.

"No, Ezra. We've been . . . whatever this is. And it's been fun. But is this what you want? And please don't make it about my dad—"

"Daisy, I . . ."

"I really like you. You don't have to be ashamed of where you live. You don't have to be rich." She reached for his hand, but Ezra turned away.

"Ezra," she said gently, realizing she'd struck something raw.

Outside, on the other side of the club, Henry stormed toward Dunkin and a group of masked men pouring oil along the pavement.

"I heard you were here tonight," Dunkin said, grinning as he opened his arms. "I got eyes and ears all over this city."

"Dunkin, go home. Now," Henry snapped. His eyes darted to the men with oil cans. "Stop that. Now."

"Come on," Dunkin laughed. "You're the best lawyer my brother could've hired. But I gotta let off steam. And hey—your rates are brutal."

"Dunkin, if you torch Malcolm's club, I can't help you. Even I'm not that good," Henry warned.

"Who said anything about burning it down?" Dunkin smirked. "I'm looting it. The fire's just to block the exits. Can't have our rich friends slipping out too fast."

He turned to his men. "Ski masks on, boys. Don't want Dan knowing it was us."

"This is *not* the way—" Henry rubbed his temples in frustration.

"I'll cut you in—five percent of whatever we take," Dunkin offered.

"Ten," Henry snapped.

"Eight."

"Seven. Final offer."

"You drive a hard bargain, *pirate*. Seven it is!" Dunkin laughed and shook his hand.

Then he and his men stalked toward the club's entrance, masks on, guns drawn.

Dunkin pulled out a match, grinning as he splashed oil across the entryway.

"Wait, wait!" Henry yelled, rushing in front of him. "There's a girl. Inside."

"There always is," Dunkin laughed.

"I've got a plan," Henry said, forcing a grin.

Dunkin, hobbling on a casted foot, limped into the club's main room. Each uneven step echoed louder than the music as he made his way toward the raised DJ booth. He shoved the DJ aside and snatched the microphone.

"Ladies and gentlemen . . . DJ Dunkin is in the house!" he bellowed.

The crowd, half-drunk and oblivious, erupted into cheers as he queued up a new track.

"Daisy, wait here. I need to call Malcolm," Ezra said, irritated, eyes tracking Dunkin's every move.

"Are you crazy?" Daisy snapped, following him.

Ezra pulled out a keyring and opened a side door, revealing a small room with a poker table and scattered playing cards. He pulled out his phone and started dialing.

"Ezra," Daisy said, snatching the phone from his hand. "If you call my dad, this is going to spiral out of control."

"Maybe it should," Ezra said. "Maybe it's time the truth came out. But maybe I'm not the super-rich pirate lawyer . . . or—"

"I'm not shallow, Ezra. You're the one with the chip on your shoulder. I don't care where you come from. I care about *you,*" she said, her voice rising.

Ezra turned away, his voice low. "Spending time with Amanda, Rob, and your father . . . I've seen what real power looks like. Real control. And I realized—I don't want to be a weakness in your world. In this life, without money, without status . . . you're invisible. You know that's true. You and that lawyer guy . . . you relate to each other on a level I'll never reach."

"You're being too hard on yourself."

"That's easy for someone who's never had to scrape for anything. You don't know what it's like to *endure*—to want something with everything in you and know you'll never have it. That's fate's cruelest joke."

"You sound like Uncle Rob," Daisy teased, trying to lighten the mood.

"And you sound like your dad—always making jokes when things get serious," Ezra shot back.

Daisy's smile disappeared. "Don't compare me to him. He's manipulative. Controlling."

"He's scared," Ezra said quietly. "He already lost your mom. He doesn't want to lose you too."

Daisy stepped closer, glaring into Ezra's eyes. Her voice dropped to a whisper. "I won't be controlled by *anyone.*"

Ezra smirked faintly. "And now you sound just like Rob."

They both looked away, the air between them tense and fraying—like two hands reaching across a widening void. Close, but drifting.

Daisy turned to leave.

Ezra grabbed her hand.

She turned back. Their eyes met. He leaned down slowly toward her—Gunfire erupted.

Ezra lunged to the door. He saw masked men storming into the club, assault rifles raised. Screams pierced the music as the crowd scattered, some dropping to the floor, others frozen in terror.

"Daisy, stay here!" Ezra ordered.

He crawled toward the bar, heart racing.

The gunmen barked orders, forcing guests to toss wallets, phones, and jewelry into duffel bags. On the DJ booth, Dunkin played along, pretending to be another frightened victim.

From behind the bar, Ezra grabbed a glass and smashed it over the nearest gunman's head. Gunfire answered. Ezra ducked under the bar, bullets shattering bottles above.

One of the attackers crept around the bar. Ezra popped up, hurling a liquor bottle into his face.

"Go ahead, hero! Save us all!" Dunkin mocked from the mic.

Ezra rolled behind a table, spotted the dazed attacker he'd struck, and yanked the man's gun. He stood and fired three precise shots. The gunmen dropped. The crowd burst into cheers.

He tossed the duffel bags back to the huddled partygoers, who scrambled to reclaim their belongings.

Then he turned toward the DJ booth.

Ezra climbed the platform and slapped the mic from Dunkin's hand.

"I *know* you're behind this."

Dunkin laughed, wiggling his cast. "You here to finish what your boss started? Rob's a big dog. You? You're just a pup. A poor little pup."

Ezra's face hardened. "Now I see why Rob doesn't hold back with you."

He grabbed Dunkin's arm and dragged him off the booth.

With one surge of strength, the massive man grabbed Ezra by the shirt and hurled him into the crowd. Ezra crashed down, knocking over two people. Groaning, he rose and charged.

He tackled Dunkin to the ground and rained down punches, blood coating his knuckles. Dunkin grunted, stunned under the flurry.

Then a bullet tore through Ezra's shoulder.

He collapsed with a cry, clutching his arm as fresh pain bloomed through his chest.

More masked men poured into the room.

Ezra bolted toward the bar again, crawling for cover, blood streaking the floor beneath him.

Smoke began to fill the club.

"Daisy!" Henry shouted, poking his head into the back room. "Get your friends. We're leaving."

He guided Daisy and her crew toward the exit, but she turned, eyes locked on Ezra, wounded and struggling.

"Ezra!" she called, running back despite Henry's warning.

"Wait!" Henry reached for her, but she slipped through the smoke.

Some of Dunkin's men spotted her and raised their weapons.

Ezra saw it too. He stood, bloodied, and shoved Daisy to the floor just as the trigger was pulled. The shot hit him again. He dropped with a groan.

"Stop!" Henry shouted, waving his arms. Smoke curled around him.

"Boys," Dunkin coughed, propping himself up. "It's time to leave."

The air thickened with smoke. People gagged and stumbled through the haze.

Ezra, gasping and bleeding, leaned against the wall to stand. He limped toward a gunman and struck the weapon from his hands. Then he collapsed again, firing at another attacker—who dropped instantly.

The last of Dunkin's men rushed him.

Ezra slid across the floor, colliding with Dunkin.

He leveled his gun at the pirate's head.

"Tell them to drop their weapons."

Dunkin chuckled, coughing. "What, you turning gangster now? Just like the rest of us?" Ezra pressed the barrel harder to his temple.

Dunkin's men hesitated, tense.

"Alright, boys," Dunkin said finally, raising a hand. "Let's get out of here."

They retreated into the smoke, leaving behind shattered glass, chaos, and a bloodied man who refused to fall.

"No," Ezra said. "Let everyone in the club go. You and your men stay."

Dunkin chuckled sarcastically.

"Drop your weapons. Now," Ezra ordered, aiming his gun directly at Dunkin's bald head.

One by one, the masked men slowly lowered their weapons to the ground.

"I'm touched, boys. I didn't think you cared about me this much," Dunkin laughed, turning to Ezra. "You're quite the soldier. Robbie found himself a good one. Say, you ever think about switching sides? My brother's always looking for talent."

"Shut up," Ezra snapped. He looked at the frightened group huddled inside the club. "Go. Now."

The crowd scurried toward the exits, smoke trailing behind them as fire began to consume the building.

"No, you stay," Ezra commanded, stopping Henry as he tried to slip out beside Daisy. Then he turned to her. "Go. I'll be right behind you."

"This isn't going to end well," Henry muttered, watching Daisy disappear through the thickening smoke.

Dunkin's laughter was the only sound left as the flames roared louder and the smoke thickened, turning the room into a choking cloud of gray. Visibility dropped to nothing.

"Daisy!" Malcolm shouted, rushing to meet her outside. Ambulances and police surrounded the scene. Amanda and Malcolm stared in horror as parts of the roof collapsed in flames.

"Ezra's still in there!" Daisy cried, burying her face into her father's chest.

Amanda ran toward the burning building, but a firefighter caught her before she could enter. She struggled violently as another officer joined in to hold her back.

Eventually, firefighters brought the blaze under control. Amanda, Malcolm, and Daisy stood breathless as stretchers began to emerge from the smoke-filled ruins.

Their hope sank as the first man they saw being carried out was Dunkin—alive.

Covered in ash, barely conscious, Dunkin wheezed through a breathing mask. He spotted Amanda and Malcolm and tried to laugh, but only a violent cough came out. He extended a soot-covered hand toward them, feebly.

Daisy spotted Henry next, being wheeled out, followed by more of Dunkin's men.

Amanda's knees buckled. She sobbed and turned away, unable to watch.

"There!" Daisy cried, pointing toward the last stretcher.

Ezra.

He was limp, lifeless, coated in smoke and ash. Amanda rushed forward, touching his face, now pale beneath the soot. The medics motioned for her to step back as they lifted him into the ambulance.

"Can you reach Rob?" Amanda asked, wiping her tears.

"I've tried. I'll keep trying," Malcolm said, holding Daisy tight. He pulled out his phone and called Rob again.

As the doors to the ambulance began to shut, Amanda ran to block them, her hand catching the doorframe.

"Wait—please—how is he? Is he going to be okay?"

"Ma'am, we're doing everything we can," a nurse said gently, placing a hand on Amanda's shoulder.

The door closed.

"The pup didn't make it," came Dunkin's hoarse voice from the back of another ambulance. Wrapped in a blanket, clutching a breathing mask, he looked smug through the ash that smeared his face. "You'd have been proud of him, Mama."

He extended his arms as if to offer comfort.

Amanda's fury exploded. She shoved Dunkin hard, turning to the nurse for the truth.

The nurse's expression said it all.

"No!" Amanda screamed, pounding on the side of the ambulance. Officers and paramedics had to pull her away.

"Slow down, Malcolm—I can't hear you," Rob said, pacing as he spoke into the phone.

The housemaids jumped when they heard a loud crash from upstairs.

Rob grunted and cursed under his breath, stomping down the stairs.

"Did you see the body?" he shouted into the phone. "Malcolm, answer me! Did you see *it*? Don't trust anyone down there."

He ended the call and marched straight to Malcolm's desk. With shaking hands, he unlocked the door behind it.

The maids paused their cleaning, curiosity drawing them toward the source of the noise.

Suddenly, a grinding sound echoed from the hidden room.

Then came the heavy stomping—like metal chains dragging across concrete, something big and angry pacing the floor.

The maids gasped and stumbled back as the sound grew louder, the creature or machine—or whatever it was—charging toward the open door. They fled in terror, having no idea what would emerge next.

Amanda, Malcolm, and Daisy's hearts sank as the ambulance carrying Ezra roared to life. Its sirens wailed, piercing the night as it pulled away.

Behind one of the other ambulances, Dunkin coughed violently, slumped on the curb. His body shook with each breath. A hand touched his shoulder.

Dunkin looked up and smiled through the soot and blood. "I'm all right," he wheezed, then broke into another harsh cough. He leaned closer to the figure beside him. "I've got a little pup that might fix your problem," he rasped.

The sirens faded into the distance. Amanda, Malcolm, and Daisy stood in silence, watching the ambulance vanish into the night—feeling as if a part of them had been ripped away, carried off with no promise it would ever return.

CHAPTER 16

ROB'S EXHAUSTED BODY swayed from pain and fatigue. Cassius stood and gently cupped Rob's face, studying the defiant fighter before him—knowing it would take far more to break him.

Cassius turned to Mikey and Mara. "I'm taking a break. This old dog will bark, though—I know it." He nodded at Mikey. "Come on. Let's see if you can send the psalmist out for some pizza."

As they left, Mara rushed to Rob's side. She cradled his head, watching his eyes flutter like he was drifting off.

"I'll never tell . . ." Rob mumbled, barely coherent, his voice slurred and fading.

"Don't speak," Mara whispered. She wiped his bloodied face and exposed chest. Suddenly, a sharp noise echoed through the warehouse. Mara jumped, eyes scanning the room. Footsteps approached.

Snapping back into her role, she quickly adjusted her elder psalmist mask. "Who's there?" she called out, voice trembling.

Amanda stepped from the shadows, holding a long sword and aiming it at Mara. "Move."

Mara backed away slowly, eyes still fixed on Rob. She disappeared into the shadows just as a thunderous stampede echoed through the warehouse. Through a small window, she spotted members of the psalmist cult sprinting in panic.

A frightened voice shouted to her, "It's Nightmare!"

At the name, something surged through Rob. His body jolted as he struggled against his restraints.

"It's Nightmare, Elder! He's attacking!" the psalmist yelled.

Screams filled the warehouse, followed by the unmistakable sound of metal clanking.

Amanda rushed to untie Rob. "Who's wearing my Nightmare armor? Is Malcolm wearing my armor?" Rob grumbled.

"First thing you do is complain," Amanda muttered, freeing one of his arms.

Suddenly, two psalmist members burst through the door, startling them both. More followed, daggers shaking in unsteady hands. Rob leaned forward, straining to see what was approaching.

A heavy stomping echoed . . . something—or someone—was coming. Red eyes pierced the shadows. A figure emerged: Nightmare.

Clad in the iconic black armor with glowing crimson eyes, the warrior's presence alone froze the cult members. Steel plates covered the body from head to toe, looking nearly indestructible.

The warrior approached Rob and began untying the ropes around his legs.

"Malcolm, get out of my armor," Rob growled. Still in his underwear, he thumped a fist against the armored chest.

The figure removed the helmet.

"Cassandra?" Rob gasped.

She grinned, then shielded him with her body as a psalmist hurled a dagger toward them.

"You brought the armor to me. How thoughtful," Cassius said as he strolled into the room, flanked by more psalmist members. "Let's just hope she doesn't torch the place like you did."

"Wait until I put it on," Rob hissed, motioning to Cassandra to remove the suit.

"Don't be so hasty," Cassius replied calmly, hands behind his back. "I know you know when you're beat, Nightmare. Hand over the suit."

His cultists surrounded them, daggers gleaming. Rob snarled, realizing they were outnumbered.

"When I kill Lucas as Nightmare," Cassius said, leaning down with a twisted smile, "he'll know it was a gift… from dear ol' dad."

Rob lunged, but Cassandra grabbed his arm, stopping him.

Cassius exhaled. "Kill them—except Amanda."

Amanda looked up, confused, just as the cultists charged with raised daggers.

Suddenly, gunfire tore through the room. Several psalmists fell instantly. The rest froze, stunned. A masked figure strode in, holding an automatic rifle.

"Where have you been—" Cassius started, but stopped when the figure threw a dagger directly at him.

A psalmist jumped in front of Cassius and took the hit.

Cassius blinked in shock as the figure pulled off his mask.

"Ezra?" he muttered.

Ezra's eyes burned.

"Well, Doctor Jonathan was right. Your reconditioning isn't complete. Back to the Blue Room with you. You still have a choice," Cassius said coolly. "Join us. Be forgiven. Become enlightened. Or die with Nightmare and his little gang."

"I'd rather take you down instead," Ezra growled, lifting his weapon again.

Before he could fire, a psalmist hurled a canister to the floor. Smoke engulfed the room. Chaos erupted as cult members fled in all directions.

"I told you that was him!" Rob shouted, turning to Amanda. Spit flew from his mouth as his voice cracked with emotion. "You all think I'm crazy! You and Malcolm!"

Amanda tried to calm him, patting his shoulder. "Whatever, Rob." She picked up his clothes from the ground. "Just get dressed. Malcolm's waiting in the car."

"No." Rob took Cassandra's hand and stroked the armored arm plate. "We finish this now."

Amanda sighed, then nodded to Cassandra. She began removing the armor.

"Don't you want to put on your clothes first?" Amanda asked as Rob strapped on the armored leg plates.

"This is all I need," Rob muttered, fastening the black sash around his waist. He extended a hand for the sword Amanda was holding. "You didn't bring any guns?"

Amanda rolled her eyes and handed it over.

"Cassandra," Rob said, pausing before putting on the helmet. "There isn't anyone else I'd rather see in the armor than you. Remember that." He slid the Nightmare helmet over his head.

Cassandra gave a silent nod.

"That's about as close to a 'thank you' as you'll ever get from him," Amanda teased, then turned serious. "Don't lose yourself."

Rob, fully suited in his Nightmare armor, chuckled. The Nightmare armor inched Rob making him look as tall as Cassius and Dunkin. This armored metal monster was like a towering all demon with a skinny sword.

With a swing of his sword, Nightmare bolted from the room, catching sight of two psalmist members sprinting by. Nightmare was a wild beast, finally unchained. A sharp slash echoed, followed by the wet splatter of blood against concrete. The cries of his victims rang through the warehouse, haunting and visceral, like souls being torn from their bodies. Blood poured like wine from a tipped bottle. Nightmare was like a vacuum sucking in the attacking psalmist cult members, effortless cutting them down and leaving them injured to suffer.

Outside, in a truck near Dunkin's warehouse, Malcolm typed rapidly on his laptop. He flinched as a flood of psalmist members burst from the building. Cassius shouted orders, leading a group of them toward a new direction.

Ezra approached the truck. "I think they got Rob," he said, catching his breath.

"I see him," Malcolm replied, staring at his screen. "He's coming this way."

The two watched as Nightmare crashed through the warehouse doors and sprinted after the fleeing psalmists.

"I'm going too," Ezra said, backing away.

"Ezra, wait— Next we need to—"

"I know," Ezra interrupted. "But they ruined my life. They took me from my family. I'm not letting them do that to anyone else." He took off before Malcolm could respond.

Amanda and Cassandra ran toward the truck.

"What's he doing?" Cassandra asked, seeing Ezra sprinting in the distance.

"Not following the plan," Malcolm muttered, opening the door for them.

They climbed in just as another car sped past.

"Yep, that was my dad," Daisy said from the passenger seat of the passing car. Jessie remained focused, gripping the wheel tightly as he chased the psalmists down.

"One crazy day," Daisy said, trying to ease the tension. "I mean, we get attacked by a ninja psycho—turns out it's Ezra, back from the dead—then kidnapped and brainwashed by some cult. It's like we're in a spy movie."

Jessie didn't respond.

"It'll be alright, Jessie. I promise."

"Rob is that nightmare creature. We know it now. That cult brainwashed your friend. Your dad pushed us out of his plan, locked us in that manor. This is all insane!" Jessie shouted, slamming the steering wheel. He pressed harder on the gas, locking eyes on the armored figure up ahead. "There he is!"

"Jessie!" Daisy yelled. "Jessie, calm down!"

The car surged forward, striking Nightmare and sending him sprawling onto the hood. He clung tightly to the vehicle. Jessie honked the horn, but Nightmare slammed his helmet into the windshield, cracking it.

Jessie hit the brakes and jumped out, gun raised. "Tell me what you know about that cult. Now!"

"Officer Handsome," Nightmare replied, voice distorted through the helmet. He advanced slowly. Jessie fired, but the bullet clinked off the armor and dropped harmlessly to the pavement.

Nightmare slashed his sword, slicing off Jessie's side mirror. Jessie backed away, aiming again. The armored knight kicked him down and pointed his blade at Jessie's throat. A shallow cut opened, blood trickling down his neck.

"Stop!" Daisy cried.

Nightmare turned to her and paused. He saw her unbuckling in the passenger seat. He straightened and pointed at Jessie—a warning—then took off toward the fleeing psalmists, his armored steps loud and haunting, like chains dragging across pavement.

Daisy rushed to Jessie, wrapping her arms around him. His neck bled slightly from the close call. He panted, eyes fixed on Nightmare disappearing into the distance.

Nearby, psalmist members crouched behind alley walls as Nightmare charged toward them. Cassius and a few others dashed into Malcolm's club. People on the street froze, staring at the armored figure moving with purpose. Phones came out. Videos began.

Nightmare's black hood and glowing red eyes cut through the crowd as he neared the club. Several psalmist members lunged from an alley, blades ready.

"Stop!" Mara barked, still wearing her elder psalmist mask.

Nightmare turned his head.

"We're too exposed," she hissed. "A fight out here will bring too much attention."

Reluctantly, the psalmists lowered their weapons but remained visible.

"Come," Mara commanded.

Rob locked eyes with her. Both stared through the lenses of their masks. As the psalmists retreated into the alley, Nightmare moved on toward the club.

"I say we go after him," Mikey said, emerging from the corner.

Mara glared. "This outsider doesn't know what he's—"

Mikey held up the psalmist necklace. "Am I not in charge?" He stepped forward, enjoying the authority Cassius had temporarily handed him. "Cassius said I had the gift of charisma. Of leadership." Power seemed to radiate from his smug grin. "Right?"

"You have the necklace," Mara replied coldly.

"Exactly. Cassius gave it to me—for now." Mikey patted a follower on the shoulder. "Let's get that armor. Let death seize our enemies. Let them go down alive into hell!"

The psalmists roared their battle cry and stormed toward the club. Mara stood back, arms folded, watching them leave.

As Mikey started to follow, Mara stopped him with a hand. "That necklace won't be on your neck for long."

"Maybe it's not for you, Mama," Mikey said with a sneer.

"When Rob kills Cassius, guess who he's coming for next?" Mara warned.

Mikey shoved her arm aside and marched past, then spun back, holding up the necklace defiantly. "I'll never have to be afraid again. I have power. Something you don't."

"Power handed to you without sacrifice always ends in destruction," Mara said.

They glared at each other. The necklace swung like a pendulum between them.

Cassius' imposing height wasn't the first thing that caught attention as he entered the club's main entrance. Instead, the eyes of the partygoers locked onto the bizarre appearance of the psalmists in their strange, ritualistic outfits.

"Take these to the roof. I'll lead him there," Cassius ordered, handing a backpack to one of the psalmists. He paused, breath catching from the run. "Then head to the convenience store and grab matches and oil. We'll stop the traitor—with his memories. We'll light a fire."

"Yes, sir," the psalmist replied, then hurried off.

Cassius motioned for the others to move just as Nightmare entered the club.

Gasps rippled through the room at the sight of the armored figure. Nightmare moved silently through the crowd, the partiers instinctively stepping aside. Despite the eerie entrance, music still pulsed, and many continued dancing—some treating the scene as just another surreal night.

Nightmare approached the bar and loomed over a man seated nearby, causing him to quickly abandon his stool. Leaning in toward the bartender, he spoke in a low voice. "You see anyone stranger than me come through here?"

The bartender silently pointed toward a door on the other side of the club. Nightmare began moving through the crowd toward it.

"Ladies and gentlemen, looks like we have a knight in the building! Great cosplay, my guy. Let's hear it for the knight!" the DJ shouted, shifting the music to a heavier beat.

Clubgoers cheered, some patting Nightmare on the back or attempting to engage him.

Metal boots clanked as he ascended the stairs to the roof. The door ahead featured a small window, revealing scattered brick structures and roofing tools. He pushed it open and stormed onto the rooftop.

There, Cassius sat calmly atop a paint-covered bucket, wind stirring his robes. The thump of bass below and distant police sirens blended into the rooftop silence.

"I've got to say," Cassius began with a smirk, "Lucas is just as relentless as you. I wish I could watch the two of you clash. But you won't be around that long."

Nightmare unsheathed his sword with a reverse grip—blade downward, hilt firm in his hand. "I'm going to enjoy this," he said coldly. "And the pain will be so excruciating, you'll beg for death."

He stepped forward.

Suddenly, psalmists leapt from behind the rooftop cover, daggers drawn. Without hesitation, Nightmare pressed a button on his chest plate. A white mist hissed from vents, blanketing the rooftop in smoke.

Cassius raised an eyebrow but didn't move.

From the streets below, onlookers pointed upward at the now-smoke-covered roof. Only the red glow of Nightmare's eyes pierced through the cloud. The sharp ring of steel was followed by a bloodcurdling scream. The gurgling sound of a psalmist bleeding out filled the air.

One psalmist tumbled through the smoke and landed hard beside Cassius' bucket.

The breeze picked up again, thinning the fog. Psalmists writhed on the ground, clutching their wounds. Blood dripped steadily from Nightmare's blade as he approached Cassius—his sword leaving a crimson trail.

Another psalmist blocked his path. Their blades clashed in a flurry. The psalmist forced Nightmare back a step, ducked a retaliatory slash, and shoved him in the chest.

Aggravated, Nightmare attacked wildly, his swings powerful but unfocused. The psalmist weaved and parried, landing an elbow strike that Nightmare caught mid-swing. In close quarters, they grappled until Nightmare struck with a brutal slap. The psalmist blocked his sword with a dagger.

Both fighters froze in a tense standoff before Nightmare shoved the attacker back.

The psalmist charged again.

This time, Nightmare met him with a steel punch to the face, then drove his sword into the man's shoulder. Screaming, the psalmist struggled, but Nightmare dragged him toward the roof's edge and shoved him off. His scream echoed until it abruptly ended with a sickening thud.

Breathing hard, Nightmare looked up. Cassius and two psalmists remained, watching intently from across the rooftop.

"Mara says you think tactically," Cassius taunted. "But we've outplayed you."

"I'll cut out your insolent tongue first," Nightmare growled, advancing. "Once you're dead, this revolting cult dies with you—and we finally get our lives back."

The two psalmists flanking Cassius sprang forward to intercept him. Nightmare, reacting with brutal precision, struck them down instantly. They collapsed, clutching their stomachs, blood pooling beneath them.

Nightmare raised his sword to strike Cassius.

Suddenly, ropes flew from both sides and coiled around his arms and legs, yanking him back and locking him in place. Psalmists hidden in the shadows pulled tight, restraining him.

Nightmare dropped his sword. No matter how hard he struggled, he couldn't break free.

"Now," Cassius said, rising to his feet. He gently removed the hood from Nightmare and unfastened the helmet, revealing Rob's face. "When we defeat your son, I'll be sure to tell him how much you helped us."

A dagger suddenly flew toward Cassius. He dodged it just in time and turned to see Ezra standing across the rooftop.

"I was waiting for you," Cassius said smugly. "The injured soldier returns to the battlefield," he sneered.

"I'm going to end this," Ezra growled. "You used me. Brainwashed me. Just like you do with everyone in your cult."

"We enlightened you, son. We used your gifts to improve the world," Cassius replied smoothly.

"You don't even believe that garbage," Rob snapped. His face was exposed now, his body still restrained.

Cassius chuckled and patted Rob's face mockingly. "Squad leader . . ." he said, glancing toward Ezra.

"I don't take orders from you anymore," Ezra snapped, charging forward.

Cassius reached into his pocket and ignited a flare. It shot into the sky, releasing a trail of smoke. Ezra stumbled back, clutching his head.

Cassius struck a match and dropped it onto a half-circle of oil behind him. Flames roared to life. Ezra collapsed, screaming, overwhelmed by a flood of traumatic memories.

"Doctor Jonathan said you might have complications with our process," Cassius said, almost tenderly. "He told me fire was your trigger. Said it'd send you back to that blaze you were trapped in. Fitting, isn't it? This is the exact place we found you."

"He can burn in hell—and so can you," Rob shouted. "Leave him alone! Fight me, you coward!"

Cassius laughed. "I am the master of fate," he declared. "I run Psalms Society. We have land, schools, and now—our greatest weapon." He motioned toward the psalmists restraining Rob.

Cassius picked up Rob's sword. "I'd shoot you, but we don't use guns," he said mockingly, pressing the sword's tip against Rob's forehead. Blood trickled down from a small cut. "Should I stab his brain? Or slice off his head?" he asked the psalmists. They shouted suggestions like an audience at a gladiator match.

Rob trembled, breathing hard. "Alright then," Cassius said. "We need to remove the suit. I'll just stab him." He began to press the blade forward.

A gunshot rang out. The bullet hit Cassius in the shoulder, knocking him back. Cassandra stood nearby, pistol raised. Blood soaked Cassius' shirt.

She fired again, forcing Cassius to duck behind a crumbling brick structure. He darted between cover, working his way toward her. Towering over her, he knocked the gun from her hands. He swung Rob's sword at her repeatedly. Cassandra ducked and dodged.

"You're the little bitch who beat on my brother," Cassius snarled. "He'll love knowing I got rid of you." His voice had changed—unhinged, angry. Everyone noticed.

"I see cowardice runs in your family," Cassandra shot back.

Rob laughed bitterly as the psalmists restrained him harder.

Cassius growled and kicked Cassandra. She slammed into a rooftop structure. He rushed in for the kill, but Ezra blocked the strike with his dagger, dazed but defiant. He held the blade firm with all the strength he could muster.

Cassandra used the opening to body-check Cassius, forcing him back. He slashed again at Ezra, but Cassandra shoved him aside and dashed toward Rob.

"I'm not stupid," Cassius said, realizing her ploy. He grabbed her arm and hurled her across the rooftop.

Ezra slipped behind a structure and stabbed one of the psalmists holding Rob. With one arm free, Rob yanked the other captor toward him. The psalmist punched Rob wildly, pressing buttons on his chest plate.

Rob shoved him away, but fluid leaked from his suit and spilled into the flames. The fire surged with a loud whoosh, sending everyone sprawling to the ground.

Ezra froze as the flames rose higher.

"Hey!" Cassandra said, turning him toward her. "It's going to be okay. Focus. Think of the people you're fighting for—Ms. Amanda, Mr. Malcolm, Daisy."

Ezra nodded, finding his center again.

Below, chaos erupted as clubgoers rushed to escape the building. Sirens wailed in the distance.

A deep crash echoed across the roof.

"Get out of here," Rob said, picking up his sword. "I'm ending this."

He walked toward Cassius, who lay beside several lifeless psalmists.

Black smoke enveloped the roof, creeping down into the club. "Go!" Rob ordered again.

Ezra and Cassandra spotted injured psalmists fleeing down the stairs, a trail of blood behind them.

"Lucas will kill you," Cassius coughed, trying to sit up. "He hates Nightmare. Mara would've told you—if she trusted you."

Rob loomed over him, kneeling beside his broken enemy. "I was never the perfect husband," he said. "I failed Mara and Lucas. But maybe I can give Mara what she asked for."

He raised the sword, his face a grim mask. "She wanted you dead. I can't wait to tell Dunkin he's an only child."

"Rob!" Ezra called. He and Cassandra stood by the stairwell as the flames spread fast. Fire trucks and police cars approached in the distance.

"This damn club just keeps burning down," Cassius muttered with a wheeze. "But the hell you'll face from Lucas—and the next leader of Psalms Society—it'll be worse. War is coming. And you're at the heart of it."

Rob raised his sword to strike.

"Rob, there's no time!" Ezra cried. "Just leave him!"

Rob snarled, then stood and walked toward the door. But instead of entering, he slammed it shut—with himself outside. Ezra and Cassandra rushed back, trying to open it, but Rob jammed a metal pole into place, locking it shut.

They pounded on the door. Through the glass, they saw Rob searching the rooftop—he found Nightmare's helmet and placed it back on his head.

The flames danced around him, but he stood tall, blade in hand. Cassandra and Ezra turned away as he brought the sword down. A wet splatter echoed from the rooftop.

Then, Nightmare dragged Cassius' lifeless body toward the flames.

"He's lost himself," Cassandra whispered, pulling Ezra toward the stairs.

CHATPER 17

BLACK SMOKE billowed from the club's front doors and windows as firefighters battled the flames with hoses from nearby trucks. A crowd gathered, watching in stunned silence as the building was consumed by fire.

Cassandra and Ezra burst through the exit doors. Cassandra placed a hand on Ezra's shoulder when she spotted Amanda and Malcolm among the onlookers. Without hesitation, they rushed toward them.

Amanda threw her arms around the two of them. "It's like déjà vu, huh?" Ezra said with a faint smile.

Amanda pulled back suddenly, searching their faces. "Where's Rob?" she asked, her voice tight with worry.

Cassandra coughed hard, her throat raw from smoke. She met Amanda's eyes solemnly.

"He lost himself."

Before anyone could respond, Officer Dan approached the group.

"I should go," Ezra said, already backing away. "Ezra—" Amanda called after him.

"I'm still in my psalmist gear. I can't drag you into more trouble." He dropped a small canister at his feet. A thick smoke cloud erupted, cloaking him.

Officer Dan stumbled back, coughing in the haze. "I have a whole damn list of questions!" he growled.

He paused as murmurs rose from the crowd. People pointed toward the club. Dan and the others turned to see Nightmare stepping through the smoke and fire. Blood dripped from the sword in his hand.

"Don't move!" officers yelled, weapons raised.

The crowd's phones came out, recording the surreal moment. Nightmare broke into a sprint. Gunshots rang out as officers opened fire, but the bullets bounced harmlessly off his armor. He disappeared down an alley, officers in pursuit.

"This isn't over," Officer Dan barked at the group before following, speaking into the radio on his shoulder.

As the smoke curled into the sky above Shiloh City, Amanda's gaze drifted away from the club. In a narrow alley nearby, she spotted Mikey. Standing behind him was Mara, wearing her elder psalmist mask, flanked by loyal followers. Brother and sister locked eyes.

Amanda silently pleaded with him, reaching out with her expression alone. But Mikey held the psalmist necklace tightly, then turned and followed Mara and the others into the shadows.

Malcolm placed a comforting hand on Amanda's back. His attention shifted when he noticed Daisy and Jessie driving away. Jessie had a thick bandage around his neck. Daisy's face was set—troubled, but resolute.

The winds of Shiloh City whispered through the charred ruins of the club, brushing over its blackened bones as the fire finally died. Crowds had been cleared, and the street was now cordoned off. In the early light, the club's scorched frame stood like a fallen giant—broken, beaten, and lifeless. It was as if the building had exhaled its final breath.

The street outside was unnaturally quiet, transformed into a ghost town by the eerie stillness.

Amanda, Rob, and Cassandra stood at a distance while Malcolm spoke with a man near the smoldering building.

"I know this place has been in Malcolm's family," Rob muttered from the front seat of a car, the door open as he rested. "But I hope they don't rebuild it. Damn place just keeps burning down."

The women didn't respond, their eyes fixed on the club's skeletal frame. After a moment, Cassandra glanced at Amanda. "Any word from Ezra?"

"No," Amanda replied, shaking her head. "I haven't heard anything." She sighed and leaned against the car. "Mikey won't return my calls either."

"He's in charge of the psalmists now," Rob said. "Maybe they'll finally leave us alone. Or maybe he'll decide I need to die. Who knows with that kid?"

"I think he'll do the right thing. I believe he will," Cassandra said, placing a comforting hand on Amanda's arm.

"Hope isn't a strategy," Rob said, shifting in his seat. "Hope means you're letting fate call the shots. I refuse to let anyone else write my ending."

"Rob, you need rest," Amanda reminded him gently.

"Well . . ." Rob tried to rise from his seat but faltered. His legs buckled beneath him, and he collapsed back down, drained.

"There's a lot of weirdness," Malcolm called out as he walked back to the group. The man he'd been speaking with headed in the opposite direction.

"Insurance stuff?" Amanda asked.

"That . . . and a pile of bodies they found inside," Malcolm replied, throwing a glance at Rob.

"I made sure Cassius was finished," Rob said firmly. "He won't stop me from finding my son. I'm one step closer."

"How?" Cassandra asked.

"Because I know he's here. He's in this city," Rob answered, his eyes distant as his thoughts drifted.

Trying to break the tension, Malcolm chuckled awkwardly and gave Rob a pat on the back. "Let's get something to eat. My treat," he said, motioning toward the cars.

"I don't think I'll be getting in a car with you anytime soon, Malcolm," Amanda teased.

"Yeah, yeah," Malcolm laughed, heading toward the driver's seat of the car Rob was in. "I'm just glad this whole nightmare is finally over."

But before Amanda and Cassandra could reach their vehicle, a group of figures emerged, surrounding both cars. They wore psalmist uniforms—but these were navy blue instead of black. And they weren't armed with daggers. They carried guns.

Rob stiffened as the blue-clad psalmists closed in.

Malcolm began to protest loudly. Cassandra instinctively reached for her weapon, but Amanda held out a hand to stop her.

The circle of psalmists parted as one of the members stepped forward and removed their mask.

"Charlotte?" Rob said in disbelief, rising from the car.

She gave a sly smile and wiggled her fingers in greeting. "Not just me, in-law."

Another member emerged behind her. He handed Charlotte his gun and stepped in front of Rob. Then, without a word, he took off his mask.

Rob stared at the man's face—his expression frozen.

The man smiled grimly. "It's been eighteen years... but fate has arrived, Dad."

JOSEPH JENKINS is a writer, entrepreneur, author, speaker, and social advocate. He works with many different medical and nonprofit organizations with writing, leadership, and management. Diversity and culture are a large part of his life, having a unique mixed cultural background, and he takes inspiration from his Jamaican mother, a former model and entrepreneur. He has received a bachelor's degree from the University of Maryland Baltimore County (UMBC) in business technology administration and a minor in entrepreneurship. Follow him @_officialjoejenkins_ on Instagram.

More from Joseph Jenkins

Freshly graduated law student Katie is living in Washington D.C. with her sister, dreaming of a future with her carefree boyfriend, David. But when the enigmatic Prince Enoch and his father arrive to combat global disasters, Katie is pulled into a high-stakes conspiracy involving worldwide calamities. As she's swept into Prince Enoch's passionate world, her attraction to the dangerous gangster Miguel complicates everything. Soon, Katie uncovers a devastating secret about Prince Enoch's father that could alter the fate of the world—and her love life—forever.

Haunted by prophetic visions and drawn to a mysterious, magnetic stranger, U.N. liaison Nia is thrust into a spiritual battle that transcends politics and borders. As the world teeters on the brink of collapse, her connection with the enigmatic King becomes a flame in the darkness—a love both divine and dangerous. In a race against time, they must face rising evil and celestial forces, discovering that their bond may be humanity's last hope—or its undoing.

Coming Soon

Lysander, a famed explorer, and his warrior daughter, Scarlet, seek a mystical gem from the long-lost Astra kingdom. In Golgotha City, they encounter Nero, a man using the red ruby's power to control fire and grant abilities. Scarlet faces a rival, Abigail, now the powerful Emerald Star, with her partner, Ronin. As a battle for the gems ensues, a mysterious force manipulates them all, setting the stage for a world-altering conflict.

Princesses Makeda and Lyssa of Sheba fear the impending power shift as Solomon's father falls ill, and his arrogant brother, Adonijah, prepares to take the throne. Amid growing tensions and the secretive threat of the Sheol organization, Makeda seeks guidance from Bathsheba, while Lyssa vows to change the kingdom's corruption. As war looms and secrets unravel, including the Queen's hidden past, Adonijah plots a coup, sparking a dramatic battle for the throne that will alter the course of history.

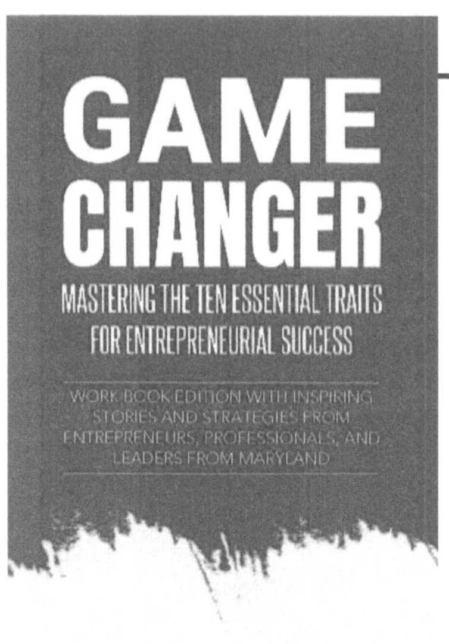

Have you ever wondered what makes men and women accomplish greatness, change their environment, and change their lives? Do you want to know what it takes to start and run a successful business and change your life? Game Changer explores the 10 essential traits for business success and steps to change your life for the better. Included in this book are stories and strategies from entrepreneurs, leaders, and professionals from the state of Maryland.

www.ingramcontent.com/pod-product-compliance
Lightning Source LLC
Chambersburg PA
CBHW030637110726
47901CB00002B/482
9798998854866